D0855834

ORANGE RHYMES WITH EVERYTHING

ORANGE RHYMES WITH EVERYTHING

ADRIAN McKINTY

WILLIAM MORROW AND COMPANY, INC./NEW YORK

It is the policy of William Morrow and Company, Inc., and its imprints and affiliates, recognizing the importance of preserving what has been written, to print the books we publish on acid-free paper, and we exert our best efforts to that end.

Library of Congress Cataloging-in-Publication Data

McKinty, Adrian.
    Orange rhymes with everything / Adrian McKinty.—1st ed.
        p.   cm.
    ISBN 0-688-14432-2
    I. Title.
    PS3563.C38322073   1997
    813'.54—dc20   96-18628
                                                                  CIP

Printed in the United States of America

FIRST EDITION

1   2   3   4   5   6   7   8   9   10

BOOK DESIGN BY GRETCHEN ACHILLES

The blots on the page are so black
    That they cannot be covered with shamrock
                        —LOUIS MacNEICE, FROM *AUTUMN JOURNAL*

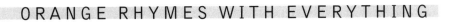

ORANGE RHYMES WITH EVERYTHING

That year, in our Province, in the town of C–, autumn came earlier than usual.

It was teeming with rain the whole month of September and the sky was a perpetual slabber of gray cloud hanging over the countryside and the sea. Concealed within it was every kind of rain imaginable. There were the hard, pounding cold fronts that sometimes had hail in them, and the damp drizzly warm fronts bringing mist and fog. Worst of all for me, though, was the slate rain blowing in from Belfast Lough, salt-tinged and almost horizontal, stinging your face as soon as it hit it.

Each day when I woke up I'd pull back the curtains at my bedroom window, and it would be the same. Water trundling out of the gutters and bouncing off the concrete of the window ledge. Wind bending the trees and howling. Mum's car drenched with pools. Everybody was complaining, especially the farmers. The storms had almost washed out the entire harvest, harsh gales driving in from the west, lashing the coast and pushing down the temperatures almost to freezing. I remember watching tv and the local weather forecasters scrambling for excuses, saying that the squalls were spillover from hurricanes on the far side of the Atlantic or vast and unseasonal movements of the ice sheets over Greenland. But with the grind of flooding and rain and cold, scientific explanations didn't seem to help. It was worse than it should have been because none of us had been prepared for it after such a balmy August. Even the metal

1

compass on our barometer seemed surprised, still pointing at "change" throughout the month of tempests.

Finally at the end of September, within the churches playing to packed houses and street preachers foretelling the apocalypse in Market Place, the storms abated. They just petered out, as quickly as they had come, leaving us all exhausted and relieved. My brother and I went out to the fields to watch men in tractors working day and night to bail what was left of the hay and make the silage.

But with the crops in, the dramatic weather over, and the trees stripping themselves of leaves, the frigid air and the nakedness of the harsh country made us all tired and listless. People wandered around like shipwreck survivors, with long faces and muttering that the winter nights were fair drawing in. Frost was on the fresh earth most mornings and there was a kind of jaundiced feeling in the hills. As if the island were one massive ocean-going craft, becalmed in a perpetual sea.

Down on the beach Sarah and I watched the gulls drifting in the sea breezes over the Lough in uneasy sensations of expectancy. She telling me that they didn't believe the reprieve was a real one. That they thought something worse was in store. For proof she pointed to the great V's of other birds flying south to the Mediterranean and to Africa, abandoning us to the future.

We were between seasons, in the transition towards winter, and to me then it was as if the very days themselves were composed of ambiguities. I was in a transition of a different kind.

I probably felt the parochial gloom more than most because, earlier that summer, I had gone to America as part of a scheme to bring Protestant and Catholic children together. Paid for by the US Congress via the International Fund for Ireland. It was my first time out of the country. Everyone got different families, and I stayed in an elderly woman's place in midtown Manhattan. I met a girl called Brigid from Londonderry, who was also on the scheme, and we had a lot of fun together. Mrs Bernstein took us all over the five Boroughs and to New Jersey, and a week seemed like a month, so crammed was it with new experiences.

A thousand hours of *Kojak* and *Hill Street Blues* and *Rhoda* had prepared us a little for the sights and sounds of the big city, but the reality was so much more potent. I absorbed each moment, each smell and touch and flavor, storing them up for the unhappy day when I had to go back home.

Unfortunately, Brigid and I had to get on different flights back because of some mix-up in the arrangements. We were sad to see each other go and at JFK we said we'd write and meet when we got home. But we never did.

All that summer I'd been restless, and after the storms it became worse. Going to school again. Girls Brigade. And all the usual political crap on the tv and in the papers. By the middle of October, though, I was slowly starting to settle in, erasing the skyscrapers and the yellow cabs and the people with different colored skins. I was getting used to the Province, thinking that it was a kind of normal.

Across the water there'd been only one obvious piece of magic which still lingered with me. That was when a crazy man had grabbed my arm and told me the number of the winning lottery ticket. The "pick four." He leaned down and whispered it to me. Hand cupped against my ear. On the corner of 54th and Broadway. 8885, he said.

He told me that he got lucky twice a year. He could feel it in his bones and he would have told me more but two cops were coming over—he hurried off, laughing like Santa Claus, and waving a big hand, as he vanished forever into the subway entrance. Brigid made me check my pockets to see that nothing was stolen.

Later I bought a ticket and we watched the draw on Mrs Bernstein's cable tv. Brigid and me. Sitting there in that big room. Her dead husband's Emmy on the mantelpiece.

A Spanish woman in a sparkled dress pulled out the numbers and, as we'd expected, it was something else. With threes in it.

But the next day it was 5558.

October was coming to an end. The last day of the Celtic year is the 31st. And my holiday photographs were back after getting lost in the processing lab. Mr Preston had me in an Art project. I was doing quantum theory in Physics. School was wick, the classes were tough. We had exams to study for. Some people were jealous of my trip, but they couldn't be jealous of me. Just couldn't.

I was in the sheugh of the year. Pressed up against my window, looking out at the street. Listening to the sad songs of "That Petrol Emotion." And slowly and with every advancing day, forgetting. Thinking that things would stay the same forever.

But when I look back, and recall that time in the town of C— I believe that there was something that happened to us. As if we were touched. As if we were spoken to. My mother, my brother, me. Something that happened. Or might have done. In those last few days up to Halloween. I was in one way of life and then suddenly I was in another. Though its hard now to put my finger on a specific thing, the days and events are all mingled together, unstrung and ragged, part of the bruised waters of a dream.

But perhaps the shift was a more gradual thing, turning us around, slowly, in tiny increments. The erosion of one slice of ourselves, the making of another. Unnoticeable, like the tectonic movement of continental plates, or like in the story of Lyr, when the sea laughs, slow and long, and all that the mortal men could see were the mirth lines on the waves.

Maybe.

PART ONE

"[T]o many, the image is of the dour and humourless Northerner, given to black moods and hard profanity, lacking erudition or insight in his choice of language. There is a grain of truth in this, since the difficulty with Protestant songs in Northern Ireland is the age old problem of the aesthetic poverty of triumphalism. The Aristotelian idea is that oligarchy leads to introversion and sterility (sic). This 'inconvenience' all too obviously manifests itself in the technically unsophisticated lyricism, the simple drum rhythms and bland story telling of Protestant anthems, which lack the subtlety of Catholic protest ballads or the beauty of Nationalist sentimentalism . . . . It is a cliché that the words 'Ulster' and 'orange' have no rhyme phonics (sic) that embrace a single word or syllable; thus "Men of Ulster" and "Prince William of Orange," the two most common Protestant motifs, are relegated to the middle passages of simple rhyming schemes, resulting in a disruption of the cadence and integrity of the composition, and a consequential loss of much of the piece's dramatic and emotional impact. Protestant composers seem to compensate for this melodic deficit by resonant drumming and lurid 'Lambeggary' which, to my mind, is nothing more than a bombastic and ostentatious display of a barely concealed desire for violence."

—PROFESSOR RUARI O'LUGHDAIGH, *ULSTER FOLK MUSIC*

CHAPTER ONE

This'll kill ya.

What?

This'll kill ya.

What?

Are you deaf? I said this'll kill ya.

Sarah wants to tell me another joke. It won't be funny. Not even close.

I need to sneeze, I say back.

Our faces are in the water. The reflection is in the playground. We're talking. Breaktime. I remember.

Forget that. I tell ya, it'll kill ya. It'll blow you away. I heard it just yesterday, so I did. Brilliant.

It's cold today. Eight degrees C, the weather man said on *Breakfast News*. It was raining this morning. The boys are running and some of the younger girls are skipping. We're at the far side, away from the buildings. The noise is the clanging of the flag. Or rather, the rope against the flagpole. The union jack is all bunched up from the wet. We are near the car park, there is a smell of sheep and cattle drifting down from the field. Someone has let down one of the tires on the VW Microbus that belongs to Mr Pilkington. Flat, it reminds me of the Mystery Mobile from *Scooby Doo*.

Come on ya big ganch.

A man with a tick is at the river fence. His head is twitching left to right like an out-of-order machine. Like a robot.

Paddy Englishman, Paddy Irishman and Paddy Scotchman are in the jungle, she begins.

The sunlight has escaped. Excaped. In the clouds beyond the hill farms. The teacher on break duty sees the man but looks the other way.

And they get captured by this gang of headhunters or pygmies or something, you know. And the chief says that there is this here ancient custom that says that foreigners can be set free if they go into the jungle and put a hundred fruits up their arses without laughing.

Her eyes are squeezed tight as she tells it. We are on the curb. Balancing. I can feel stones under my feet. And beside me: grass frog, a crushed Coke can, a bottle of de-icer. A vocabulary of natural objects. In my mind's eye I can see the cows. Through it the visual bulletins and the squashed up face of my friend. Bored, the teacher turns her back. Avoiding a scene with the man. Vigilant of nothing. The sky is a panorama of motion. The dry days are gone. Green waves of cloud swarm into the mass of white. Like the riot police.

I am dirty. Black are the racks on the back of my hands, and the curve of my blazer no one sees.

And if they laugh they get killed.

Her voice is high. As if to an audience. She is telling me this as if I was young. That's the way she sees me, I think. I am older by six months and in the summer I will be a year older. Sarah is skinny. Her breasts are tiny levees above her protruding belly. She looks as if she is with child. I heard of a girl who didn't know she was pregnant until she went into labor. This isn't the case with her.

The trapdoors of her eyes are like moonlight, and there is a line of a slug trail as she talks. Unattractive, but not hideous. I am being critical as I look at her and I stop and think: as if I'm one to talk.

Are you paying attention wee doll?

Of course, get on with it.

Theatrical expressions and the joke is a story of her arms. Reflecting. In the puddle. With a penny sunk in the middle of it. Rings are forming from the drops of rain. The man is having trouble with his fly.

So Paddy Englishman comes back with a hundred grapes and he starts putting them up his bum.

The perv at the fence is here for the second time in a week with a bag that says: pharmacies. We are the closest to him but I don't want to look. As if I could actually see the place where his willy is. There are creatures in the water as we walk and stay tighter. She has not seen him, caught up in the story of the jungle. Free of wires he is like a puppet trembling for the gap between his legs. Just as he's about to flash us, a boy sneaks up and throws a handful of mud at him. The cry is almost manic.

Ya wee skitter, the man shouts.

The wee boy turns with a grin on his face. And if it isn't sleekit Pete. The man runs. His getaway documented in laughter. Over the stream and the football pitch. One hand down. Peter is a star, and I remind myself to give him a break over his next misdemeanor.

And he's getting there—ninety-six, ninety-seven, ninety-eight, but suddenly he starts laughing and they have to kill him. And Paddy Scotchman comes back and he starts putting raisins up his arse.

We're beside the boghole. It occurs to me that I've heard this before. Down, the boys are playing football. A couple of muckers at pitch and toss, throwing silver against the low wall of the shelter. Gambling. Someone quivers from glue sniffing. And the game is rigged but the stooge doesn't have a clue. I recognize him from the lockers. Cold on my tongue. Wig, they call him. Because of his hedge-like hair. The bent coin wins every time. But Wig's too dumb to see.

And he gets up to ninety-eight and the same thing happens, he starts to laugh and can't stop. He's rolling on the ground laughing. Now the old chief boy of this tribe wonders about this and he asks Paddy Scotchman what's going on. And Paddy Scotchman says: Och aye I nearly got there, but then I remembered that Paddy Irishman is out there collecting melons.

A circle of kids are running tig. Last off ground is on. Flecking the curbs. A blur of movement for the bicycle racks. Like small animals. One passes near. His shirt ripped and off center. His trousers held up by a wire belt he's made himself. Uncheap Dr Martens. He's a pochle of his own design. Here the rigid sky is a smudge of amber. The boy has a moustache of hot chocolate. Frenetic, he weaves from an outstretched hand.

Dja geddit? Dead funny huh? Collecting melons. Dead funny? Huh? Eh? What do you think? Huh? Huh? You're not laughing. You don't get it do ya? You don't get it.

A raisin isn't a fruit.

The clouds blacken and I can see the first spits on the lens of my glasses. It has turned a lot colder now. Sarah's black hair is being blown about.

Oh Jesus, she says smiling.

But it isn't, I say back. We're both in the game, I half want a fight.

It doesn't matter.

You said they had to go and collect fruits.

It's not important, that's not the point.

She is starting to sound pissed off. Her teeth are gritted and her eyes are narrow with faked up anger. In a good way.

It's not funny.

It is funny, you're just too thick to get it.

Aye I am?

Aye you are.

Aye I am?

Aye you are.

Aye I am? She punches me on the shoulder. Not hard, she is careful around me. Everyone is so careful. I punch her back.

Anyway I've a better one.

Aye you do? The boys are up from the football pitch. Running with their blazers and wet shirts. Ties flying over their necks. The ball smeared and kicked ahead.

You never know how to tell gegs.

Who says that?

I do. She cocks her head. And I wonder if I have a reputation for mucking-up jokes. I dismiss it. I don't want to start getting paranoid.

Do you want to hear it or not?

Alright.

Paddy Englishman, Paddy Irishman and Paddy Scotchman are about to be executed.

Why is it always "Paddy" Englishman and "Paddy" Scotchman?

That was my question, she knocked it from me. I was saying it last week to somebody.

I don't know. Did I interrupt you?

No.

Right then. Ok, so Paddy Englishman gets asked if he wants the guillotine or the firing squad. And he wants to die an original death so he picks the guillotine.

What's a geeotine?

Shit, you don't know what a guillotine is? And you're calling me thick? Where are you from wee girl? Stupid central?

I was just asking, alright.

Ok, fur theck cuntry peeple, hi better hexplane, I say doing my best cultchie accent. She grins.

Halright, I continue, it's like a beg theng. A beg theng with a blede hon it. Like a beg knife. Jeez, boys, like a trecter you   11 know. You put your heed in through this here hole boy and then and thes tother thing, like the blede falls down on ya and cuts off your heed, iss on runners or somethen and it . . . shite in an ice-cream, wee girl, there's no point in me telln the geg if ye don't know what a guillotine iss?

I think I do know. It's a gillatine, right? Like they had in the froggie revolution in History and everything.

You don't say gillatine. You say geeotine. My god. Jesus. Kids today. It's tv that ruins them if you ask me.

Look did I do French? You smell garlic? I don't think so. How am I supposed to know that? And anyway that's the way Mister Rook says it, so he does.

No way he does.

He does so. Ah bugger there's the bell.

Ah no. I've J-J-Jabba next.

That's a new nickname right? Why do they call him that?

From *Return of the Jedi*—the ugly guy.

He is pretty ugly. Come on we have to go in. It's the bell.

Yeah, I say reluctantly.

Come on, it's just as well, it's starting to rain you know.

But you're not going to hear the joke.

It's probably stupid anyway. Come on I'm getting wet.

Shhhiiiit.

Come on, it's pissing, everyone's away in.

You go on.

Everybody else is away.

Go on and I'll see ya in there.

She shakes her head at me like a disappointed older sister. Her hands fretting at her hair band. Mine shoved in my pockets.

Tell ya wee girl, you're weird.

Go on and I'll catch up.

Alright see ya later alligator.

See ya. Wouldn't want to be ya.

The rain on my skin.

You there, get in this instant.

The sneeze is back. The need. I run. Arms outstretched. Horizontal. The rain on my fingertips like a small world. Water at the cuffs and the hem of my skirt. My eyes big and blinking in the drops. Sometimes I am more mature than others.

Wheeeeee, I say delighting in the sound, a different key in the downpour. My feet in the puddles. Stamping. The bell ringing in the background. My legs, disjointed and slow. I am alone in the playground. I yell and run. My body moving like an engine oscillation. With a dull rhythm.

Come along, get in. Something in her voice. She draws a reluctance after her. Incendiary and subdued. I know what it is. The tangible facts and a scunnered expression on her face. A lean woman in a woman's suit, hands on an imaginary waist. She sees me as a character from a Dickens novel. The limping girl.

Do come along.

Eyebrows fluttering like a blue moth and her gestures a study of impatience. My skip on the patio is a deformed harmonic and I'm damp up to the top of my white knee socks.

Well aren't you clever. It's teeming out there. Teeming. You're soaked. What class do you have next?

I look at her. Mrs House is definitely annoyed. Her lips are pursed and her finger is tapping at her watch.

Physics.

And who's that with? Mister Ross?

No. Mister Pilkington.

Well ... well, just get along then and dry yourself with something.

Jabba, a pushover and she knows it. She floats. For a second. In a dress from the seventies. A misery in purple. A bruise of   13 daffodils on the belt. Appropriate somehow. I think of Toto and Dorothy.

What with, miss? I say, trying to rile her.

Oh dear . . . anything. Dry your hair at least.

Her accent tickles me. She's English. Trapped here by marriage. Poor woman. Like a petty official of the Raj. Her hand reaches up to the top of her forehead. I follow it. Her hair is elaborate, piled high on her head like a braided haystack. It goes up nearly half a foot. It reminds me of a London policeman's hat. I stare and don't move. Transfixed by the effect.

Go on, she says, tempus fugit.

Crazy with a capital "k."

I run down the corridor to the sixth-form toilets. It is windowless and painted military green. The naked strip-lights are depressing. A leaf comes off my back. My watch says ten past. I foresee trouble. I pass my locker and the double doors of the Physics block. I stop and have a look, the class is already in. Bollicks. I grab my bag from where I've left it at the door. It's the only bag not inside the class. I run across to the bog, skidding on the floor.

Half the world is slidey.

I shove open the bathroom door pushing hard on the double hinge. It squeaks open, the brush on the bottom, bent in half, rubbing on the floor tiles. It is empty and windowless. The light is harsh.

There are four sinks and a giant single mirror that runs along the back wall. I face it. My black curls are ambushed flat by the water. I look like a fugitive. A young version of my ma, skin like paper and eyes the color of water.

Decorated near the reflection are all sorts of things. Lipstick iguanas, a violin and a mask of crocodiles. Two cloven hoofs are on the glass. Libelous graffiti and a cancer of petty insults. Scent marks in biro. More on the back doors of the toilet.

Libidinous and profane. The cleaners don't scrub them off. I don't blame them.

I push the button on the blower but it fails. I push again and this time it whines into life. Pulsing hot air down toward the floor. The drawing on it is of a stickman rubbing his hands. I tilt the funnel up to the vertical position. The hot air caresses my face. Pushes up my fringe. I bend my head so it will flow onto the middle of my scalp. The machine picks up a gear. It rattles noise into the empty room. It's spooky in here. Shadowy. With the tube blinking. The cement is frigid on the bare wall, the ceiling migraine gray.

The word Hemlock is scraped into the door. A rock band, I suspect. It appears again on the foam tiles just above the cubicles. Where smokers hide their fags. Flies sniffing at them and at the dog ends in the bowl; and elsewhere, a wasp, crawling and recrawling up the window.

The scent is of pine and strong church mints. To overwhelm the nicotine. I lean on the edge of the washbasin. There are roses along the perforations in the porcelain. The air is blowing. Nice, like a mild sirocco. The ends of my hair begin to dry. The heat is good on my face. I open my mouth and suck in some of the hot air. It tingles. My sinus jags and I remember the sneeze I repressed earlier. The door opens with a kick. I see a foot below the condensation on the mirror.

Jaysus, ya glipe, you're all wet.

It's Louise, big, on a runner from something. Tight in her navy jumper. Square, she is, with eyes like butts in an ashtray and her teenage lived-in face like that of a truck driver. Maybe just a truck. I like her. She's an oul lag. Before the bathroom door has even closed the cigarette is in her hand. Silk Cut. Easy hits.

What're ya mitching? I ask.

Mazz.

Maths?

Aye, Mazz.

She breathes long.

D'ya want a fag? She offers me a cigarette, it looks very white in her pink fist. I shake my head. Chubby fingers in a V at her mouth. She exhales. Smoke like a gray familiar on her shoulder doing Brownian aerobatics. I watch it disperse into the low ceiling. Her fingernails are chewed and fenian green. We pause in the quiet, after the dryer kicks out.

Made in Cock, the amended sign says. The long sigh of the moment is delicious. I cough on the tobacco and her breasts heave sadly in her jumper.

Mathematics. I say the word.

Uh huh, she says. She hoists her arse up onto the sink, her socks at her ankles. White briefs curious on those enormous thighs. Her legs are blue and white. Masculine. She grunts like a beefy transvestite.

You're mitching Mazz? I say, bewitched and switching into her lingo.

Yeah.

You get Bald Eagle, aye?

Nah, oul Monkey Miller.

You don't like her?

No, she hates my guts.

She hates everybody's guts. She does.

A slouch of smoke. Blue arms and a vein running down her chubby arm. It's all blue, like a sea, and the river. She pricks up her ears at a crack outside, ready to fire the cig into the toilet bowl. The cleaning spray comes on. The water rush bubbling through the pipes. It has an impact. I need to piss now. I look at her and go to the cubicle. I open the swing door. There is a gap to see out, at the top and bottom.

Did ya hear what Keith said to her? I say to cover the embarrassment of silence.

Which Keith? she shouts, as if I cannot hear her through the door.

My cheeks are red now, as I get some warmth in them. Outside its still raining. Water pouring down the frosted glass. To the gutter and the bogstreams. I pull up my skirt and let my whips fall to my knees. I sit.

Keith Simpson.

There are so many bloody Keiths in this school.

Keith Simpson.

I let the pressure ease on my bladder. The tension gives me a high. Like a chili pepper. A trickle of urine through my urethra.

Oh that wee shite?

You don't like that Keith? Are you wired up, he's a hunk and a half and he's nice too.

Keith Simpson you're talking about? Not Keith McGahern? He's nice too.

I pull off a sheet of paper and wipe myself. I slip the paper into the bowl and stand to watch. It absorbs the water and transforms. I throw in another two sheets.

Keith Simpson's too pretty, she says. Like Donny Osmond, so he is.

No. You're taking a hand out of me, I say.

Would I take the piss?

Yes.

I'm not.

Aye you're not?

I look around and I'm suddenly dazed for a second. It isn't the walls, it's just the artificial light.

I blink.

Her hand is scratching at her ankle, through the gap I can see it as I turn. The last piece of paper sinks. Falls beneath the surface and folds over on itself. My urine has a yellow tinge today. From the jaffa oranges. I pull up my whips and tug my skirt into place. The paper is now in the U bend. I grab the lip of my jumper and pull it down over my finger. With my wrapped finger, I let the lid fall and press the handle on the cistern. The flush splays cheerfully and I open the door again.

She smiles with the face of a tv preacher. Happy and content in our mitcher's guild. I go to wash my hands and then I change my mind. I can't be arsed and the peer pressure is not there. She blows a smoke ring and I can't help but smirk through the whimper of the hand dryer. She must have pressed it as I flushed.

You really don't like Keith? I say dragging it as far as it will go.

No, she replies, emphatic and a little bored.

Sure?

The tongue almost out between my lips.

Anyway, she says exasperated, What about him?

Ok you want the story?

Uh huh.

Right, well.

I want to disengage, but I want to make her laugh. The story will make me later still.

Think it was about a week ago. He was in a class with her. And she was in a mood, and she says that she wants complete silence. Right? So everybody there's keeking their whips. (You know how scary she is.) And Keith's desperate for a fart. And he's a big fella, you can't deny that, so finally he caves in and explodes this huge fucking belter. And he looks down and starts writing. Dead fast. And Jim Purdy he's sitting at the front and he hears this enormous load drop behind him and he laughs out loud. And she, Miller, turns round and sees Jim laughing and she was all angry so she was and she yells at him and sends him down to the office.

Who Keith?

No. Jim.

Wee Jim?

Aye.

Oh bet he felt wick. That's pretty funny.

Yeah. I can just see Jim's face.

I pull a mug and we both laugh for a moment.

So, how was your trip to America? she asks, after a pause.

Well you know what they say about America, I reply with the first part of the line I've rehearsed.

What?

It's a lousy product, but it has great advertising.

She looks at me.

Who says that?

Me.

Did you make that up?

I think so.

Oh, she says and then if she's just getting it, she starts to laugh again.

I laugh as well, inspired by her enormous breathy guffaws.

But then I slip in a note of discord. A wee half a cough. She understands and doesn't try to help. She smiles a sleekit grin. Mocking even but without any real malice. She's about my only ally in the bottom class.

The terrace beneath the extractor fan vibrates and sings. The fan cuts out.

So where's your wee pal?

My wee pal?

Aye you know, what's her face?

Judy?

No, you know, Sarah, the good-looking one, she says. Sarcastic, probing.

Talk about the pot calling the kettle black, I tell her.

She chuckles and catches some smoke the wrong way.

And between coughs: Are you staying here?

I dunno, I say. It is a lie. My hair is dry.

Well what are you doing here? What's a lick like you doing missing classes?

Who says I'm a lick?

I do.

Aye ya do?

You are and ya know it, you're too afeared to show it. Arse licker. Big wet lick.

Jeez Louise. Easy up. I have a delicate disposition you know? I say with a hint of tension in my voice.

She shrugs. Outside there's the wild wind and in here the sheugh at the back of the sink is burbling. Her fat lip relaxes. Aware that this could become a sore topic. Her nails are jagged and leave a white mark on her face as she scratches. We're old pals. We went to the same primary school. Wee muckers together. Though I never really see her. It wouldn't be cool for her or me. We're in different classes and she's in the bottom stream. S and I'm in P. S for spastic we say. P for prick they say.

I better go.

I knew it, you lick. You've never mitched a day in your life.

What about that time in P-5 when the pair of us snuck out to see *101 Dalmatians* at the town hall?

Jesus, I remember that.

See?

Yeah I suppose you're not too bad.

Nope. Anyway I'm off.

She winks at me and I open the door.

The smell of tobacco and lemon scent is behind me. I go out. The spring catches and the door closes in two jerky movements, wheezing shut. My feet are small on the plastic surface of the ground.

The tramp across the corridor takes forever and I count seventeen of the big floor tiles. I stand outside the class and stare in through the crisscross window on the fire door. Jabba is at the front. His jacket is on the seat and there is a sweat stain on his back that looks like a face.

Laura sees me peering in and looks over at Jabba significantly. Shit, the wee git. I have no choice now and open the door.

Sorry I'm late, I say automatically. My forehead is bristling with embarrassment. The lesson has stopped and all eyes are on me. On my back. I walk past the front desk to the second row. My stool is empty. The room is still. Everybody looking and then someone blows their nose. I breathe-in comically. My eyelids are half down for protection.

The weather is teasing at the window. Chaos in water droplets. Frozen. I focus on the periodic table on the far wall and walk to my seat. My legs move, one in front of the other. I skite round the overhead projector and make it to the window. Jabba has a dilemma now: he can't say anything bad to me, but he can't show himself up in front of the class. I hear him stutter, still looking at the floor. I sit on the stool and reach down for my bag. I feel my skirt wrinkle under me, my whips work themselves into the crack of my buttocks.

Wu, wu– he begins.

I pull up the bag and place it on the bench. It's a blue army rucksack like everybody has. It says "Undertones," "The Clash" and "R.E.M." in big letters on the front. On the back is a sewn-in Harley patch. My hand touches it as I reach in and drag out my exercise book and Winnie-the-Pooh pencil case. I leave it open on the desk. It forms another barrier between me and the talcy faces of the others. Inside, I can see my English and History books. My journal and my Polaroid camera.

Wu, w-why . . .

I open the book and break the spine. I reach over for my pencil case. My hand feeling the smooth surface of the bench. It is warm. The wood is like a person under my palm.

W-why, why were you l-late?

I look up. Under my hair. The front row has turned to look at me. The boys on the other side of the room are making faces behind Jabba's back. His hand is resting on the bench beside Laura. A few inches away. The sweat stain on his shirt carries through to his shoulder and his armpits. His tie is a dead emerald. The lenses on his specs like the bottom of a jam jar. His lips seem out of sync with his speech. For a moment I think he is an alien. I push my glasses up my nose.

I take a breath loudly and say: Mrs House told me to dry my hair off before coming to class.

He pauses, his finger running the length of his shirt sleeve. Hair and cotton covering the transparent nerves. His mouth opens. The blood vessel on his temple pulses.

W-w-well I suppose that's o—o—ok then.

The town is damp and broods on the slab of gray water. A sea mist on the Lough. The wet belly of the all-weather pitch and the hockey nets lying against the crossbeams. Gravel on the surface like volcanic sand. Black and unpierced by angles. Then up a little: the grass embankment, the ivory football posts and an amputated horse chestnut where someone has tied a dreary-looking swing.

H—H—Heeeather are you sta, staring out of the window?

Heather spins and looks at him. She isn't, but I am.

No sir, she says.

I, I hope not, because this is g-going to be a very difficult class. I wa, want you all to pay attention.

A helicopter comes over the low shoreline. Like a slater

from the naked body of a tree. It comes slithering over the ashen clouds. Jug, jug, jug, it goes. It's a war machine that absorbs all the other sounds of the afternoon.

It's coming closer and all the boys want to turn and take a look.

I'm thinking of something else. In a frenzy of motor neurons. I can feel the fetus of the sneeze at the bridge of my nose. I tap it with my finger to make it go away.

Pay attention, Jabba says to the whole class.

I can't. My eyes are brown and syenite, under a perfume of curved lashes. I can see them in the silver-backed reflection of my pencil case. Beside the rubbed-out cheat notes. The binomial formula. The instructions for integration by parts. They're there in pencil, from my last test. Tigger is on the obverse side. I have kept this metal box so long it's gone from cool to childish to cool again. Cheating is easy for me. In a reverse of the Middle Ages, the impression seems to be that the halt are somehow touched by goodness. I stroke the soft metal. The chopper's engine boils over as it stammers over the school. Pencil on aluminum. Ideal. I can smudge it with my thumb, at the first sign of trouble. Leaving nothing and never get caught.

Looking at my hand now I can see a skelf in my thumb. From my wooden ruler. I pick at it. I am finding it hard to concentrate today. It's because I'm thinking of Art with Mr Preston. The day after tomorrow he wants me to stay behind, for the project.

Jabba is setting up the overhead projector. Playing out the wire and three-pin plug. Everyone wonders if he's going to get electrocuted like he almost did once last year. I look outside. The field is a dour verdigris and a man is marking the goal lines with opaque powder. He is wearing a flat cap and his hands are bold and pronounced in his yellow gloves. The soles of the man's feet are white and treading on the chalk. One of the caretakers. Big fella, it could be Joe. Re-marking the touch lines for the next game. The grass is soft. Cold blades that are muddy and inviting. The pitch is a bridge of green between the town and raw edge of the forest. Organized now that he has marked it, hemmed in by the mossy banks and the damp snow lines of the edges.

The class lights dim slightly by themselves. I yawn carefully. Heather is being disciplined. I shake my head and wait until the teacher has turned his back.

It's spitting outside. Small rain. The radiators beside me moan and the helicopter is just a pulse in the murmur of science equipment. It chugs over the sodden roofs and unnerves the swaying ravens on the trees. I shiver and think to myself that it's good to be indoors.

N—n—now that, eh, everyone is with us wu, w-we can begin.

Someone coughs.

It's di, di, difficult to know wu, w-where to start. With your maths ba, background ma, most of, of you should be able to k-keep up. Ha, how many of you are doing A, A-level maths?

A few hands go up.

About half of you. G-good.

I look out the window again. Below us is the big Stalinist housing estate of Sunnylands. A misnomer if ever there was one. It's sturdy and working-class but going the way of the ghetto as the badly built houses fall apart. It's a place for boys in hoods to play with homemade guns. I'm in Victoria estate, which is better council housing but is coming down with the bad element. I try to see my house but it is way behind the Map of the Universe and the sneeze is teasing me again.

Qu, quantum physics, is the, the, the—

I look back at my reflection in the pencil case again. A

bump in the metal distorts my nose, making it more upturned than it is. The rest of my face is obscured by maths.

Qu, er, this p-part of Physics is a m–m–more philosophical branch of the d-discipline.

Teasing. The pencil is in my hand. The point, sharp and brittle. I write Quantum Physics on the inside cover of my new notebook.

My thumb is marked from the graphite. A black scar on the gray line of my fingerprint. The shavings are on the floor. My lower back is sore. A numbing, irritating pain. I'm getting it from sitting on a stool. My fingers are long, the nails chewed horizontal at the end. My brow is lined with tension.

We all know that our b-body is made up of p-particles, fundamental particles of mat, matter.

The rubber at the end of the pencil is flat and almost gone. It is black from pencil erasings. I should just score out my rough work. My face is like a dam. The pressure building, shit, I really need to sneeze.

But quantum physics t-tells us that w-we c-can't know the p-position of these particles at the same time as we know their veh, veh, velocity. The position of these p-particles therefore is more cor–rectly described as a probability distribution. Nothing is certain in this field. Not even where s-something is.

He is at the board. His stutter evaporating in the subject. We're looking at the round bald spot on his head.

It could be drawn on a graph and the distribution would f-form a bell shape whose w-width corresponds to the pr, probability of the particles' position.

The polished wood of the desk is reflecting the lights. I bend forward and can see the blurred abstraction of my head. There are no features in the brown stain. My head is tilted back and my fists are tight from repressing it. The nerve ends dragging at me, the sneeze crying out to be born. But I can't, I don't want to attract any more attention to myself.

In today's class, we w-will discuss the works of H-Heisenberg, Einstein, and B-Bohr, all f-famous, famous.

Someone sniggers at the word Bohr and passes a note back. I don't want to read it and pass it on, my sinuses are going crazy.

Finally I just can't resist anymore. I shift round in the stool, away from the others and with my fingers in a fan beneath my nose, I carefully extend the blunt end of the pencil into my left nostril. I shudder as I feel the cold metal of the tip and the softness of the rubber. I'm in the back left hand corner of the class. Nearest the window. I can force the sneeze with the pencil without anyone noticing.

F-famous n-names.

My head is turned towards the outside, my long hair concealing the half of my face that is visible. I nudge the pencil further.

T-today and for the next week or so I want to look at what is called the p-principle of nonlocality.

I can see it despite its closeness. I only bought it last week. But it is not new anymore. It is thick and red with the letters HB embossed in gold, half chewed beneath the rubber. The sun is out again, playing cat and mouse.

You can wa, write that down.

My forefinger and thumb are on the tip, maneuvering it carefully through the ridges and bumps of my left nasal passage.

Non, new word, locality, all one w-word.

The end is way in and coaxing the sneeze. Tickling. But, I'm losing it. It's all too much. I try to focus on something else. The windows are gray, dirt thick at the corners. A spider's web broken on the handle. Paint chipped and lying in the curtain rail. Outside the rain has temporarily stopped.

Locality, local w-with −ity ah after it.

I'm getting too much resistance so I gently remove the pencil. I insert my finger and hoke out most of the nose pick,
gathering it together in a neat pile in front of me. I slide the
pencil back in. The snot sits beside my Flintstones sharpener
like a dino dropping. Except the scale is all wrong. The girl in
front moves. She bends down to scratch her leg. The sun glints
off my case into my eyes. I blink. The girl in front sits up
again. The sun a lightness beyond her shirt. I cannot remember
her name.

I lean on my elbow and let the room drift to persuade the
sneeze. It's all there. The lazy smell from the gas taps at the
back. The heaving cupboards. An ether spill at the work bench.
The computers all along the side wall, dusty and silent. Fifteen
people in the class. The air is moist. Nine boys, six girls. My
desk has a sink at the end, brown and white porcelain. Ah here
it comes, I've pulled it back. A huge burn mark up the side
where, legend has it, somebody emptied in a bottle full of white
phosphorus. Ah yes yes, a wee bit further. It's tingling. Donkeys'
years ago the person did this, when the room was new and such
things were possible. Coming. The present incumbents, a dull
lot by comparison. There is a corresponding burn mark on the
ceiling, though that could be coincidence.

I stroke the pencil against the membrane and I can feel that
it's nearly there. The tree sways and leaves displace themselves.
A seagull is at the window. Yellow on its beak and wing tip, a
black eye against the gale. Oh shit. Now I'm losing it again. I
have to think about something else. The girl beside the girl in
front is Laura Bennet. Laura.

Risky. That's a side of myself I don't want to encourage.
She's sitting in the first row. At the bench right in front of the
teacher's desk. Her choice. No one made her sit there and her
eyes are fine.

Now I, I know a lot of you think this is p-pretty abstract

stuff. And there is only a s–small chance it's going to come up in the exam. But I still think it's wa, worthwhile to do it.

In my English class Judy Wilson sits at the front because she has trouble seeing the board and is too shy to get glasses. Why else would anyone sit there? Unless they wanted to suck up to the teacher. I look along the bench. The other girl sitting at that front desk is the new girl who is Laura's friend and will sit wherever she sits. She's a transfer from another school. It's slipping . . . go back to . . .

Laura sits there, at the front, only because she's a lick, a teacher's pet. Definitely. Yeah that's it. Come on ya bastard.

But they haven't asked a qu, question on it for the last two years, so its p–probably got a better chance this year. Heh heh, here we are talking about pr–probabilities already.

My thighs and my nose are working together. Can't think about it. The pencil is way in. I look long at her. The sneeze has nearly taken me over.

When it comes to the m–measurement of sub, sub, sub-atomic particles, the apparatus needs to be v–very acute.

Can't deny she is isn't pretty. Beautiful in fact. A button nose, delicate, that wrinkles at the top. It's nearly there. The inside skin is stretched, pinpricks on the nerve endings. Like a red hot poker.

B–because the a–act of measurement changes the thing being measured. In m–most cases of course this will not m–matter (n–no p–pun intended) because the object wa, will be big.

My breath is held. Chest half out. Her eyes are hazel I remember, wide and gorgeous. My lungs tight. Frozen. I'm getting a heavy head. A pounding. My throat is dry. The sneeze is almost . . . The pencil is way up. I move it further. A fifth of a ruler. Twenty bastard centimeters. Her eyebrows are rakish and light brown. Her hair cut in a bob that hugs her face.

But electrons are s-small. No wa, wonder therefore that touching an eley, eley, electron is going to alter it.

An inferno on my nerves. I have to trick it. Think about L . . . Shit. Two more inches. Christ, the tip is nearly in my bloody brain. Her cheekbones . . . high. Up there. Her breasts form two perfect curves in her sweater. Her legs, tanned, show, in the gap between her white socks and the bottom of her skirt.

The nature of the f-fundamental p-particles is d-diff, d-diff, d-diff . . . some say impossible, and many physicists have seen this as some kind of d-defeat for the goal of Physics. The goal of p-perfect description.

Her hands are hugging her arms. They move and cup themselves above the eyes she uses to. Flirt. Parched. With the boys, and the male teachers. A little further. Male teachers. A hum from the pipes. Some of the female teachers too. Hum, just a wee bit . . . Her shoulders are relaxed in the back of her sweater. The sound of a . . . Frigging . . . Ugh. Hum, frigging humming bird.

My head is bowed. My hair waved in front of me protectively. The pencil deep. Bloody deep. Faakin deep. I can feel it. Tickle. Hurt. The sneeze. Come on you little . . .

Einstein for instance ar, argued that although the a-act of measurement itself changes the p-particle being measured. It was l-like using a sledgehammer to separate grains of sugar; and that in f-fact all we needed was a b-better measurement tool. In h-his famous dictum he sa, said, God d-does not play d-dice with the Universe. Things f-for him are n-not random b-but ordered, p-predictable.

What the hell is he talking about? A voice.

Jane beside me, whispering.

Ahhhh. Christ. I don't want to talk. I'm on the fucking verge. The motherfucking verge. I nod with the pencil still up my nose, my hair a wall between us. Jesus, turn away. Please. Jane. But she doesn't. My lungs are about to explode.

He always goes really dead slow over the easy stuff and then like a bloody train over the hard stuff.

I cannot leave her unanswered. I've screwed it. It's gone. Shit. I breath in hard, filling the vacuum. My face lightens. I take out the pencil feeling the sneeze slip away. I shake back my hair, pulling a strand out from behind my glasses.

Yeah, I whisper, breathing out. Damn, damn.

You see Kate, she's reading so she is. Reading a bloody mystery novel under the desk and drawing in her wee book when everyone else is taking notes. She's effing smart that wee girl. Probably do faaking alright at exam time.

Yeah.

An' oul faaking pervy Jabba. I mean he always goes really slow over like long division or something like we're retards. And then this, Jesus.

Jabba has seen her whisper.

Ok, no, er, t-talking there.

She turns round again.

Fine, now f-for the rest of the class I w-want you to copy down the f-following e-example.

The chalk squeaks on the blackboard and falls in a dry powder onto the floor. The room is the sound of writing and the clank of the central heating. Finally, and again shielded by my hair and hand, I get the pencil up my nostril. My nose contracts, I draw in the warm and musty air. My shoulder hunches forward. I close my eyes, my lips part.

Ah. Ahh, ahh . . .

The sneeze comes and takes me by surprise. Not loud or violent. I merely say the word, puhh.

A few drops scatter on the desk. Mucus runs down the pencil end. Heads turn but then turn back. As if I am invisible. Unteasable. Mr Pilkington's hand jiggles on the board. The sneeze feels good. Relief. So good I want another. But it isn't worth it. I glide out the pencil and clean the end on the edge of the desk and wipe it with my fingers. I roll together some pick between my thumb and forefinger. I add these couple of grains to the pile of snot in front of me. I sit for a minute. And then without thinking I flick the bogey with my middle finger. It arcs through the dust thermals, disintegrating. But the aim is right. The remains hit Laura in the center of her bob. I wince. Sit frozen, but she doesn't even feel it. I laugh a half a snigger. The shot is so good I want to tell someone. I'm keeking my whips. I look over but Jane is reading and the room is quiet. I lean back in the stool and gaze over to the far side. Feeling that the boys, if they knew, would celebrate my triumph of a flick. But the boys are working to a man.

Disappointed. I lean forward and focus on the blackboard. A residual tremor from the sneeze runs down the longness of my spine. Jabba is writing equations. The overhead projector is running, unused. Casting a white shadow onto the wall. He has forgotten about it.

Finally I get out another pencil and begin to copy the example. It is the first thing in my new book. I mark the paper. A 4H soft. My nose itches. My fingers write. The sun jukes back behind the clouds. Avoiding us. I yawn.

Suddenly the window panes rattle and I know the rain is on again.

CHAPTER TWO

He slept. Bigger than the bed, lying on his stomach with his hand resting on the floor.

He dreamed.

He was falling.

To a strange place. A chasm was opening before him. Vertical cliffs were on four sides, sheer and impossible, like prison walls, constructed from cheap concrete and sanded to gray perfection. Pillow smooth. Fiberglass smooth.

His body was electric, charged while he'd been in flight. Like a Vandograph generator. Unretarding at a rate faster than 9.8 meters per second per second. Miles gone by in an instant.

He tumbled like a skydiver. Spinning. Over and over. He dropped by a man strapped into a barber's chair. Past children wearing animal masks, and further still past animals wearing the faces of children. A bear tracked him as he fell. Sightless and clumsy, its claws sought him out in the asphalt dark. Huge swipes of air, missing him. And bass notes from the cliffs shoving him away, like anti-gravitons. An iceberg push. A leper push.

And still he plunged, on into the center of the world where nothing moves and you fall forever. His curls flowing out behind him, the air resistance pulling off his clothes, faster, the gases grinding at him, teasing out the hair on his body like a vacuum pump, shaving him, follicle by follicle and piece by piece. Yelling and falling and unbecoming, until at last, in the cold worms of light, he looked and saw. He was naked.

He was a child.

He was . . .

The city woke him. Its early morning whine of traffic. Cockroaches crawling back into the walls. The dank room seen through a gauze in front of his eyes. A pipe lay smoking on the asbestos floor. Daylight squirming in through the window. Reluctant. Sores wept on his face. His cheeks were hollow and his belly, empty for days, was growling. Garbage beckoned, bullets lay drying in the yellow sink, blue smoke crawled up from the street. The sun was rising over the East River. And then there was knocking. Events replayed themselves for him:

We have a warrant.

We have a—

The door opened and the room changed.

It became empty and a dull brown. Only the sunlight was the same. He was confined, softness all around him.

Uh.

Lifted. Carried.

Two men were cleaning the shit out from between his legs. He wanted to howl.

How we this here morning? We gonna behave?

The plastic on the shower door reflected like a looking glass. Strong arms held him under the water. Different colors. Sanctified movement, every gesture significant—like in a mystery play. A tautology of freedom. If only he could put it into words. The water was cold, his reflection bedraggled. He twisted in the grip on his shoulders. There was soap in his hair, and more running down under his nostrils. The shower was warming up.

See doesn that feel nice, didn we tell you that would feel real nice.

His reflection: his ribs were gone, his belly fuller and he was strong. From nowhere a smile curled at his lips.

Lovely warm water wash those bugs outta yo hair.

A smile curving in the glass, forty degrees off the horizontal.

The men talking to each other. In language that was far from the talk of his from the Old Testament. The way his people spake.

And the men rubbing hard on his stretched skin as if it were two sizes too small. Water absorbed into the thin rag.

Make you nice and dry, hey up, just gonna put you up here, oh you gettin' heavy and, oh oh, I think we miss a bit.

That'll do, I'm not drying off his goddamn balls.

You do it righ, else there be trouble.

The bench was cold now, the straps taut and harsh. Circulation cut off to his fingers, they whitened, growing pale. The tube slipped down into his stomach. It was painful, choking. Dying here, Jesus can't breathe. Can't you.

There we go.

Please, can you see that, can't, I can't breathe.

That's good, real good, you eat that all up. Vitamins is what you need, make you big and . . .

A trouser snaked up his leg hugging him securely. The crotch tightened between his buttocks. Arms behind him. Tied. The door thudded in the wispy light, playing havoc with the dust lanes in the sunlight. Circling in a holding pattern round a terminal building which was really only a speck of damp on the floor.

So what you think?

Giants for my money, Jets haven't got the stamina.

What you know about stamina?

What do you know about anything?

More'n you.

The voices faded with the footsteps.

He hunched himself up onto his knees. Balancing, he eased

himself onto his feet. He stood on his toes and strained to see the color of the sky. The bags sewn into the end of the trouser made staying upright an effort.

He felt like a gymnast on the balance beam. On tiptoes he could see the form of a white cloud through the misted safety glass. Blue behind it. Definitely blue. He let himself drop onto the cushioned floor. He felt his face twitch into another grin. A floor polisher started up outside, blaring noise in under the door and through the gap, he could see it. A big brush turning round and round like a solar system.

Next door on cue the tapping had begun. A jagged wee lament. Tap tap tap tap tap tap tap tap. Eight taps and then a pause. Twenty one, pause. Fourteen, pause. Seven, pause. He blocked up his ears, but the tapping wouldn't go away. A corrosive equilibrium of noise. Persistent. They were spelling out the word hungry. Again. What would they know about it. For my people the past is everything.

His fingers dug deep into the wax, making a noise like the sea. His arms locked behind his head, crossed over. His left forefinger the plug for his right ear and the right forefinger the stopper for the left.

He lay on his side, his back curved into the fetal position. Eyes tight shut. Opening them occasionally to stare at the two sources of light percolating into the room, a slit under the door and a swathe of muted brightness through the dirty window.

It seemed that he only lay for a moment but it was enough for the sun to track a third of the way across the sky.

Then it was dark another time.

His wrists trembled. Like the mane of a pony. Mane, main. Young. Wasn't there once a horse? In the nursery rhyme about the sheep.

The light was all ambient now. The particles reflecting from the angles on all the other surfaces before bouncing into his iris. Taking the long way or as if they were the exertions of hawsers. He couldn't keep them out, not even with his fists. Like they were homing missiles. Cruise or Exocet, killing him with senses. It was a rain of information. About the padding on the walls and the wireless fittings. Or the ricochet man from *Murphy*. Or the blank page from *Tristram Shandy*. The stuff they were always trying to learn him in school. All them prophets and all them Kings and Queens. Shit-eating Ezekiel the only one he liked. And all of that was years ago.

The tapping had stopped, the corridor was noiseless. An aeroplane screamed overhead, heading northeast. His shoulders were sore. Like someone had kicked him.

His hands were the color of onion when the door opened again. The room had stayed constant. The plastic bed. Sanded. The floor that absorbed condensation. The somersaults of flies. The orange padding with bite marks in it. The metalized hum of the air vents.

The same old feet in the doorway. Four, in regulation steel toe caps. Prescribed by good old Dr M.

Mmm, mmm. Smell tha, bes cup o caw you-er ha.

He looked and saw that it was still blue outside and this made his mouth open. Blue, he would have said. If he could.

Cryin like a baby. Sip o this.

The two men sat him up in the special chair. His arms still tied behind him. A palm behind his neck, tilting his head forward. A finger pushed his tongue down. The coffee was sweet and burned the roof of his mouth. It tasted new and got rid of the rubber feeling in his throat.

Jus way here till yourn doctor comes. Whol bunch today.

I don't know why ya talk ta that fucking idiot.

A bundle of features, khaki slacks. Dalai Lama in a white

t shirt. A ginger beard. He let his head rest in the hand, buoyed up on the sugar rush. He sat still on the chair, biding his time. The door was ajar, he could see three men and a woman walking down the corridor. 100 yards off. All dressed in white. The students and the professor. They turned into the first room. A roulette circumstance.

How would they feel? Today was the day because of the indigo sky. How did they feel? He was like Princip and Oswald and Jimmy Ray. Castlereagh before the razor. More school stuff.

The first time's the hardest. After that it comes like slicing bread. He had topped a few in his time. And it was nothing.

Fucking idiot.

Watch yo tongue, I warn you bout yo language.

The white man in the crew cut winced. The spaces under his eyes were cold. Ready.

Now was the moment.

As if by an act of will the electric light embedded high in the ceiling flickered off. He grinned.

Sheeit. Jesus, where'd the light go?

The man's voice became disembodied and lost in the tepid light from the corridor.

Goddamn thing. I'll get a—

Wait a minute, sometimes it come back—

The tube stripped on for a second, flickered and then buzzed off again.

Shoot, Jesus H. Wouldn ya know it. What with them doctor comin.

That fu-riggin light. I'll sort it out.

The second man went out and came back with a stick he used to open the high windows when he was on his own. It was frightening. He'd seen it before. A boat hook. Sharp. The door was open. Sky still blue, the clock in the corridor ticking loudly.

Chalky pressure on his face. Arms reaching up, stains under the pits.

The man tapped the fluorescent tube with the stick and the light did pirouette back on, but only for half a minute and irregularly, chained to an epileptic current that strobed static down onto all three of them in the room. Random flares. Or so it seemed, for with each flash he could feel the air charge. It was a signal. A message. Like when the ark called out to Samuel.

Now you done it. Broke it. And watch yo carry tha thing for?

To open the windows.

We never open no windows, we got air conditioning.

Hey. Maybe it's just good to have a big stick around sometimes, the white man replied, laughing. With these mothers you can't be too careful.

The door was half full of doctors. The clock disappeared behind one of their heads like an eclipse, the second hand was flowing past 35, the minute hand stuck on 27.

Lemme have another try.

The stick thudded into the light again and in response the tube spasmed back to normal, spreading a flecked and garish luminescence onto the brown floor.

See whaddid I tell ya.

Lucky.

He closed his eyes. The men were whispering now, the doctors were nearly in the room.

And how are we today? I bet you any money that'll be the first thing he says, classic ice breaker.

Put tha thing down yo scarin him.

I'll bet you a dollar.

Shuddup, wha I tell you bout that thing. Look at hisn face. A lousy dollar.

The coffee cup lay by his side, still hot. Cigarette smoke drifted down from the supply closet.

Four qwarters.

White styrofoam and sweet black coffee. He went to take another sip. He spilled it over his leg and yelled.

Sheeit. Now look wha he's done. Hol on. Lemme jus free yo hands thur.

The man unbuckled his arms. Slipping the plastic grips out from one another. His shoulders relaxed and retensed. His hands free, he cupped the styrofoam and tasted the coffee. Holding it carefully. Thumb under the bottom. It tasted good.

Wdja pu tha stick down.

Their chatter marching ahead of them into the room. The doctors were almost here.

Four lousy qwarters.

He could hear them talk. Nervous. Speaking about other patients, clothes, small things. Small. Like—

Ok ok a buck, lean tha thing agains the wall.

The white man laid the boat hook against the back wall. His hands twitched. Free from the restraint. It was close.

The doctors entered in single file and formed a semicircle round him. The one with the beard cleared his throat heavily, absurdly, as if about to sing.

Now this, gentleman and ladies. Oh, no wait a minute, all gentlemen today? Uh no. This is a uh– if I remember correctly. Attacked four police off, where is my . . .

Mornin Doctor Fletcher suh.

Good morning.

Fletcher looked down at a clipboard and paused. One of the other doctors, the nearest to him, had scar tissue all down his right cheek. He was picking nervously at a whitehead on his neck. Another shuffled in his black loafers.

His name is tut, tut, uh, let me see now.

The whitehead popped, oozing a small amount of pus onto the ball of the doctor's thumb. Eight feet. And four more feet. The ticking clock. The coffee. The hook. And it was turquoise on the far side of the glass.

The loafers squeaked on the vinyl floor.

I can't find the thing.

John Doe all we have I thin suh.

Oh yes of course. Names are not as important as people, I find.

Nearly kilt two FBI and did a man in jail. Crazy.

Yes well that's for us to ascertain. It's a continuing thing. He smiled and drooled out the side of his mouth.

The white man's beeper sounded. He looked at the black man. The black man turned to the doctor.

Needed below suh.

Go, go ahead. We'll lock up when we're done.

The black man hesitated.

Go, the doctor said.

Ok.

The two men went out, their shoes making tiny sounds along the floor.

And that left: An old man. A girl. Two boys as fragile as reeds.

The doctor slapped the clipboard at his side. Gray hair in his beard. He leaned down into the steam of coffee. A smile showing the dental work on his back teeth. His breath was mint.

And how are we today he said. A hemorrhage of doubt moving suddenly across the fading line of his face.

His hands the color of a Coca-Cola can. And free.

He laughed.

His feet in the black loafers smudging a vermilion trail leading back to four people dying in the room. Three men. One woman. With a hole in her head the size of a tennis ball.

The keys jangled beside him and he was panting. He was not used to exercise, though he had kept his body on automatic pilot, in good condition, like a software program that checks itself. And all of it for this moment.

Running was like a dream of running. His legs taking big strides. Past the cell doors. The keyholes. And the giant windows. Outside the lake and trees. Almost bare. The car park. The driveway and, just beyond, the outline of the city. It reminded him of the bright angels and the dingy streets of that other city. On the Farset river flowing under High Street. Mingling with the Blackstaff. The Albert Clock with Albert perched, ready to abandon the tilting ship, and the *Titanic* memorial shadowed by the very gantries themselves.

Suddenly he stopped and took a second. He was breathing in great gasps. Blood was everywhere on his fingers. He was in a panic of exhilaration. Still carrying the hook. He dropped it on the floor with a fat gulter of noise, heavy in the silence before the alarm. There was a sound behind him. He ran down the corridor panting, away from it, stopping to smash the Perspex on the clock. The clear plastic fell in shards onto the freshly polished corridor. He ripped the thin black second hand from the casing and slipped it into the pocket of the knocked white coat. The minute hand said thirty-one. But the plan didn't work. For all the time that he had been in this place, from the shower to the room, he'd thought that the chronometer controlled the environment and now he found it was vice versa. He stood disappointed, watching humanity move.

A bell, high and shrill, started up. Like a drill, except people were running into the building. Security. Damn. He was off again. He could see them through the windows as he ran.

With a crunch, at the end of the corridor, a set of double doors sealed themselves. In response to the alarm. He skidded to a halt in front of them.

Jesus.

It was early in the morning in the gap between the shifts. The guards were few. He had hoped to get away.

Not now.

The door was collection-plate thick. Warped from the clang of stretchers. He shouldered the tiny gap between the doors but nothing moved. He stood back and studied them. Looking for a flaw. They had circular windows laced through with wire. Unbreakable. He tried anyway. Smashing at them with his elbow and then running back for the hook. It bounced off like a javelin. Clattering on the corridor. He pushed at the lock but the doors were secured with an electronic dead bolt. He stood uncertain. He couldn't go back the way he'd come. Ahead the corridor was empty. Above him was the tiled ceiling. Big foam tiles, perhaps a gap big enough for him to hide in. How to get up there though? There was nothing to stand on. And if he hid, they'd find him sooner or later.

He should have made sure that the men were dead. It had all been so fast. Easy, even. A blur. He was an old old pro, and they had been barely awake.

But someone must have lived long enough to call or press a button, and soon there would be guards all over the place.

He sat down on the floor by the locked door. He stroked the stubble on his face. He hadn't gotten his shave yet.

Sirens were coming up the tree-lined drive now. Men with guns. He could negotiate his way out with a hostage, but that never worked. He sat down on a different part of the floor, away from the window. He felt in the pocket of the white coat for the clock hand. He came across another object, a box of cigarettes and, deeper in, a cigarette lighter shaped like a pistol. He lit a cigarette and smoked, his red fingers in a satisfied V up at his mouth. The nicotine hit him fast. Jeeezus. Everything was a little clearer now.

He blew out the smoke and it stuck between the doors. It hung like a tiny atmosphere. He let ash fall onto the yellow floor. He stood up and walked to a storage closet, but the door was locked. He looked outside. Time was going because there were at least six police cars out there now and more on the way no doubt. And SWAT teams and riot gear. The bastards. He shoved against the door in frustration. He kicked it and drop-kicked it but it hardly buckled.

He stood up again. It was strange, he was trapped in the building. The snare of coppers tightening and yet it was still blue outside. Still blue. Blue. He checked. Yup.

It didn't make any sense.

This should have been the time.

He closed his eyes and growled to keep the peeler noises out.

Later. A symmetry of drift above and below. Dogs and piers and a barking man. Yelling outside in the plaza. His face on the floor. On the cold of it.

In the quiet after the alarm had ceased he could hear everything. Talk and engines. Feedback from an amplifier upsetting the birds. The air-conditioning. It most of all. Monotonal, purring a single note of charged dryness. In time to the pepper lines of boxcars under his eyelids. He could hear the plumbing, dropping in the petrifying water tanks above his head.

He could hear and it was all a clue.

It would take him a minute or two to fit it all together.

The shoes were tight on his big feet.

As were all the dead man's clothes. He lay with his back on the crisp floor, his ear chilled on the pale surface. His hair sticking to the waxy remains of multitexture cleaner. The smells were of disinfectant and cigarette. One sterile and uninviting, the other warm, burnt and comfortable. He took long sucking heaves on the harsh tobacco. It was feeding him and he could not cough.

He sat up, stubbing out the last of the smoke on the grain of the wall. The doors were heavy and made of steel. They had been painted white, which had faded to a kind of cream color. The paint was chipped. He scraped at it with his fingernail and it fell, seared and cracked, onto the sober floor.

In frustration he pushed again. Nothing moved. He stood up and looked out of the window. There was an arsenal outside now. Four different kinds of police and the SWAT boys moving in. He scratched the back of his head, smearing it with someone else's blood. He felt in the pocket for the lighter. No one could see him up here but they would have a fair idea of where he was. He eyed the cops through the glass. More were arriving, hustling for cover, and lining up the sights of their weapons on the formless mass of the building. It seemed a lot of trouble for one person.

The guards and the nurses must have all run out to let the cops take charge. Maybe they'd thought it was a full-scale riot.

Maybe they were just chicken.

He singled out one of the cops in his head. A man in a crouch, in a blue flak jacket. Blond hair under a helmet. He pulled the trigger on the lighter and said, pow.

Bang bang and you die.

Figures sleeked their way to the front of the car park. A special team. With tear-gas guns. Preparing for an assault. He had to think.

And then he remembered. Weekday nights. Dark at four. Running back between the alleys. The good and the sacred and the love of stones. The wall of a hundred bricks. His brother telling him the joke about the shoplifter. Who lifted shops a few feet off the ground. The two of them in the entry, playing.

He remembered and then he knew what to do.

At the narrowest part of the corridor, where the wall bulged out to accommodate the pipes, he climbed up towards the ceiling, straddling one foot astride the other. His legs were just long enough. Harder when he'd done it before, when he was a wain. Racing to the top of the terrace's entryway. Back against one wall and his feet against the other. Shuffling up. With a piece of chalk. The first to stroke the red-brick roof was the winner. Graffiti scrawls on top of each other, stories. The entry had been narrow, it had been fun, chalk was always on the mortar, what with, games and the names of would be sweethearts. These walls were smooth and awkward. Characterless. Someone was speaking through a loudspeaker outside. The voice was garbled. He'd never tried this splits-fashion before, it was harder than it looked. He was like a demented pair of scissors cast into life. With nowhere to go but up. The pressure was on his knees and groin. His eyes were bulging in their sockets. His shoulders groaned.

He opened his eyes. The wall was fingerpainted red. A vertical staccato mark that sanctified the surface. Baptizing it. He was at the ceiling. Barely able to stay.

Three feet from the smoke detector he flicked the lighter. He had narrowed the flame. He couldn't keep his legs taut much longer. His arms hurt. The flame was almost touching the detector. His foot moved. Slipped. A 747 was landing, its wheels braced, flying low over the city, taking up the whole of the window. He hit the floor. The tail fin carved its way through the blue. The loudspeaker was drowned out in the wail of aircraft engines. Something exploded above his head and water poured down onto him. Cold and stale, not like the shower. Fifty pounds of water, spraying. He lay for a moment, his hands whitening.

An alarm went off and suddenly every sprinkler system in the building erupted.

He kicked at the door. Second time, it opened. He ran back down the corridor the way he had come. Back to the room and picked up another set of keys. He jogged back. He opened as many doors as he could. In a minute there were yelling men everywhere. Most of them naked. Screaming in the rain of water. Some crawling. Fighting. Frankie Bacon crossed with Lucian Freud. All from the horro page of his big art book. He held the door open for them and they followed him like the Pied Piper. Through the doors and along to the top of the fire escape. In half a minute everyone was drenched. Washed clean.

A team met him at the bottom of the stairs. People in shapeless uniforms with guns and wearing masks. Tear-gas canisters had been fired into the building. Someone pointed a German assault rifle at him. Water was cascading off the walls. Halon was belching out on the bottom floor. Behind him was a scene of panic.

Doc, you better put this on, a man said to him, holding out a set of goggles and a hose to breathe.

A fat man fell over the banister with a crash. Others started screaming. He put on the face mask.

Jesus. Don't anybody shoot. Shit, is there anything we can do, Doc?

A burst of automatic fire tore through the air-making pock-marks in the ceiling. The screaming men grew even more hysterical.

Don't shoot goddammit, Jesus.

He walked towards the glass doors and the exit.

Doc, where are you going?

He held up his left arm and, with his right he mimed a needle going into it. He pointed back at the men.

Getting some tranquilizer? the lieutenant asked.

He nodded.

What do we do with all these guys?

He pointed towards the exit.

Ok, the cop said. Get these crazy fuckers out of here. And keep your eye on 'em. And for Chrissake don't shoot.

He walked. He saw everything. Men were lying on the ground in discoloring sweaters, struggling with the sights on their weapons through the halon mist. One of the doors was cracked. The shards lying in front of him. The black loafer treaded between the feet of a spread-eagled cop, cracking on the glass.

He pushed the door open. His arm gleaming in the doctor's coat. He was nearly outside. Nearly. For the first time in . . . He noticed that the shard was in the shape of Tasmania. He looked up. In the car park the fire service had arrived. A skull and crossbones flying from the lead tender. He took off the mask and stepped. Stepped.

And then he was out. He breathed. The sunlight was dazzling. Swarming reflections on the chrome. People running like stagehands. Frenzied. Yelling at each other. Two men wrestled at a fire hydrant. The air by contrast was placid. Warm and rich. The smell was of the city and the river.

A memory tide that almost knocked him down. He angled ninety degrees, and checked himself. He was really free. Breathing, checking his wet clothes for blood. Not too much. The coat concealed it.

About him. The ballad of weapons. Faces. The fuzz of a dog.

He stopped.

He vomited coffee.

The grass. A sleeve. A lagoon of clouds.

Ugh, he said.

He looked up.

The building was behind him and under the unseen constellations of the sky.

Hunger lightened him and he knew that he was falling. The great bear tracked him as he fell.

CHAPTER THREE

Cats and dogs. Out of the black sky. Cold, salt tinged water hammering off the platform.

It's pissing down now.

I didn't bring my coat.

You didn't?

Nope.

Heh, heh. That'll learn you.

The wind is up. Whipping at my legs. Both hands, white. Holding down my skirt. I see a curve of a rainbow. An arc of water along the sheugh. A locomotive is belching out diesel fumes and leaking oil onto the famished concrete. Someone screams at the back of the line. There's a rumble of thunder, and in amongst the ambush of people there's a high-pitched jarring yell. Like teeth on a blackboard. I turn. The screamer is one of the McDowell twins. Spinning, making frail protestations to Johnny McGurk who has grabbed her from behind. In the last of the daylight. Tugged at her hair.

On the ground beneath me is the chorus of feet. The white socks and the wee black shoes. Wrappers. Two lines of legs and a broken trolley.

Johnny and the girl weren't seeing each other. But they've clicked. She is laughing and trying to grab at the jumper he's brandishing, matador fashion.

Olé, Johnny says, doing his best to make it sound sexual.

The ferry train has finished disgorging its passengers, who

walk out quickly under the ornate awning and then begin running when they get out from under the cover, going down the steps and into North Street. One woman slips and nearly goes on her arse. But her arm goes out and she rights herself. A group of kids is coming up the other way under the old North gate, hurrying in the storm and going even quicker now that they see the train.

We are waiting on the platform. At any moment the guard will let us through. I look at the ground, at a hundred pairs of regulation black shoes fidgeting among the guano and the litter. The younger kids are yelling. Waiting. The cries like songs of tiny expectation.

It will be a mad rush, I say.

I know. Jesus. Do you want me to keep you a seat? Sarah replies.

I nod. The guard's arm falls and the scramble begins. Sarah with her long legs and lanky frame, elbowing the younger boys out of the way. In a tide of rain, she runs down the platform. In the lead pack of girls.

Go on ya girl, ye, I shout after her.

Someone bumps into me and almost sends me flying.

Ya wee skitter, I say half-heartedly.

I watch the melee until they reach the carriages, everyone pushing and shoving, soaked in the rain and the dirt and the yellow light of the violent dusk.

I walk to the edge of the overhang. Just out of the downpour. Another foot and I will be up to my thighs in rebounding water. My hand is in my pocket, touching my keys and a flower of tissue paper. Sarah is not doing so well now. Fighting to get in through the doors of the carriage.

I'm standing in the dry, enormous drips teeming down in front of me. The wee muckers are rougher to her. She's getting drenched. Pushing through as best she can. As she tries to get ahead of a group of younger boys one of them pulls up her skirt. The wee shites. She turns to retaliate and they are past her. In front of me the rivulets are pouring under my soles, sour and clogged by garbage. There's a magazine page that someone's scrawled on—Mrs Thatcher wears a wig, the felt tip says and for a moment I wonder if it's true.

There's more thunder and I look up as the station lights gutter on. Sarah has gotten a seat at the back of the smoking carriage and waves to me through the window, her arm above the hubbub and the fumes.

Still in the shelter, I hesitate. From a feeling of contradiction. The guard's face is plain and absolute. Bored beyond belief.

I watch the alternatives, idling between them. As if the two are unambiguous. To stay or to go. To be dry and miss the train. Or to catch it and get wet. My hand sways. It's really pissing down in front of me. Like a wall. I follow my fingers and swing into the downpour and out again like a pendulum. It is beautiful, the rain. Hard. Ricocheting off the bent aluminum. Like tracer.

I put a socked foot out, and then an arm. I pause and feel the refrigerated day. The guard is looking at me. His beard bristles.

Come on, he says. It won't dissolve ya.

I shrug and run. In an amble. Like a cow with BSE. My hair wettening. I am the last one on the train. The guard waits. I reach the end car and step up into the carriage. I angle round. The bearded man is cut away above the brow. Where his hat is. I close the door, behind me, one arm through the window. It slams into the locking mechanism. The guard blows the whistle. With a jolt the engine pulls away. I can see the station moving through the black diesel fumes. I lean in.

I stare down the aisle to see if I can spot Sarah, but the train is bunged. Boys and girls between the ages of eleven and eighteen. In the land of eyes. And hands. In the same dark uniform.

Half the younger kids are standing, hanging from the ceiling grips. And playing. Like chimpanzees. And for others the floor's awake, and the seats are used as toys and battlements. A few brave souls are doing homework, only to see their exercise books grabbed and tossed about.

I look along the row of crew cuts. Some of the wilder boys have initials carved in them above the back of the neck. And with all the craic it's difficult to pick Sarah out. The carriage sways and I reach my hand up to the plastic-covered pole. Ridges fit into my palm like goose pimples. I try again to spot her but it's hard to see. No one is able to keep still and there are people smoking now.

Give it back.

No way.

Please.

No way wee girl.

My head is swimming. The air a snow of slobber and insults and a heaving mass of excited wains. Some at the nectar of sweetie bags or at the window. Some talking. Others mummified or fighting. And where the groups of boys and girls meet, still others, showing off and flirting. I walk forward from the door. In front of me two second-year boys are swapping *Back to the Future* trading cards and a girl is picking bubble gum out of her hair.

I don't want another DeLorean, I've four already.

Aye but yon's some car. Belfast-made you know?

Aye I know, so was the *Titanic*.

Another ginger-haired boy is getting the Indian burn. The excitement building now as the train gets faster. And then I see it: a hand waving at me with a ring on the middle finger.

Beside it the terrace of the buildings slipping and chugging away towards the city. The train moving with a fair rock from side to side. The hand is connected to a blazer, bunched at the shoulder. Limpid and trembling at the same time. The blond hair and smile belong to Sarah. Her face slightly asymmetrical. She is sitting at the back with the smokers, right enough.

Shit, I say, ungratefully.

I sling the bag over my shoulder and begin to make my way down the aisle. I grab onto the handles at the top of the seats. They are cold and made of steel with the grease of other people's sweat sticking to my fingers. I lurch with the carriage. The younger children are messing. Playing gegs on each other. Ladders of games and practical jokes. Attention getting. I am tensed for something and walking balanced. I slink and breathe between handholds. But no foot comes out to trip me. No hand grabs at my pony tail. Everything is a shattering of noise. And I know. It is not because I am older. No one so much as sticks out their tongue or throws their hymn book. I am ignored. Ahead of me two boys move aside from politeness. Even. I step into the gap like a creature unable to be seen.

Sorry about the smoke, Sarah says moving her bag off the seat she has been keeping for me.

It's ok.

What's up?

What do you mean?

What's wrong?

Nothing.

Are you sure?

Nothing's wrong, ok?

Alright.

I sit down opposite her. We are beside two boys from about the third year. Both have razor cuts, fags grubbed in their fists. Trying hard, but they don't seem older than about fifteen. One of them stares at me. Green eyes sleekit. Narrow. Blond face hair, in an almost goatee. Lips and a tongue big and flared, fat on his cheek like a baby's.

What're you looking at wee doll? he asks.

We pause. The train rolling. Aquatic mouths moving in and out. His friend nudges him with his elbow. His stretched hand out. Dirt beneath his fingernails. Sniggering. Eyes bent up. Neither is wearing a uniform. They could be any wee hood from Belfast. Out from the bodegas, taking a train ride to find some trouble, and either prod or taig. Impossible to tell yet.

Are you talking to me, ya wee fuck?

Aye, he says and pausing for effect, surprised to see a fucking camel talk back.

He laughs. His pal is already in stitches. Sarah is red. Immediately. My hands whiten. The air so tense and tight it could rip the barnacles from the back of a boat. I am angry. I look at her. She is embarrassed. Beyond belief. I know what she'll say to her ma: Dead affronted, so I was. I stare at the boy again. His nose is small and off center. A bent-tooth smile. There is a scar below his eye. Hardly a knife, at his age. He is chubby. It does not detract from the general impression, and despite the fact that he's from the city there's something tangible and unsunk about him. He is not unattractive.

Ash is falling from the cigarette and blowing back onto his trouser leg, a breeze from the top slide window.

I breathe in through my nose. The floor is filthy with chip packets, coke cans and sweetie wrappers. The sound behind me is an introverted bedlam. I can see one of the twins pleading for her pencil case back. In the window. A group of boys is using it as a football. One of them is Johnny, his loyalties torn in two. But he can't lose face. Judy McDowell is close to tears. The train bumps over a set of points. A girl yells. Someone laughs like Popeye. Pandemonium and the two wains in front of me are like oul Moloch and Belial. Bad lads.

Oh my God you're such a hard man, I say, and wait until he has turned to look at me. Picking on a girl with glasses.

Fuck, they don't come much tougher than you, boy. Do they? Jesus, I'm tremblin'. What are you gonna do next, hit me?

I say all this snide with the muzzle finally off. For the first time today. Letting it all go.

Maybe I faaking will, he replies.

Aye and maybe I'll straighten your fucking teeth for ya before ya get a bloody chance.

I'd like to— he begins, his cheeks contorting, with a kind of rage.

Christ don't make your face go like that wee lad, you're ugly enough.

You're one to talk.

I am, but Jesus I tell ya I've seen abortions more attractive than you, so I have.

Like faak ya have.

I look at Sarah and back at him. I want to reassure her. But her head is way down.

That's your comeback? Like fuck you have? Oscar Wilde lives. Jesus. Tell ya if beauty were cities, you'd be Beirut.

He says nothing. I'm still thinking.

I mean, what are you like, wee lad?

I turn to Sarah again. Now she is looking at me, concern on her face.

Here's a fella, I say, nodding my head over at the boy, that got a bit too much of the oul ugly stick when the bad fairy came acalling. An' yer man there what's he laughing for? I've seen better looking creatures on the bottom of my shoe.

Aye you have? the other boy says and then says nothing.

Aye well you're one to talk about ugly. You look like you've got the fucking Cave Hill on yer back.

Nasty.

An you're one to talk yourself, slab. You're so fat I bet your ma irons your shirts out in the fucking street. Who makes your

57

y fronts? Boeing? No wait a minute. I apologize. You don't wear them do ya? Not when you're living up in Bellevue Zoo picking the fleas out of your fucking arse every morning.

He hides a grin. His friend is quietly appalled at the way things are turning out. Sarah is almost in tears. Her lips are quivering. Her face is the color of tomato. I want to lick my finger, touch her cheek and say tssss.

Rainwater still runs down the inside of the carriage, but it's easing up.

I'd rather pick fleas out of my arse than go round like the Hunchback of faaking Notterdam.

It had to end there. Not because I am hurting. It is my stop. The train is slowing. To the left is the hospital, surrounded by oaks, ivy-clad in a smothering of trees. A fence, and then the field where the swings used to be. The sound is the open beaks of birds and the disc brakes.

Dumb, I shake my head.

The new fold housing. I turn and look through the other window and I can see the Lough and the graffitied platform of the Halt. Remember 1690, it says. And UVF. And a homily about gray skies south of the border. The rain is coming down in torrents. But lessening. I see the power station and the beach. Seaweed comes in with the cold. A thick smell. I'm half exhilarated by the talk. I see the fold in his jeans. The broad back under his jacket.

Dumb, I mean, Jesus. I've seen amoebas smarter than you.

I stand. The doors open.

Least I'm not a faaking camel.

You seem to know a lot about animals. Probably because your ma fucked one to have you. What she do, screw a beached whale or something, fatso?

I have to brush past him to get out. The atmosphere is less menacing. I bump Sarah. The boy is smiling despite himself.

Mask down. And it is infectious. Only the two of us know we aren't completely serious. Sarah is showed up, a beetroot face, and murmurs like incantations coming out of her mouth. His mate is looking at his laces. Sickly yellow on his neck. I lean out of the window and open the door. The sea air is bracing but I feel bad to leave Sarah there with the two of them.

Give me a ring, I say to her. The boy looks at me and opens his mouth to say something. Conciliation is in his sweet green eyes. But he changes his mind and turns away. I step out towards the wet concrete. As the train squeals and shudders to a halt.

I am on the ground. I turn to close the door. But his hands are in the gap. A scar on the left runs along the forefinger all the way to his wrist. Both hands are on the frame up to the knuckles. Doing nothing, strong. The other doors are opening. His hands move. A wounded circle. Masculine. I cough. Our eyes meet and he slams the door.

Cunt, his friend shouts after me. Brave now, that the carriage is moving once again.

Wee fucking shite, I yell back. Unsatisfied. And watch as the train heads towards the headland and the power station. Four other kids have gotten off. They walk by me standing there paralyzed, and clonk up to the footbridge. The rain is only spitting now and from the sky. I can tell the evening is clearing up.

I stretch my back, rotating the shoulders. I look over the water at the yellow cranes of the shipyard. Giant even here. Seven miles up the coast. In the city. The sun is behind the clouds. Almost down. Dusk is here already. The wind from the shore is bitter. I walk to the bridge. The plastic from a six-pack is lying on the ground. I kick it with my left foot.

A grayness off the Lough. Unmoving, it is a thirty minute portrait of the water. Gulls come to the slope of breeze blocks.

There's rubbish on the sand and driftwood run aground. A box marked: oranges. I took pictures here once. I stand on a paper and a rolled-up cigarette. The smell is burnt diesel and overnight piss at the train shelter. Pictures of a man and woman having it away on the beach. I step up and my sole clangs on the metal. Each landing place is ridged with corrosive bumps of cast iron. I left the photo roll in my drawer, undeveloped. And now it is gone, thrown out, I expect.

A dead jellyfish is in the corner of the stair. Wet and on its back. The eyes dug out.

The night's fingers are on the islands in the sea. The lighthouse sweeping up the horizon. Divis Mountain blistering. The sun unclimbing over its horns.

At the footbridge there is a terrace of grass. The metal tie of rocks and coral. In a unison of iron. Crystalized leaves, the odor of earth and clay. The sides are sheer and painted green and high to prevent people jumping over onto trains. Or dropping things. Like shocks and cut-off razor wire. And stones from in between the sleepers. Not that it does stop them. I sling the bag onto my shoulder and put my foot on the first step. A tear runs down my cheek, much to my surprise.

I focus on reading the graffiti. They've painted the bridge with a special solvent so that spray paint doesn't work anymore. It's all names in biro or felt-tip. Or scraped in with something.

The red-brick road bridge is where the creative stuff is. Catholics must die, Fuck the Pope, No Pope Here . . .

The words Rathcoole Kai have been scored out with a wavy line of black paint. Someone has attempted to write the word wankers over the word Kai.

I look at the water as a breather. It's dark out now and it is only four o'clock. In the rock pools contaminated oil drums have mingled in the shore, and in the divots diesel floats and laps itself. The sun is behind the Knockagh mountain and the sea is sad and quiet.

Back to the graffiti. It makes me think. Rathcoole is a dive four miles up the railway line. In another turf. A worse place than this even. A prison of burnt-out shops and highrises. At a junction of pepper moss and sewers. Full of wee hard men. UVF and UDA.

I had to ask what the Kai meant once. Sarah told me. It was too obscure even for me. It means Kill all Irish.

Brains being not their strong point, I suppose.

I put my right foot on the second step. Water is dripping down the grating. Glazed and dirty. I read the scratchings: Mike and Sharon. TLND. Alison loves . . . Now my back is sore again. I walk up three more steps. On the County Down side of the Lough the stars are coming out. And beneath them, the red lights of Bangor and the Copelands that hyphenate the shore line. Andrew and Rhona TLND. Never forsake . . . Kill all . . . I touch my hand against the metal and run my finger over the words. As I step up. Marty. Gail. True Love Never Dies. Letters weaving nocturnes. It is not easy to think about love. Among these people.

I'm so slow at walking that now above the lamps of the dual carriageway the stars are thick. Bunched like vertebrae. And jungle shadow. Marking lines in the heavens like faraway roads. Places to escape to.

And I can see now that there is nothing melancholy about the water. Darkening. It's me. I'm on a downer from the argument in the train. Everything was going fine. Until that final "cunt." That hurt.

The wee skitter. The wee bloody . . .

I can barely take a breath.

The bloody wee shite-brained wee bastard. Wee minging dirty, wee piece of crap. Wee piece of . . . piece . . . of . . .   61

I breathe out and unclench my hands, doing it quick to make a clicking noise.

Suddenly all the street lights come on—the way they would for Arthur Fonzarelli. They've come on as I was looking at them but I can't be arsed to make a wish.

My socks are way down at the ankles. The fingers of my left hand are turning blue. In the cold. Bad circulation probably. Hair is blowing round my neck and shoulders and from here I can see the last of the train slip round the bend of Black Head. Two blinking faces on the last car. I rub my eyes. Headlights. It's almost silent. The roar of the traffic kind of anonymous as it comes up to the main rush hour home.

To the left of me now is the house that's pitched on a tiny cliff over the sand. Someone has a bulb on in the hall. Small threads of saffron fusing the ground of curtains. The window shakes its branches. I like the house. It has two nibbled eaves and an outside chimney of red brick. Like a nose. A homely place. I can smell the turf burning in their grate. I've often wondered who lives there. A single wire droops from the slate roof to the wood-stained telegraph pole. The wall is an off-white and the roof has curves like an eiderdown. It's like something from the nursery rhymes.

I walk on the horizontal part of the bridge, touching the collection of rainwater on the handrail. I used to dream about owning that house and building a massive bay window to look out to sea at the parasol of islands, the fat container boats and the new and shining ferry ships.

Another train is coming from the opposite direction. Its hooter blowing. Like a coyote. I circle round wet cardboard and the smell of meths. If I lived there, from that house window I could have seen all the way over to Scotland. If I also had binoculars. Bi-noc-u-lars. The back door opens into the early night. And a woman pulls in a cat-shaped cat.

Multiplications, salt fumes and the singsong of automobiles. Conflicts. Keith Simpson told me that he can see Truro from his house on Islandmagee. Past Ailsa Craig. At the throat of Loch Ryan.

In the waters of the sea.

And I believe him. It's only seventeen miles over the North Channel. And the reverse is certainly true. When I was in Galloway. From the harbor at Portpatrick, or the hotel on the hill. Playing bowling. We could see the buds of the glens and the Antrim Mountains. On the peninsula. And Kilroot, the chimney bright on that clear day. I saw it myself without the scope. The regatta in the summer. In the heat. The beads of phosphorus over the cobalt ocean. Out from the pub with my belly full. My hand up to my eyes, leaning on the rail, I could just see the finger of smoke. On the iguana back of hills. Delicate. Down from Slemish and Tor Head. Ash from low-grade fuel oil. Burning. The chimney huge in the crucible of landscape. I laughed. It was like an upturned hand giving the whole mainland, an insult.

Sarah says that from her house she can see people playing golf in Scotland with her daddy's telescope. Always takes it too far that wee girl.

At the end of the bridge I let the bag fall off my shoulder and carry it in my right hand. I swing it over the metal. The bottom d of adidas brushing against the ground.

My shoe takes the form of the pavement and I am off the metal surface and nearly at the road. Under my feet now is a new, weird kind of tarmac, smooth and spongy and in front of me is the broken sea wall, recently mended with fence wood that has been all roughened up and scrawled over. The hole in the stone has been there since the accident, when someone drove down the hill at eighty-five and through the traffic lights. Which anyway were red. The car, a souped-up Fiesta with a horn that whistled "Dixie," aquaplaned and fractured through the stone cladding. He yelling and the horn playing and it almost made it over the railway tracks into the water. But the wall was too thick. And the momentum not enough. The driver was the brother of a friend of my brother's. He had been drinking all evening at Dobbins Inn: Harp and vodka chasers. Pissed up, and after a row with his girlfriend, fogged up emotionally. It was an accident and not deliberate, the paper said. Saying that, maybe to avoid a scandal. But who knows for sure?

I walk up to the edge of the road. The cars are tight and moving faster than they should. The train passengers who were up ahead of me are still waiting to cross. Along the incline on the other side of the road, traffic is backed up to the police station and the castle. All down the Marine Highway. Jammed.

Now that I think about it, there must be something seductive about a car in the water. A familiar object in an unusual place. Two years ago a Volkswagen washed up on the beach. And on Christmas Eve a woman drove off the end of the fisherman's quay into the tide. In front of the boozed-up Saturday night Chinese take-out crowd who cheered her the whole way down the pier and then did nothing when the car sank like a stone. She did it after a fight with her mother about marrying a black man from the university. Took her dog with her, someone told me. Though none of that was in the paper either; but afterward everyone in the know was saying how sorry they felt for the poor dog.

I stand on the edge of the road behind a couple of fourth years. And clear my throat significantly, but they don't move out of my way. Normally I would think nothing of it. But the fight on the train has unnerved me. I push past them and stand beside a man in a suit. To reassert my authority. Cars whiz by, one stops to turn to the right. An outrageous driver in a blue Ford Escort overtakes the sitting car on the outside. We all have to step back to let him through. There are only inches between his bumper and the curb. His wheels skid.

Fuck, somebody says and we all move up again.

The light goes orange and then red and I walk over. The chipped stones are like tiny axe heads. The cars wait. Suddenly and for the time it takes my legs to cross, I need to shit. There is a pound coin on the ground, spotted in the sand and granite. But there is a load in my arse the size of a redwood, and I can't think about anything else.

I ignore the cash and walk quickly past the corner house with the alsatian and the new timbers on the side wall. Painted black, Bavarian style. There is a palm tree in the front garden and ivy on the hard stone of the south-facing portico. Eclectic is the polite way to describe the effect. I walk past the Residential Home on the opposite corner. The pumice stone wall has been lowered to let the residents see out. Barbed wire is in its place. Zer vill be no escape, I say to myself. To my right is the car park. Large potholes filled with rainwater. Beat-up seventies cars and a Range Rover. The supermarket and the adjoining shops are busy. Especially the chippy and the off license. The offy. Where ma sometimes goes.

All around is darkness and the rain is definitely over. The queue for the chippy is out onto the pavement. A couple of boys are sitting under the Big Light and drinking.

I look over into the McGuires'. Their big white horse is there today and his chickens are feeding in the mud. His yard is junked with tires and bits of cars. Mr McGuire has hung an arc light from the phone line and is working at an outboard-motor engine. Swiping at moths, in his Ozark overalls. He waves over at me and I wave back but I speed my pace up as I feel the stool begin to work its way down my bowels. Jesus, it's a monster and it's almost in my whips.

Hey, Mr McGuire says, and I point at my watch to show I'm in a hurry. He nods to show he's got the message and goes back to his motor.

Mr McGuire has been building a boat in his back yard for as long as I can remember. Once, about five years ago, I asked him what for. The Ice Age, he said. We haven't mentioned it since. It's our secret, I think. But at the rate he's going I'm sure the ice'll be here by the time he's done.

Ahead of me a woman crosses the road from the fold housing. And behind her, huge rooks lift off from the trees at the old almshouse, to the left beyond the shops. The building is nineteenth century gothic surrounded by chestnuts and limbless sycamores and a cast iron fence, two kids high. We are surrounded by old peoples' homes and hospices around here. Because of the sea air, is my theory.

Frustratingly, a Cortina stops me from crossing the entrance to the car park. I can almost feel the turd come out. The driver waves me over and I practically run all the way to my front gate. The hedge is trimmed and scraping at my hand. A Pepsi bottle has been shoved down the hollow of the concrete pillar. The top of the pillar is lying in the garage. It has been shoved off too many times. None of us wants to keep putting it back. Not my brother nor ma, and I don't have the strength. I push down the kinked handle and walk up the drive to the patio. My mother is in the kitchen.

Hello.

The tiles are gleaming. At the cooker something is boiling in the pot. Potatoes. Shapeless meat is under the grill. The kitchen is small. In the middle of the room, the breakfast bar rests on a single aluminum pole. The washer lies broken at the bottom of the shaft. A newspaper is open near the fruit bowl. She is standing at the sink washing the bone-handled knife. A crack runs up the grip. She uses it to peel the spuds. It was a wedding present. The last of the set and is useful for nothing else. Her hair is redder today than before. I close the door on the wing. Her eyes are puffed. I can see the peels of onion on the table. But I know it isn't that. The picture of my da has moved.

Hi mum.

I drop my bag in the kitchen and start to pull off my coat.

Did you have a good day in school?

Can't talk, I need to go to the loo. The coat comes off my arm and I push open the door in the bathroom. It's vacant and I am about to enter when I remember. I go back into the kitchen and get my bag. Oh God. I am almost getting a masochistic pleasure out of this. I close the door. Pushing the lock on the handle. I pull up the seat and hoike up my skirt. I pull down my panties and am surprised not to see half a clump already in there.

I sit on the toilet and in the three seconds before I finally shit I experience a masl of pleasure. My teeth gritted. I squeeze my bowels twice. The scats are spread out like polka dots.

When I have done, I stand up. I reach for my bag and pull out the camera. My arsehole is itching so I go fast. I wrap the camera around my wrist and pick up the toilet brush. I arrange the half-submerged turds until they are evenly distributed throughout the bowl. Eight egg-shaped mounds floating in the artificial water. Fake blue. The texture is dense and rich. They took like a cluster of drumlin islands in Strangford Lough. I set the brush back in its lemon holder. I turn on the flash and wait a second. The warning light winks off. I get down on my knees and, getting close, I take a Polaroid of the arrangement. I set the camera down on the lime-green carpet. I watch the picture develop itself. And wipe myself off with the Inversoft bathroom tissue. It takes four intense wipes until I am done. I wipe a final time and check to see if the paper has discolored. It hasn't so I toss the scrunched-up tissue into the bowl and press down on the handle. Gushing indigo water takes away the paper, the urine and the excrement, leaving only the photograph as evidence that it was there at all.

The phone rings as I come out.

It's for you, mum says.

Hello.

It's me.

Hi Sarey.

Hi.

I sit down on the carpet. The paper bumps in through the letter box. The headline is still folded-up but the first three letters are MUR.

Sorry about the stuff on the train. Are you alright? She asks. Concern makes her voice go all tremolo.

Yeah, it's me that should be sorry. I should have just ignored them. Did they hassle you once I got off?

Nah.

I lift the phone off the table and set it on the floor.

You were wild.

Who me?

Aye you. Your head's a marley. Them lads couldda had knives or anything, so they could.

Ach they were just wee messers.

Well anyway you gave as good as you got.

Don't I always.

Yeah . . . So you're alright?

Yeah.

Is your mum ok by the way?

I don't know, why?

Nothing?

What?

Nothing.

What? I say getting frustrated but not upset. I am still feeling guilty about the ride this afternoon.

You always think something is wrong with somebody, I do not say.

What?

Well, nothing really, she just didn't sound, you know, she just didn't sound like as cheerful as she usually is.

Aye you might be on to something. I think she was thinking about dad.

Your da?

Uh huh.

I thought you said he, er . . . Sorry.

Look it doesn't bother me. I never think about him. He's dead as far as I'm concerned. I don't care.

There is a silence on the line. I can hear the static.

Neither of us wanted to bring this up. I've only talked to her about this in confidence. She feels bad repeating it to anyone, even me.

Ehm, well tell her I was asking for her, won't ya?

Yeah I will.

Ok I better go, dinner's nearly ready.

Alright, talk to ya later at GB, you are going aren't ya?

Yeah.

Ok.

See ya.

See ya, wouldn't want to be ya.

I put the phone down and set it back up on the table. As I do so it rings again. I pick it up.

Hello, the voice says.

Who is it? mum shouts.

It's my teacher, Mister Preston, I say with my hand over the receiver.

Hi, I say shyly and close the kitchen door.

69

I was just calling you to remind you to bring your stuff for Art.

Oh . . . yeah.

You hadn't forgotten had you?

No.

Good, that's it.

Ok.

Goodnight.

Uh, goodnight.

Don't let the bugs bite.

Bye, I say and put down the phone.

I'm going up to my room, I shout but she can't hear me over the noise of the water boiling and the sucking of the extractor fan. My face is red in the mirror. Ma has left my coat outside the door. I take it and carry it down the hall. I stop outside my room. My brother's door is on the right. I walk past it and push on the handle of my door. A plastic sign says: Do Not Enter. The room is cold, so I set down the bag and close the window. I pull the blinds and switch on the tv. One channel is showing a promo for a new Woody Allen film. I've seen every previous one and there are a few scenes of New York that get me interested. But the promo ends and I have to start getting changed out of my uniform, switching the channel to a Bugs Bunny cartoon. I loosen my tie and fold it on the desk. It's the one were the gremlin has taken control of the plane. The plane's a Dakota. I unbutton my white shirt. Before I forget, I put the photograph with the others in the bottom drawer of my desk. The gremlin has sabotaged the controls and set it on a collision course with the airfield. Bugs is turning every shade of green and flattening. I set my skirt on the bed and pull on a pair of jeans. I put on my blue sweatshirt. I open the top cupboard and place the skirt and tie neatly on the shelf. I throw the shirt and socks in the corner and lie down on my bed. I reach over and grab a handful of the photographs. Just as I do so the aeroplane that has been hurtling towards the earth stops in mid-air, a few inches above the ground. Bugs is perplexed by this. But the gremlin laughs. The plane has run out of fuel and cannot pummel into the runway by the strict rules of cartoon physics.

Your dinner, mum shouts threateningly. It sounds like "you're dinner." I imagine her in cannibal get-up, and grin.

I sit up from the waist and walk to the kitchen. I settle down to eat. It is sausages and mashed potatoes. With scallions and milk in them. Champ. My hair is everywhere. Tangled.

You're a pochle, she says.

I make a hole in the center of the potatoes and drop in a knob of butter. It melts and oozes down the side. Mum is smoking and looking out the window. My brother is late. She can't see anything because it is pitch black outside. I listen. The silver paper in the grill is crinkling. The wind has died.

And the tv is still blaring in my room.

CHAPTER FOUR

Slaters, clegs, midgees. Insects everywhere. It was the first thing he noticed. Crawling over the weeds and the uncultivated flowering plants. Wasps, striped on the pollen, and flies. Bigger than bog flies, or horse flies. Mosquitoes were hovering close to him, attracted to the smell of blood on his lips. He let them land on him, feeling nothing.

He was leaning against the back of a tree. Thirty yards from the lawn dotted with police cars. It was very bright outside. There were new colors: aquamarines, golds and ocher. He was sensible to everything and still dripping wet, sitting on his hands.

Whoowee buddy is that some scene.

Blinks of two seconds or more. A man squatting on his honkers in front of him. The man fazing in and out of vision. The blades of hammers, pumping in his head.

Shit, I tell ya, that's crazy. You know, no disrespect or anything, but I knew something like this would happen. All them loons in the one place. Inevitable. We're too easy on em. Hey are you ok, Doc, you look kinda woozy. Are you ok?

He nodded. Behind the man was only cartoon violence. Cartoon dialogue come to that.

You know it's probably the tear gas, some dickless shit panicked and let off a couple of cylinders. You'll be all right. I've seen it before.

He nodded again. And smiled.

We can take you over to the hospital, the man said. He was

in a red uniform, with a baseball cap. T shirt. A paramedic, he imagined. Not a peeler.

He shook his head and tried to say something. But it was hard to speak, to get new words out. Hard.

Ok, whatever you think.

The man pointed with his thumb.

I'll be over there. If you need anything just holler. The man stood up and blocked the sun. Almost turned.

He picked a leaf off the ground and felt it. Touched it against his cheek. It had the smell of gasoline. He put it into the top pocket of his white coat.

Just lay under that tree, Doc, and I'll check back with you in a while. Gonna have a lot more serious injuries in a minute if this bullshit keeps up.

The grass was soft and pliable under his back. Bending like peat soil. Ants were scrabbling everywhere in the shade. Car engines snarled through the air. He put his hand up to his eyes to see better. It was a scene of anarchy. Men and women in an assortment of uniforms were running aimlessly, swearing, most with weapons drawn, still expecting trouble. Some of the mental patients were walking delirious in between the police cars and the fire trucks, panicking to be outside in the natural light, and already—to cap it all—the tv crews and news teams were showing up. Vans with aerials on the roof. A couple of camera crews looking for people to interview. More fire tenders honking their way down the driveway.

The paramedic gave him a tired look and shook his head. He was right it was bollicksed up now but soon it would start to get organized and the cops would be coming over to check everybody out. He wouldn't have a story.

It was time to go.

Crazy, the paramedic said, giving him the ok sign and walking back to an ambulance, leaving him alone.

He sat just for another moment. Easy in the shadow and the protection of clouds. Dogs howling somewhere. Or people. And the sound of a helicopter now, landing at the back of the institution. A noise like a Bell Huey. He stood up and scanned the car park.

It wasn't an easy decision. Flashes of memory were coming back to him. Cars were cars. But he had rules for everything. Scenes spilling from behind the courtyards and the terraces. On nettles and deadly nightshade. A rudder of movement behind him, more yelling and the sounds of confusion. Ethically there wasn't much between them. In the great hall of capital. GM, Ford and Chrysler were all antisemites. Then there was Nazi VW, BMW and Merc. And of course the Japs. The oul boy from Ship Repair said they were the worst, he'd been on the Burma railroad. And brought in as clear-out detail after Hiroshima. His legs had been wasting away for years. Evil wee yella bastards. He walked, falling and righting himself with every step.

He wanted a Brit car, but there wasn't a Jag or an MG among the lot of them. Not that he could see.

An elongated Toyota was the nearest car to the exit and, forgetting about his friend from the shipyard, he decided that that would have to do.

He walked over to the car and stared inside. The door was locked. Inside, the wheel was free. No club, no chain and it even had a radio. He looked around. All attention was focused on the building. He paused for a moment and checked the sky. Animals dead and alive spinning in circles around the building. A few hundred feet up. A slobber of cloven hoofs and sulfur. He shivered. They were up there, but there was purple behind them and that was fine. It would draw them like a net and it was ok to go on. When his eyes opened they were gone.

He put his palm against the hot roof. There was no trick. He hesitated for just a second. Unsure. In mid-hit. But then memory took over. He drew back his arm and then slammed his elbow hard into the glass. Laterally, arcing it backward. The window smashed. Fragments spraying onto the seat and others embedding themselves in his coat. He winced as glass cut into his knuckles. The car alarm went off with a loud whooping noise. He froze for a moment, his hand in through the window, but no one turned. One particle of glass had grazed his cheek. Blood was running down into his mouth.

He fumbled for the lock on the inside of the door and pulled it up. He opened the door carefully with his left hand. He crouched down and hastily began picking most of the bigger fragments of glass off the seat. He threw them on the ground and sat down. The car was baked hot and smelled musty. He searched in the glove compartment and found a flashlight. He picked it up. It was silver and said "Rayon" on the side.

He took it in his right hand and thumped it at the plastic on the steering column. On the second blow the plastic covering came right off.

Like he'd done a hundred times before back home, he fused the wires in the ignition system. The engine growled into life and the alarm canceled itself. He did another check to see if anyone was paying attention, but the noise of the helicopter was drowning out everything else. He put his hands on the wheel and slipped the car into gear.

He sat there for a moment, eager to get away but disorientated. Hours and days were decomposing in his head. Bleeding incidents in front of him. Images of violence remembered. He was rational enough to know that things would be hard coming off the medication. He looked in the backseat to see if there was anything he could use. There were papers that he couldn't read and an action figure. He took it in his hand and held it in front of him. It was a toy soldier in a commando uniform. With a jet pack and a gun and arms and legs that moved. He picked it up and dug out the bead eyes with his fingers, blinding the soldier, and then with the lighter he melted the plastic over where the eyes had been. He set the toy up on the dashboard and, satisfied, put his hands back on the wheel. It would be his totem.

Driving was easier than he thought. He angled out of the car park and swerved the Toyota over onto the mowed lawn to let an ambulance pass him on the narrow drive. A purple asterisk and a snake flashing by him on the side. A man in a black uniform was lowering the metal barrier at the end of the road. He rolled the car at five miles per hour and waved into the wooden box. A cellophane pane separated him from the security guard. His face was dark and lined, gray hair poking out from underneath his hat. Fine hair like copper wire. The radio was on, playing commercials. He looked over at him and knew he had to say something. The guard glanced up, his eyes, tired and bloodshot. With the remains of the car window wound down both men could see the other clearly. A look passed between them. No glass showed in the window. Both men smiled. The car smelled of hot leather. The barrier rose and he drove out onto the road.

Driving on the highway was more difficult. The lanes moved fast and ineptly. The cars were big and clumsy. Trucks thundered by him shaking the vehicle and sucking it near to the huge wheels. Horns blared beneath him. Brakes screeching all the time. Taxis weaving in and out.

Through it all it was hard to see. A conflagration of buildings laced the skyline. The city was close. He was moving fast and wanted to move faster to see how far he could go. But his foot skulked from the gas pedal. Easy up and resting. Toes clenched in the tight shoes.

It was like being in a fairground ride. With someone else in control. Or like he was driving for the first time with all the other cars his enemy. He drove quickly until he was sweating too much to see. His face in the mirror the color of alabaster, his hands cold and damp. Ahead the road was closed in by yellow lanes. A field to his left, brown and expansive. So large it made his neck twitch. White clouds touched the ground behind an empty stand. Men in padding and uniforms squatted in lines facing each other. They ran and then some took their helmets off and he saw that they were only boys. The ones near the fence had paint on their faces. Lines under the eyes. He turned back to look at the road in front of him. His shoulders were starting to shake now, and he felt hungry. All those wall taps he'd blotted out. He needed to stop the car. He spotted a turn-off up ahead and pulled the car off the highway into a tree-lined street.

He'd driven into a suburban picture. It was quiet. The leaves were gold here. He slotted the car behind a white Mercedes. The sun glinting off its hood, harsh and garish. The lawns were neatly parceled and trimmed. One or two had sprinklers making rainbows in the air above the grass. He put the stick shift into neutral and let the engine tick over. He found the pack of cigarettes and lit one, smoking it down quickly in desperate, gasping breaths. His hands were really trembling, red traces under the fingernails, rounded where he'd bitten them down. He threw the stub out of the window. The engine coughed but righted itself again. He checked the fuel gauge. A quarter full. A man was painting the timber frame of his house. Black paint. He was halfway up a ladder. The house was mock Tudor. The brush moved in tiny sweeps as if it were working on a canvas. The man was moving slowly, taking a full minute to descend another rung. A child was playing with a basketball in the house next door. A small kid with red hair in a t shirt and baggy denims. A net was nailed above the garage door. Not once did the basketball make it into the hoop, not even near to the ring. He watched the child for a moment and then leaned his head out of the window and sniffed the air. The smell of cut grass caught him like an uppercut. Dense and singular, he drank it in like spring water. Another old man stopped beneath the ladder, wearing slacks and a porkpie hat.

Afternoon Henry.

Hey Frank how are ya?

Not too bad, busy day huh?

Yup.

Been at it all morning?

Uh huh.

Mmm. Taking it right careful.

Sure am.

What, er, what type of paint are you using there?

Oh I don't know, stuff I always use.

He coughed from some residual smoke in his lungs. He leaned his head back into the car and put the radio on.

You're listening to the Accu weather forecast on WCBS, weather reports every ten minutes. Today sunny, with the high at sixty-five, low mid-forties. Clouding over tonight, the chance of precipitation: twenty percent . . .

The basketball bounced all the way to the road, trundling downhill towards his car.

Be careful, David, someone shouted from inside the house. The boy ran and caught the ball. Shamed, he turned and walked back, his head slunk on his chest.

You know with one coat you . . .

Well I've always done two coats and never had any reason to complain.

It'd be quicker that's all as I'm saying. What with the rain coming.

Rain coming. Are you sure?

Tonight I reckon and all of tomorrow.

Well I don't know about that.

He pressed a button and the radio was tuned to jazz now, which he could only ever take in the evenings, back when he'd been blitzed and wanted to faze out to something. He turned it off without hunting for a better station.

The afternoon sun fell in a heavy accumulation of light. Fine dust was stirred on the road by a passing truck on the express-way. Leaves gathering in the gutter, fresh and untainted by decay. The old men talking, the boy playing, traffic dead all down the lonely street. Still air folded itself tight over the car, pressing hard on the window. He could almost feel the wind-shield buckle under the oppressive sky. A chill had moved amongst the trees making the big oaks sway in a gust that had no wind.

For no reason a dog sleeping on a porch rose in hackles and slipped into the shadows in the lee of the sun. It wasn't a sign. But he moved his hand down to the brake in any case.

The engine was idling fitfully. He gave it half a boot of gas. Over loud, turning the head of the man with the paintbrush. Being more careful now, he eased it into gear and drove slowly past the boy fumbling for the basketball in a rose bush. The flowers had all been pruned, the ball was the only color in the garden at all. The street ended in a cul-de-sac shaped like a V. He put the stick shift in reverse and let the clutch out carefully.

He backed halfway into someone's drive and turned the car around. The wheels skidded on the gravel. A sign said: Protected by Lion Security Systems. Drops of rain were starting to fall and the man with the brush was climbing down the ladder. The boy had gone indoors leaving the basketball on the driveway. He put the car into first and drove back along the street looking

neither left nor right.

The car moved for an hour until it came to water. An inlet decked with reeds backed onto large wooden houses with elaborate chimneys made of stone. He could see birds near to the shore. They had long necks and large wings, he didn't know what they were, except that they weren't swans. The wind sprayed across the water without order or law, making the birds uneasy and shiftless. He pulled out the wires on the starter and as the engine died he opened the door and walked over to the trees. It was wet and his feet sank into the moist grass at the side of the road.

He urinated and sat down on a trunk at the side of the bay. He cleaned under his fingernails with a broken twig and sat, smoking and throwing branches into the water. Memories were starting to come back in patches. Replaying events. The images in his head like snippets from channel surfing. He tapped the side of his temple and walked back over to the car.

It was silent and getting late by the time he decided to head on again. The trees had become now spectral figures in the evening landscape. Wasted and sharp, hominoid branches swaying like hanged men. He'd been sitting on the hood, dull light squandering into the evening from his cigarette end. It was colder now. The sun was going down behind the mansions on the sound. A woman with blond hair appeared on the road walking a dog. She was wearing a blue sweater and jeans. A woman. He stopped smoking and looked at her. He grinned and stretched his arms. She moved over into the middle of the road when she saw him. Her body gravitating towards the last fragments of the street light. The dog, a border collie was sniffing at the ditch running long and narrow at the side of the tarmac. It was filled with organic debris and the scent of all the other dogs.

The western sky was reddening, the higher clouds absorbed into the sunset behind her head. On the water the birds were precipitously making noises. Squawking and flapping, settling down for the night. She walked by, ignoring him, head held up and looking ahead. He could hear the eager breath of the dog as it passed not ten feet from his back.

He was staring at the water, but out of the corner of his left eye he could see the woman turn her head slightly. Checking out him and the car. Memorizing the plate. He glared and waited until she rounded another bend before he climbed back into the vehicle. He fused the wires, turned the heat and the radio on and headed back along the lane to the highway.

A hundred minutes later and he was nearly out of gas. It was full dark now. He was stuck in the seat. Freezing. He'd been driving in one direction, turning back and heading in another. He was messed up. Not sure what to do. Where to go. He needed to stop and walk again in the night air. To get a grip and warm himself.

He was in the poorer parts of the suburbs. He parked outside a clapboard house in a rundown neighborhood. He got out and locked the door pointlessly, and lit himself a cigarette. The hairs on his neck were bristling. He was cramped from sitting. He curved his back and rotated his right shoulder. With one hand in his pants pocket, the other holding the cigarette, he walked slowly along the street, trying to take everything in.

The homes he went past were made of low-grade lumber. Wood that was white and pale yellow, paint, flaked and torn. On one a sign said: Warning Atak Dogs. Some of the doors were open, light pouring into the blackness of the street, music from tv commercials alluring in the silence, like the stories he'd been told of mermaids enticing on a shipwreck.

It was chilly. And yet he went on. Reluctant to go back to the car just yet. To return to the helter-skelter. He paused outside a small house with nine door bells, names in Italian, he looked in at the ghost of the tv set and the ruined curtains. He stared for a moment and then sloped away.

A group of black kids were under a streetlight on the corner, the only light he could see that worked. They looked at him, white and out of place.

You los mista? one of them said. He shook his head and crossed the street. The smell was of exercise. They faded behind him, taken in by the dark, and the night sounds. He went by another junction and the houses got cheaper as he walked. Glass in the windows gave way to cellophane and then that gave way to plywood. The frames boarded up and scrawled with graffiti. Some were almost shacks and where people existed at all the figures moved, silent and circumspect in the bulbs strung over garage doors. Shadows. Their rubbish in their yards, their cars pickups and big domestics, most at least ten years old, battered and tired looking.

He came to the end of the street before some railroad tracks. The grinding noise was the sound of an ice plant. Sandwiched uncomfortably between a couple of rundown warehouses. Three empty trucks were parked outside. Hot air belched from extractor fans. The machinery was exposed and looked antique. A thin fence separating the sidewalk from a conveyor belt and a clanking generator. Lights were on inside the plant. He could hear voices and a radio.

A carpenter's shop on the other side was closed, but a sign outside said: free wood. He crossed and took a look inside a long rectangular bin. Logs and the hacked-off remains of doors lay untouched. It was no good for planking and clean-air laws didn't allow burning. The wood lay good for nothing.

Frost was slipping in amongst the houses. He could feel it. He dropped the lid and turned back the way he'd come.

A slender drizzle was falling over the town now, scurrying the kids indoors. He began to see things clearer as his eyes adjusted to the dark and the lazy gatherings of light. Pumpkins sat on doorsteps and skeletons hung on vines, swaying gently in the rain. Witches stared toothless and flat from white screen doors. Masks and costumes peered out from every crevice. For the first time he realized what time of year it was. How long he'd been away.

He coughed, the night swallowing up the water vapor from his lungs.

His feet crossed under the street light again. A black girl in an open doorway raised her hand. She had heard him snort.

You got a light mister?

A what?

A light, you got a light?

He came closer, she was leaning on a patched screen door. Someone else was inside.

Sure I've got a light.

The white of her cigarette fretted in the porch. She smiled.

You some sort of a ambulance man?

A what?

A doctor, you some sort of doctor?

He smiled back.

No I'm not a doctor, he said bringing the lighter-gun out of his pocket. She leaned into the flame, taking a sensual pull. The house was musty, there was more than one person inside. The girl was pretty, her eyebrows arched up crazily, her eyes were smiling all the while.

I better go, he said. I'm looking for the way out of town.

She didn't understand.

Tie-n?

Town, looking for the way out?

Tie-n? she said again. The accent was the trouble.

I want to get back on the highway. Her mouth curved down. Someone sneezed inside. The air was warming him. She glanced back, barely a look.

You turn left on Center and then head all the way down.

He remembered the way he'd come.

Thanks, he said, and turned, the lighter feeling heavy in his pocket, walking away from the warmth and into the chill. When he looked back she was gone.

He'd spoken. The radio was dull in the background. It was easy now.

Call 1 800 LAWYERS if you've been hurt in any way. We're open New Year's Eve at midnight . . .

The return route was empty, though it wasn't late. He hugged the middle lane and steered for the toll road. He had a single note. He stroked the stubble on his chin and watched the road side strip by like junkets from the pictures. He was heading back. The car was warming up despite the ice pouring in from the open window. He liked it this way. The faster he went the louder he needed the radio.

No really if you are losing your hair take it from me this stuff really works. I've tried it and I wouldn't just say that.

Take it from me, he said back to the radio.

Even if you're bald or just thinning on top, Actihair's new biological formula actually strengthens the uh tissues in your skin and promotes new hair growth.

The wind was rushing in his ears. His hands were numbing. His mouth was set in a fixed grin. Tiny insects sprayed against the windshield. He slowed as the row of booths reared out of the night like squat molars on a giant. The car rolling into the jaws along its curving asphalt tongue. He had no need to wind down the window. The engine was in first, his foot resting on the clutch, he was revving it gently. The man had a moustache, thin and drooping at the ends. His shirt was stained with sweat, a fan heater was baking the air inside the booth. Moths flickered against the Perspex, dog-fighting and ramming up against the transparency. A notice pinned inside the window said: One Thousand Dollar Reward. For Information Concerning Toll Booth Robberies. The rest was in small print.

He paid the toll and drove on with an idea.

He stopped the car ten minutes later at a road side hot dog stand.

The man inside turned a lazy eye and a fat cheek towards him. The radio warbled easy listening.

Whaddya want?

Give me all of the money and don't try anything, he said pointing the pistol-lighter at the man.

Ok uh—

Give me the fucking money or I'll blow your fucking face through the back of your fucking head.

T-take it easy, man, I'm getting it. Sweat was on the fore-head of both men, one counting, the other straining his foot on the accelerator.

That's all I got, the man said passing through about a hun-dred bucks, his hands shaking.

That'll do for now.

He wanted to accelerate away. Wanted to. Instead he slipped the clutch and climbed out of the car.

Get out.

Man, p-please.

One more word and I'll blow you away you sorry fucker.

The man came out of the door holding a bottle of fruit punch. Not knowing what he was doing.

Drop it.

The bottle fell and didn't break.

He motioned for the man to lean forward, as if to whisper in his ear. With the butt of the lighter, he clubbed him on the head. The man fell against the metal walls of the stand, breaking the wooden Snapple sign. His fat wobbling. He looked like Super Mario. He glanced over but the man's Ford was empty.

He got back into the car and lit a cigarette.

Jesus, he said.

He opened the door again and got out. He went back to the man, where he was lying on the verge. Moaning softly but only semi-conscious. He kicked him behind the eye. Twice, until blood started to come out of the socket.

He climbed back into the Toyota, slipped into first and drove off into the blackness ahead of him. In a few seconds the dial said fifty-five, the lights of the hot dog stand falling behind him like a movie set, artificial and contrived. It was the most he'd spoken in a long time and he felt exhausted. Speech was the hard part. Nothing else. Nothing.

Tenebrous lanes and highways stretched out before the car in a black and silent world.

To the right were the wounds of buildings. And vapid countryside. There was a possession taking place within him. He regaining himself and seeing things. Taking himself down a road that, he knew, would narrow to a series of incendiary dramas to be played whatever way he went.

But there was really only one place.

There in the shapes of the bogs and hills, in the noose of scrub and trees, a place of voices and whispers, where the dark was a sound in his mouth and where no light fell.

He pawed the wheel and threw out words to the radio, profane and unholy:

I killed them. The fucking fenian bastards. Bastards, bastard, bastard. Jesus. Killed. Topped. Shit. Oh shit. Shit.

He closed his eyes and opened them.

Whole regiments of birds in the night sky and the blood pumping like a steam piston in his head. He could feel it under his temples. His eyes were stinging and it was hard to see. Brine in them.

And all around the salt marsh talking, heaving gloomy portents in the glare beyond the headlights.

A kiss of wheels. An overpass. A cop car.

He slewed in off the highway and followed a minor road that ran parallel to it. A gas station appeared on the bend beside a sycamore tree. An incantation made it still be open.

The engine died under the neon sign. An old white man in blue overalls walked from a shack near the office, smoking. He was wearing a baseball cap with the insignia of an airline that no longer existed. He was possessed by logos, like a racing driver. His shirt was owned by the oil company, his dungarees by Goodyear, his rubber shoes by Ford. Shit, under Chapter 11 bankruptcy the hat wasn't even his. He leaned in the window blowing in a sweet tobacco smell.

What can I do you for? Dentures staining yellow and eyes still blue under the incandescent lamps. Country was on in the office, crickets were singing over on the far side of the forecourt.

The lighter ached in his pocket.

Just fill her up will ya? And I'll get a pack of cigarettes from inside.

Go right ahead.

Petrol smells rejuvenating his frozen nostrils. He watched the old man fill the car, with the dog-ended smoke still hanging limp out of the side of his mouth.

He got out of the Toyota and walked over to the building. He turned and stood for a second gander, his fingers wrapped around the handle to the office. He pressed lightly on the door. It creaked open, the smell of the heater nauseating. The meter on the pump was clicking up to double figures.

You want this filled right up son?

Yeah fill her right up.

The pump gurgled. The station was quiet. The highway droned softly a half a mile away. The crickets and wee cratturs giving voice to their usual lament. He felt the leaf he'd put in the top pocket. It was still fresh. The moon was glinting between fast-moving clouds. It was green but with a hint of blue. Blue. He entered the gas station and walked to the cigarette stand. He chose a pack of Marlboros and a pack of Camels. He was hungry but knew he couldn't eat. He grabbed a can of Coke out of the refrigerator. The proprietor was hanging the hose back on the pump. The scene looked unreal out there with all that illumination. A fantastic bleached island in the slabber of darkness.

Rain was on there for a little while, the man said coming back in through the door.

Yeah.

Couldn find a key for your gas tank.

No.

The man smiled. Always keep me a master key, can open just about anything.

He smiled back.

Well lemme see now. Eleven dollars and fifty cents and, uh, well let's call it an even fourteen dollars.

He counted out the notes and left an extra couple on the counter.

Thanks.

Thanks yourself.

Their eyes met.

Where you headed son? You don't look so good.

To the city, he said, only just realizing himself. He had to get back. He had to get really back. This place wasn't for him.

The city? Only I wouldn't be asking but there's a big road-block up the highway, best avoided I'd say, all sorts of delays, police, uh, you know.

He nodded and smiled at the old man.

Thanks again, he said and headed out into the cold. He closed the door and sparked the engine. Waving back to the man as he drove off.

The road was a little wider than the car. Driving with his fists. Nearly blind from withdrawal pangs. White lines keeping him in place. An aeroplane ticked off the miles overhead, lights on like a UFO. Papers rustled on the back seat. The radio was on religion.

I tell you folks at home. I tell you in the name of the Holy Spirit. The Lord is knocking at your door. Knocking. And the Lord aint no salesman.

With his tongue he moistened his lips tasting blood and ash. The air condensing in front of him and the car heading toward that race of people who dwelt like weirds, long and strange on their bartered island; the lights of their city pulling him, diaphanous and coul and so bright as to dim the stars themselves.

He rubbed his eyes.

The Lord aint no postman. The Lord aint no gas man. Jesus is the only man you'll ever need. I tell ya the Lord Jesus Christ. Knocking. Aint no UPS man. No meter man. It's the Lord Jesus Christ. Lord Jesus. Lord Jesus and he got one thing to say. He got one message. One simple message. Ye must be reborn. Back in the womb, the womb of the Lord. The womb of love and the blood of Christ.

He was tired but already he could feel himself. The fine lines under his eyes. The blurred features. And his hands remembered. Semtex. Durex. Fuse wire. Piano wire. The men behind the wuyur . . . The wind matted his hair. The car moved by itself.

Ye must be born again.

CHAPTER FIVE

In front of me is a Pepsi, a penny chew, a Twix, a packet of Monster Munch and half a Bounty bar.

I can't decide what to eat first. I'm in an enclave of indecision, and, for a second, I'm stuck there, like the donkey in the story who starves because he can't decide.

The noise of industry is next door. Children running. Yelling. Playing tig. My room is quiet. I'm alone in the side office, sitting facing the window. Darkness coming through the frosted glass. I have laid everything out in front of me. In order of size. All I bought from Leathum's before ma gave me a lift in. Half my tuck money, gone. In the tangle of sounds, someone is playing on the piano. Thumping the keys in a scar of ugly notes. Through the plasterboard walls I can hear nearly everything.

Be careful with that you big ganch, a woman shouts.

Ach miss you're dead boring, so you are, a wee girl says back defiantly.

My mouth is salivating with expectation. I haven't had this much raw sugar in exactly a week. I'm still not sure what to take first. Whether to start with the crisps or the chocolate. Animal fat or glucose. Aesthetically the Twix is most appealing, with its gleaming wrapper and, inside, the long, carnal rectangles of caramel and chocolate, but I want to eat it slowly, to save it for last. The Monster Munch has the best texture and the best noise. But all that salt. My hand hovers over the table and finally, I reach out and pick the thing that isn't food: the straw that came with the Pepsi.

I grab it between my finger and thumb, ripping off the top of the paper covering. I pull it halfway down the tube so that it is dangling over the end. Someone is being disciplined next door:

Come on Deirdre. You'll break that, so you will.

I won't.

I will not tell you again.

I put the other end of the straw in my mouth. I take a deep breath and blow, firing off the paper. It floats and buckles in the air but it only reaches to the edge of the table. Near the hinge of the pull-out extension.

Alright less of your messing, we're supposed to be starting in five minutes, so we are, a male voice growls.

Five minutes. And I've still all my sweeties to eat. A flood of urgency goes through me. With the side of my hand I skite the paper off onto the floor, accidentally knocking the Twix over with my arm. It clatters onto a jagged line of chrome that's been peeling off from the central heating pipes.

I bend down to pick it up. My lower back leaning in my shirt. Ruffs on my blazer chasing each other. Under the table I can see that one of the kids' pictures of Jesus has fallen down. Drawn in crayon, Christ's skin a weepy salamander. Desert and camels in the background. The big head of an ass munching at palms strewn decorously at the feet of the Lord. It's a bad picture, drawn without perspective, the houses and temples balanced above Jesus's head like a weird hat. I pick up the Twix and throw it back on the table. I'm thirsty. So, keeping the straw in my mouth like a cigarette and getting my finger under the ring, I pull open the cola. I thought it was settled but the Pepsi still fizzes out of the opening towards the rim. I sup to prevent it spilling over the sides and making the whole can sticky. When it has stopped foaming I put the straw into the drink and suck out a whole mouthful of sweetness.

Seeing the camels has made me think of exotica so I grab the Bounty bar. Half already eaten on the way in.

Settle down, settle down, get your uniforms on, please. Hurry up everyone.

The taste of Paradise, it says on the side. The blue on the wrapper is the color of the ocean. 300 calories. Milk. Artificial Flavoring. Cocoa butter. I push aside my bugle and eat the Bounty in two bites. It doesn't transport me to a tropical paradise like in the tv ad, but it's still good. I take some more Pepsi. In the room beside me people are getting ready now and a big gulter of laughter comes through the door. I rip open the Monster Munch and eat a couple of corn puff monsters. These are big and golden with a cheesy flavor. They're very salty so I have to take a large swig of Pepsi. I shovel in some more crisps and blow with the straw, listening to the bubbles at the bottom of the can. I have to stop this after a while because it takes the fizz out. I scrunch up the Bounty wrapper and shove it in the pocket of my blazer, getting a little piece of coconut on my finger and licking it clean.

I peel off the paper on the penny chew. Underneath, it is orange and green and some of the wrapping has stuck. I put the whole thing in my mouth and suck on it. Not minding the wrapping because, like the rice paper on a nougat bar, sometimes the bit you're not supposed to eat is the best. Besides I've always thought that paper tastes good. I've eaten some already today. Earlier on, before I came out, I ate some newsprint. Ripping off and chewing the corners on the tv page of the *Belfast Telegraph*. Its soft and dissolves on your tongue, and it's chewy, like gum. Ma was pissed off though. It annoyed the divil out of her when she found it.

Your head's cut wee girl. There's bleach in that you know, she said. They bleach the pulp, with chemicals. So they do.

I finish the crisps in a few greasy bites and wipe my hands on the side of my skirt. I lift the Monster Munch packet up to my mouth and pour in the crusty bits at the bottom. I still haven't got all of them so I tear open the thin plastic swaddling and dab my tongue into the yellow remainders. When I've licked up every last bit, I fold up the bag and put it in my pocket too. I take another sip of Pepsi; its warmer and flatter now and not so good. I swallow the last of the penny chew and start on the Twix. I have a special procedure for eating a Twix bar. I'm rushed today but I still follow the drill. I break it open and take one of the bars in my hand. I lever it horizontally into my mouth and bite off the caramel coating all the way down its length, leaving only the biscuit behind. I chew the caramel, swallow, take some more Pepsi, and break apart the biscuit bit. Into three edible sections. I lick the chocolate off the bottom. Faster than usual. And munch the cleaned biscuit down in a couple of quick bites. I take another sip and then repeat the whole procedure on the other finger. When I have eaten the entire bar I gather all the wrappers together and put them carefully under my seat, under the leg of the chair. Squishing them flat.

I drink some more of the Pepsi and pour out the last of the remains, before trying to crush the can in my two hands. This hurts a bit and there's a pain along my spine even though all the pressure is on my arms and shoulders. My mouth makes a noise as I squeeze the can and, with eyes popping, I gaze at the writing on the wall in front of me. A huge poster in purple felt tip.

Ugh.

Do not withhold discipline from a child, it says. For, if you beat him with a rod he will not die. If you beat him with a rod you will save his life. —Prov. 23, v. 13.

Bullshit, I say, grunting and finally the can collapses in on itself. Pepsi leaking out onto my palms from the rip in the aluminum.

When it's totally compressed I take aim and toss it onto the top of the cupboard in the far corner. It bounces off the ceiling and settles there among the dust and the rolled-up billboards with the faces of black children from the missionary stations in Malawi.

About half a second after I've got rid of the physical evidence Bobby Pike comes in.

So how's it coming along? he asks.

I pick up the bugle and wave it.

Just taking a break, I'm a wee bit blown out. Been practicing hard so I have.

Oh er, ok, of course, he says apologetically. Before a wave of skepticism passes across his fat face. I am not concerned. My tongue is tingling from the sugar, and my head feels light.

I haven't heard much at all, though, he says suspiciously dabbing his fat face with a hanky.

I told ya I'm blown out, so I am, my lips just won't pucker together, I have to wait a minute.

Ok ... but parade's starting in five minutes and with Mrs McConnel coming and everything, you should be ready, so you should.

I will be if I can get a breather for a wee while. I can't practice, like, five seconds before I'm supposed to play.

Ah, ok, well that's good, just uh, and fix your uniform.

He goes back into the main hall. Straightening his tie. I smooth out my skirt, pull up my gray knee socks and put my hat on. It is a thin cap with tassels down the back. Navy blue with the Girls Brigade logo on the side, and a small 2 which shows that we are the second company in the town. The first company is the Methodist GB which is down at the end of High Street. We're one of the two Presbyterian brigades. The Episcopalian, Baptist and Congregationalist churches also have a GB. The uniforms are all the same. Only our hat numbers differentiate us. Pretty much every church has a GB except the Catholics. They don't go in for the GB or the Boys Brigade, preferring the Girl Guides or the Scouts because there's no religious element. Bobby told us it's because they're not allowed to do Bible study without a priest. But he's an Orangeman or something, which probably means he's full of shit.

Whatever the explanation, there are no Catholic GBs at all. Although there are a couple of Catholic girls in our GB. Sometimes they get hassled, or get the piss raked out of them. But not much.

My hair is tied up in a ponytail and dangles over my school blazer, which I've brushed and cleaned for tonight. The buckle on my belt has been shined with Brasso and the leather polished with stainer. I pick up the bugle and put the strap over my shoulder. I pull on my white gloves and my haversack. I look absurd and stupid and maybe that's the real reason the fenians don't have a GB. But then again, as ma once said, the Church of Rome isn't noted for its sartorial modesty either. I think she got that phrase off the tv. Or the radio.

Bugger, I say, tripping on my lace.

I walk into the parade room. It's just a standard church hall next door to the church itself. The lights are dim and through the stained glass I can see the street lamps outside. Five groups of girls are lined up on the badminton court. Four to a squad. At the beginning of September I used to have a squad of my own, but they all drifted away after their initial enthusiasm wore off.

I slow march to my spot. Arms not swinging, the bugle held at my side. I turn and face the officers standing at the front of the room. Five elderly women and one chubby man. At attention. Legs together, feet thirty degrees apart. Arms by their sides, their thumbs pointed down. The air is heavy with expectation. But I'm not nervous. It all seems ridiculous somehow. That grown people should be doing this.

The room is small and gloomy. A stage, plastic molded chairs, an out-of-key piano. Yellowed bulbs, all as old as Benny. I twist my neck to take some of the tension out of my black tie.

Mrs McConnel the special VIP from England is standing beside Bobby. He is the only male in the room and looks out of place beside this elderly slim woman, wearing her dark uniform like a mourning dress. He looks over at me to see if I am settled. His fingers restless and moving like Oliver Hardy's. I look at the cowlick under his cap, his azure nose and the gap between his teeth. I give him a tiny nod of the head.

General salute, he says.

I pick up the bugle, having a momentary flash of fear that I left the mouthpiece in the other room. But it's there. I bring the bugle up to my chin and rest it on the cleft. I purse my lips for the fourth note. The officers raise their right hands to their eyebrows and I blow the general salute. Without missing a note. Perfect in fact, except for the final phrase, which is a little rushed because I'm out of breath. Out of practice. I finish on 2. The officers' arms drop to their sides again. Long way up, short way down. Mrs McConnel starts to pray. Everyone bows their heads.

We thank thee oh Lord for this night and gathering us all together at this time . . .

It's very tedious so I try to think about something else. The bugle at my side comes to mind. I try to think of old tunes in terms of the numbers. "The Fields of Georgia" starts off 4, 3, 3, 3, 3, 2. "The Pipers Son" is 1, 3, 5, 4, 4.

The notes are numbered 1 to 5. I have learned all the tunes we play from memory. Twenty in all. None of us can read music, learning by copying the older players. But now that the number of girls is falling off, the band plays less and less, and there's no one to teach. I am one of its last four buglers. We don't do marches anymore. The only times I really get to play are at funerals when I do "The Last Post" and "Reveille." I don't even like to do that because it can be bad and embarrassing when, in the cold, the whole bugle goes flat. You get blamed. And no one believes you that it isn't your fault.

I stroke the saliva off the rim of the mouthpiece, and put it in my pocket. I clear my throat. One of the younger girls is having a coughing fit.

And in thy name and thy everlasting glory, Amen.

Bobby grins, pleased that it all went well. He wiggles his head nervously in my direction. I bring the instrument down to my side and stand at ease. The Captain, Ms Moffett, leads Mrs McConnel on an inspection tour of all the squads. They briefly stop in front of me.

Good show, she says in a cut-glass voice that reminds me of Mrs House and Mr Preston from school.

Yeah, that was good work, so it was, Ms Moffett adds.

I'm the Lord's instrument, I think about saying, but she moves along before I can.

After inspection it is badge work. Sarah and I have got all our badges so we can slip outside and get something. I'm not too keen tonight because I'm already stuffed, but she wants to go.

You didn't think you'd have to play the oul buggley tonight did ya? she asks as we walk down the stairs of the church hall.

Nope.

You were good though.

I am the master. It's not practice you know. It's skill.

Aye well don't give up the day job.

Not much call for a traveling bugler these days.

Don't think there ever was.

No.

We walk outside into the street. It is cold. I button my blazer over. A line of cars is at the traffic lights. There's a queue at the petrol station.

Where do you want to go? I ask her.

I fancy a pasty at Elsie's.

A potato pasty?

Aye.

Aye I think I could go for one too. If I have another bar of chocolate I think I'll puke.

It's a bit far away though.

Ach we've got plenty of time.

You know some night we should slip into the pub.

Aye right, in these uniforms.

We dander along Albert Road and turn onto West Street. It's a control zone at this time of night. No cars allowed in case they've got bombs inside. All the shops are closed and there's a big yellow barrier across the road. The sign on the barrier says: Police No Entry. It's only about nine but we're the only people walking on the cobblestones. It's safe enough though, since there hasn't been a real bomb in the town center for about five years, but even so very few people come out after dark, except to walk their dogs or go to the pub. All the shops have been closed since five.

I stop and look in the window of the Record Rocket.

D'ya like "The Smiths"? I ask her.

Nah, they're wick.

Ever heard anything, they did?

Oh wait a minute, "The Smiths," I thought you meant the "Pet Shop Boys," aye I like them. They're good.

They are good. The "Pet Shop Boys" are wankers.

You know who I like?

Who?

I like Sting.

Uh huh?

He's good, he's dead cute.

Tell you who's cuter.

Who?

Michael Stipe.

From "R.E.M."?

Aye.

Aye can't see it myself.

You know Louise thinks Keith looks like Donny Osmond?

Donny Osmond? What's she in, a time warp?

I don't know.

Anyway I like your man from the uh, I can't think of the name of it, the "Bangles."

The "Bangles" is an all-girl band, shit for brains.

No it isn't, the drummer's a man, so he is. I think.

I don't think so.

Ah who cares. Hey do you know Sting sometimes stays with his grandma up the coast?

Sting?

Yup. A couple of miles up the coast from here in a wee house by the sea. His granny's from around here.

Sting?

Yup.

Are you sure?

Heard it from Jane McConnel.

Jane McConnel? Never heard of her.

Wee girl from my road.

Yeah? How do I not know her?

Doesn't go to our school. She's from Scotland.

Scotland?

Aye, she's my neighbor, just from a wee bit down the road. She's at a school in Belfast. I think.

And she's Scottish?

Yup.

And you play with her and everything?

Uh huh.

Jesus, you're like the UN, so you are.

Yeah, we have an Ethiopian family in the attic, refugees, quiet lot, don't eat much, always going on about Bob Geldof.

Yeah we used to have Vietnamese refugees in our house but they went back home, said Northern Ireland was too violent for them. Poor loves.

That's funny.

Not as funny as your face.

Yours makes the Ayatollah look good.

What are you saying he's ugly? I personally go for that religious fervor thing. Adds depth to a man. And that beard. Stylish. Beards are coming back.

Sometimes I feel sorry for me.

Aye me too. Anyway your wee pal knows all this stuff about Sting?

I don't know, she's probably talking shite.

Probably.

Probably, I agree, and we slip back into silence.

We walk past St. Nicks church. It is dark with only the lights from the harbor and Marine Highway sneaking up the   101 alleys. I look over at the shutters but it is too gloomy to read the graffiti. Sarah is walking in time with me, slowly. The echoes of our feet bouncing off the walls all the way down to Market Place.

When we get to High Street there are a couple of kids outside the pub trying to get in.

Look at them wee muckers, younger than us, I say.

She says to me under her breath: Forget that. Don't say anything. Look over there. No, over there.

I look over to the other side of the street but I can't see anything.

No over there, there, she says and discreetly points over at Taylors barbers.

Oh my God.

In the shadows by the Ulster Bank, Frank McConkey is pushing the empty wheelchair of his dead wife, with nothing on but one of her old summer dresses. His feet bare, his head bent over looking for cigarette butts. He is talking to himself, muttering. Rust has seized the brake on one of the wheels, making it scrape uneasily along the ground. With each feeble shove the whole thing clanks loudly, like an out-of-tune steel drum.

I see it now. Jesus. It's Frank McConkey, I whisper to Sarah.
Uh huh.
God he's like your man in *Psycho*.
Oh that's a sin, she says, half laughing.
Didn't he push her around in that thing before she died?
Aye but look at him now.
I tell ya, he's wired up that oul boy.
I know but you shouldn't mock the afflicted, Sarah replies with no special emphasis on "you." But I'm sensitive about these things and slip into a minor huff.

Why shouldn't I? I want to ask. But Sarah's laughing and I

smile too. I decide to skip over the remark and start walking again.

Come on we better get going to Elsie's, there might be a queue, I say to her.

Yeah, sure, she says. Her voice not revealing whether she knows I've changed the subject deliberately.

We walk past Dobbins and round the corner of the post office to Elsie's Carryout. There's nobody inside. We both order potato pasties and watch one of the girls boil them up in the deep-fat fryer.

Are you going to finish that joke? Sarah asks out of the blue.

What joke?

Paddy Irishman, Paddy Englishman, and Paddy Scotchman were gonna be executed.

That joke, ach it's not funny.

Go on.

I'll tell ya it later.

Bet you don't.

Ok, I bet ya I don't.

There ya go, that'll be a pound, the woman says.

For both? I ask.

Aye.

I'll get it.

I give her the pound coin. We take the pasties off the counter and help ourselves to salt and vinegar.

We walk back along the sea front. I can only eat about half of the pasty before I start to feel bloated.

I'm stuffed, do ya want to finish this?

Ugh, Sarah answers shaking her head in disgust.

Thanks for the vote of confidence in my standards of personal hygiene.

Don't mention it.

We sit down on one of the benches near the castle. The

night is cold and the water is calm. In Belfast the lights are on above the hills. We can see the trains on the railway line, making the turn from the Bla Hole. Behind us traffic is light on the highway. I get up and walk over to the wooden litter bin. I put my chip paper inside and drop the lid on the smell of something burnt. I walk back and sit down beside her on the bench. She's restless.

We don't have the time to stay long, she announces.

Catch yourself on wee doll, they'll be ages yet.

No, we better get back now.

I'll tell ya the joke.

You will?

Uh huh.

Sarah makes herself more comfortable, leaning back in the seat and taking tiny bites out of the pasty. The smell of excessive vinegar over her fingers.

So Paddy Englishman gets the choice between the guillotine and the firing squad and he takes the guillotine and they drop it but it crashes and there's a big bang, and it seizes half an inch above his head. Like it just stops there. Stuck. So they have to let him go. Cos that's the rule.

What sort of rule is that?

Now don't start with me, wee girl, it's just the rule, it's the law. Ok? Like in your joke when I didn't interrupt you.

Alright.

Ok. So. Where were we? Oh yeah. So, Paddy Scotchman gets the choice between the fire squad and the guillotine and he also picks the guillotine. The whole thing shudders, the blade drops, there's a big crash, and the blade stops a couple of inches above his head. Same place, stuck. So Paddy Scotchman is out of there too. Free. So Paddy Irishman's up next and they ask him what he wants. And he thinks for a minute and he says: Oil take the foiring squad that ting doesn't look soife to me.

You were right.

What?

That wasn't funny.

Aye and like you can do better.

Oh yeah you're the bloody joke master, able to judge.

I thought I was pretty good today.

Wha? she asks, not knowing what I'm talking about.

On the train, snapping out those lines like nobody's business.

Yeah yeah, with them boys, sorry about all that, she says, somber and regretful as if she were to blame for it. Coddling, and it makes me annoyed. I sit on my hands and want to tell her, but I can't.

Look don't worry about it, I say gently. She is looking at me inquisitively. I tell her the truth.

I sort of enjoyed it.

She smiles but I can see she doesn't believe me and thinks I'm putting a brave face on things.

Honestly I did, well . . . almost, I begin to say into her doubts.

If you say—

Look, let's just forget it.

Ok.

She takes the final bite out of her pasty.

D'ya wanna go?

Sure.

We walk back, walking up Lancastarian Street, past the row of butchers shops. A long cut to waste more time. When we get back to the church hall nobody has noticed that we were gone. The officers are having tea with the VIP. The girls are getting ready to play murder ball. One mat is at one end of the

105

hall, the other mat is up on the stage. Murder ball is simple, it's like rugby without any rules. Sarah and I both sit it out. She reading *Great Expectations* and I watching the game until it's time to go.

Sarah's mum pulls up in the car at ten-thirty and I walk out saying cheerio to a couple of friends. Sarah climbs in the front.

Remember to put your seatbelt on, Mrs White says.

I will. I reply, buckling up.

So how was it tonight? she asks both of us.

It was good, I say.

And what did you do?

Natin.

Nothing?

She didn't do nothing, she played the bugle, mum.

Mrs White turns round and looks at me. Her bob brushing against her cheek. Her lips are long. Her brown eyes, more attractive than Sarah's.

You played the bugle?

Uh huh.

Good. You're a very musical young lady.

Yes.

And you do art too, isn't that so?

Sarah giggles and I laugh, there is something funny about the way her mother says things. Mrs White turns back round and puts the key in the ignition, looking at me in the mirror.

We drive home carefully along the Marine Highway. Past the Chinky, past the cop shop, and over the railway bridge. Mrs White turns along Victoria Road and stops the car outside the front gate of my house. I get out feeling happy.

Thanks a lot.

Don't mention it.

See ya tomorrow, Sarah says.

Yeah.

I run round the side of the house and wave as the car backs up. When I get in mum has gone to bed. I change out of my clothes and climb in between the sheets. I fiddle with the picture on the black and white and watch *Newsnight* and the late-night tv shows before turning it off. I quickly brush my teeth and pee and then turn the bedroom light off. I lie back in the bed but I can't sleep. I am thinking about Islamic militants taking over the world. I am worrying about President Ray Gun. The Russians. The Chinese. A shooting in West Belfast. I'm burnt out. Tired all over. I lie on my back but it's still sore. I think about going to get an aspirin, but I don't. I turn on one side and then the other. I try hard to doze off but the images of violence are playing endlessly in my head. I think about football teams to try and keep them out.

At one in the morning I hear my brother arrive home. The car coming too fast down the driveway. The engine raging, Enya blaring out of the speakers. Headlights on the other side of the curtains. The engine slinks into neutral. He turns the radio off. Then the ignition. The engine dies. Up the park a dog stops barking. His seatbelt unbuckles. I hear the car door slam. And now there are only footsteps and a jingle of keys in the husk of silence.

They drop.

Shit, he says and as he bends down to get them money falls out of his pocket.

Shit on a stick.

He picks up what he can find in the dark and walks over the gravel to the front porch.

La, la, la, he starts to sing from the song on the stereo.

The deadbolt turns in the lock. The front door opens and 107 the bottom of it squeals irritatingly, from the friction of rubbing against the welcome mat. The air pressure in the house changes and my bedside lamp rattles on the bookcase. The light in the hall goes on. My brother wipes his feet on the plastic mat. He steps off. The floorboards groan. He belches. The front door closes and I know now that it's ok to sleep.

CHAPTER SIX

He left the car forever in an empty lot downtown. Garbage
and graffiti were on the walls surrounding it. Someone was
looking at him cautiously. A man in rags.

Don't think you want to leave that there mister, he said.

It's ok, it's not mine, he explained.

Oh.

Vapor was pouring out of the metal gratings on the sidewalk.
Subway trains were running loud and dissonant under his feet.

How much for your jacket? he asked the man.

This thing, Jesus, I picked it out of the trash, it aint worth
nothin.

I'll give you ten bucks and my white coat.

The man grinned, his breath smelled of malt liquor.

It's a deal then.

The jacket was stale and dirty but didn't smell too bad.

The shoes were pinching his feet as he walked, but the
slender pain helped keep him awake. It was long past lights out.
A man was sitting cross legged under scaffolding. It was impossible to tell if he was white or black. His clothes belonged on a
scarecrow. Great torrents of rainwater, cold and rust colored,
was running out of a gutter down onto his head. A sign in front
of him said: hunry and homeles. The man was quiet, swaying
a little and bowing his head. Nodding as if in agreement with
the thoughts of those who passed him by on the other side.
The loafers leaked water. His toes were wet now. He reached

into his pocket and gave the man a five dollar bill. The man nodded and mumbled, hardly seeing him.

He walked for a while and on the far side of an avenue, lights were on in a food store. He crossed over, running between a limousine and a yellow cab. The cab honking him. The crossing said: Don't Walk. He stared through the glass. There were white people inside. The aisles were stacked with fruit and vegetables: rare fruit, exotic vegetables. Women in expensive looking coats pushing around miniature trolleys. Tiny four wheeled devices that looked as if they belonged in a doll's house. A window display was made up of a ring of caviar. Two different kinds, dark and light.

He pushed open the door. It was warm inside. He grabbed a basket and held it tightly in his hand.

You have to try this, a woman was saying, it's amazing, I had it over at Susan's and she told me. It's so good for you and fat free.

The two women were pointing at a bowl of Baba Ghannouj, both small, heavily made up. One in furs despite the rain.

You can really taste the eggplant and the lemon.

He walked by them, past degutted salmon and shark. He paused and stared at an artfully arranged octopus. From a display he grabbed a coffee bean and put it in his mouth and sucked on it. The flavor was rich and smoky. It made him thirsty and he wanted to eat.

Can I help you sir? A man beside him was asking. Tall, standing close to him. A young man, hair cut short on top, with a ponytail. Eyes narrow and black above the blue of his suit.

I was just looking at the, uh, couscous.

Yessir, but I'm afraid I'm going to have to ask you to leave.

Leave? I haven't done anything.

I know sir, but we are closing and I'm afraid I'm going to have to escort you to the door.

110   The man pressed lightly on his crumpled jacket.

He marched back along the rows of marmalade and preservatives and dropped his basket in the rack by the door.

Outside the rain was easing.

He pulled up the collar on his jacket and stood and rubbed his hands for a moment.

He looked down. A hundred cigarette butts lay underneath the grating. A doorway was ajar beside a scruffy deli. Silhouettes moved in the crack, small, like dwarves. Kids playing with a plastic gun. Their faces soiled and greedy for attention. He bought a soda from a stand and drank it down in one.

In the slickness of the evening an array of headlights slithered down the thoroughfare. Smudged and weary in the teeming rain. The wet was all over the sidewalk like oil. He lit himself a cigarette in the illumination from the gaudy window displays. A helicopter flew overhead, barely audible in the paroxysm of traffic. In front of him steps led down into the subway. The underground world seemed suddenly more appropriate.

The train came long and whining out of the tunnel. Metal glinting on the side. It was a third full. Only two people got off. He got on and walked along the car until he stopped opposite a black-haired woman in a business suit. Tawny. Her skirt was pale green and ugly. She had dark eyes, reading under heavy upturned lashes. She was beautiful. He sat down two seats away, opposite.

Don't touch my bags, don't touch my fuckin bags, muthafucka. Muthafucka, a man was shouting at no one in particular. Bug eyes and huge hands, swollen from frostbite.

He studied her as she read. She was so unlike the nurses. Not cynical. Her face was concentrated on the book. She was biting her bottom lip. And as she turned a page her eyebrows rose at an acute angle to her nose. Brown and soft.

Muthafucka, what I tell you bout my bags.

It intrigued him. Her right eyebrow arced on a higher gradient than the left which meant that the area displaced by the curve would be greater. It was an integral calculation that only he noticed.

My bags, who's been messin with my bags? You a muthafucka and you a muthafucka, yeah, you right there, you. You I'm talking about you. You a fucking alien. An alien. I seen you in *Alien,* the movie. Fuckin Sigourney Weaver, man. I seen you coming out that gut.

She was reading a book with a black cover, a title he couldn't see. From the design he could see it was a Penguin classic. The shouting man was tiring, his voice smothering out his words, hoarse and bitter.

I know'd it, you a fuckin alien, man.

She yawned delicately behind the book, her teeth tiny like a spider.

Oh man I know'd you.

The train pulled into the station, decelerating rapidly. She placed a bookmark carefully at her page and rose. She had in her hand a small sports bag he hadn't noticed before.

I know'd you man.

She stood at the doors and walked through them quickly when they opened.

Muthafucka.

He got up and followed her. She crossed the platform and walked up an incline. At the top she turned left and descended onto another waiting area. It was busier here, hot and lined with people. The sound of running water was overhead. She stood a few feet from the rail beside a man tapping at his watch. Her hair blacker than the dark at the tunnel's mouth. He stood ten feet back. A transit cop was talking to a girl with a clipboard. They were both smiling. He stepped closer to the edge of the platform. A mouse skittered out from underneath the overhang and sniffed at the siding. She had her book in her hand again. A quarter of the way in, reading, the bookmark tucked in her fingers at the back cover. Someone coughed. The mouse leapt back to where he couldn't see it. Two lights appeared in the tunnel. The sound of the train came afterward. The book went back down to her side. The brakes squealed, high and absolute. Easing diminuendo until the train stopped and the guard signaled for the doors to open. She sidled along to the nearest entrance and pushed her way second onto the carriage.

Inside he had to stand. The whole platform had got on the train. He read the billboards one by one.

The Aids Coalition, helping the community to help ourselves, call 1 800 HOT LINE.

Beside this ad, a fist with the word VOTE tattooed across the knuckles.

Have you witnessed a crime? A cash sum could be yours. Call 1 800 6 ACTION.

A man with his arm in plaster—Unexpected Medical Costs?

She was sitting four people up, beside a white man, tight in his suit. Bald with bags under his eyes. He was fat and she was squeezed against the partition.

Los ninos de Cristo, a sign seemed to say though the words were drawn all over.

Bodies were pressed close to him. It was crowded and yet it had to be near midnight. Perhaps because the trains were so infrequent at this time. His hand held onto the steel support. His knuckles whitening on the bends. At the next stop a lot of people got off and he sat down. Three away from her. She was holding tightly to the bag, as if she were afraid of something.

A Jamaican man got on, cleared his throat and began to talk in an accented voice that he recognized from his time in Coventry. He was very tall, holding what looked like a metal box. 113

Ladies and gentlemen a famous man once said that music is the food of the soul. Many of you need that there food of the soul. Hungry right? Tonight, right here, right now, I'm going to feed you.

Her head was up and looking at the man.

With my music. My poetry, muze-ic-al, po-et-tree, I hope you like it.

The man bent over and opened his box, pulled out a flute and began to play. He looked above her head at new advertisements.

If your partner is hurting you, we want to help. The partner abuse line is open 24 hours. Call us night or day in complete confidence.

She was looking back at her book. Not reading. The man's long fingers raced over the instrument, testing its limits, reminding him of a Kick-the-Pope band warming up.

The man played a scale, ascending it in strange harmonies. Melodic but atonal.

Her hand was in her pocket. She pulled out a white, crumpled tissue.

Notes escaping from the instrument seemingly at random.

Holding it between her finger and thumb.

At a high note the Jamaican man changed the tune and began to blow furiously, concentrating full on the sound. She was half watching. The music was darker now and not unlike a left foot prison ballad. It was unsettling. He hadn't heard anything like this in a long time. An asymmetry of notes, complex and disturbing. The man's eyes were shut, deep set, his body swaying to the music.

The tissue was up at the woman's nose. She was watching the flautist now, and he alternated between the two of them. They could have been brother and sister. The carriage was tense. All faces, concealed or not, were on the player.

The train pulled into a station, but no one got on or left.

As if it were part of the enchantment. Finally, in the midway point between two stops, the tune fell away, diminishing softly until it was nothing more than the sound of metal rattling on the rails. A couple of people applauded. Most turned away. The man came round with a plastic cup. A ring of coffee visible on the bottom. Someone threw in some silver. A black man in a suit put in two dollars. She put in some quarters and went back to her book immediately. The man faced him.

Hey that was good, I liked it, he said.

He reached in his pocket and felt underneath the lighter for a bill. He gave it to him without checking what it was.

Thanks man.

The next stop will be 96th Street. 96th Street, the announcer said. Passengers should remain on the train for 103rd Street. This is the one to—

Not me, the man said, I'm getting off here.

The atmosphere was one of reprieve when the Jamaican climbed off the train lugging his flute box like there was something heavy inside. The way a mime artist would.

An obvious undercover cop got on at the next stop, fat and white and surly. He was chewing gum. He started hassling a sleeping kid in a woolen hat who was hogging all three seats. It seemed a waste of time.

Get up, I want to sit.

Gey your own seat, the kid said, his words slurred.

Fucked up huh?

He tugged the kid to his feet. Not on this train you don't.

The kid pulled the hat low over his head and looked at the undercover. He didn't speak.

Get the fuck off at the next stop arright? I said arright?

Ok.

At the station the cop pushed the boy out ahead of him onto the platform. A whole lot of people were getting off.   115

He stood up. The cop was close, his breath smelling of onion and mint to cover it. He bumped into him as the cop got off. Hard.

Sorry, he said.

Take it easy bud, the cop said and stepped out, shaking his head.

Dumb fuck, the cop said as the subway doors closed on him, the boy standing on the platform.

As the train pulled away he sat down again, the policeman's wallet heavy in his pocket.

They were alone in the section. She had caught his eye once and had looked away abruptly. Their eyes locking for no time at all. It might be enough though. She would know that he was following her if she saw him again. He had to be careful.

The journey was not a long one. He read some more of the signs: Ugly feet? We can help. The NY Foot Docs. Call toll free on 1 800 1 N-U-F-O-O-T.

Add a new chapter to life. Learn to read on tv.

U too can buy a new smile.

If you need a lawyer fast . . .

She was standing. Two white men in double-breasted suits stood between him and her. Carrying briefcases, reeking of aftershave and whiskey. The door opened and she left. Her legs swaying slightly in the tow of her skirt. He got out of the car and watched her skipping up the stairs, sliding step on step with a lilt in her walk like a dancer's. He waited until she was through the revolving metal barrier before following her out onto the street.

The area was not bad. A large Baptist cathedral was on the left. Polished marble buildings on his right. An institution of some kind. Probably a bank. She was heading north. Lights led uphill. He touched the gray marble with his hand, feeling the

smooth texture on his skin. His fingers too were gray. And cold.
He unclenched them and shoved them into the crowded pockets
of the jacket. He pulled out soiled tissues and a half a candy bar
and let them drop slowly onto the damp pavement.

Clack, clack, clack, her heels in the middle distance. Traffic
was light. The wide boulevard nearly deserted. Pale men walked
alone or with dogs. Two women were laughing on the cathedral
side. High and childlike. Intoxicated. She stopped at a Don't
Walk sign even though there were no cars. He slowed and slunk
his head. The sidewalk was smeared with the dark stain of chewing gum. The gutter was swept clean. She crossed and passed
an open grocery store on her left. Fruit was stacked outside.
Melons and oranges lacking color in the meager light. He was
thirsty. She was slowing, tiring or getting closer to home, he
surmised. If the latter it was just as well because he could feel
himself getting weaker.

He didn't want to lose her but as he passed the shop he
couldn't take it any more. His thirst was like woodsmoke, gnaw-
ing and seeping into crevices of his mouth. His throat ached as
if it had been filled with ashes. It must have been the effect of
the cigarettes. She was up ahead, not far, a taxi passed her slowly,
dim and yellow, in a blur of indolence. In a guess of probabilities
he decided that she was going to go straight on. It would be
ok to juke quickly into the store. He pushed on the door. The
heater was on. His head was light and he felt close to passing
out. Inside it was narrow and convoluted. The shelves stacked
high with cans. Processed meat and bagels in a trough. Loud
Islamic calls, masculine and violent were coming from a radio
tuned to short wave. A butcher showed him a flash of gold. His
sharp features turning, softening, dissolving into the ironies of
naked girls behind his head. He was leaning against the wall. In
the corner he could see four standing refrigerators, stocked with

117

beer and soda pop. He opened the door, seized the first can and bolted to the counter. He paid and ran back out into the star lit avenue.

Outside it was quiet and the woman was still there, a smudge on the black chalk of the horizon. He narrowed his eyes and pulled the can open. He was about to take a sip but before he could the shop's door opened in a wake of light. The store owner striding over, his hand holding something.

A folding thing, severed. It was a walking dream, the man like a grim demon grinning. Thirst was making him crazy and there were lights everywhere. The man spoke. Semitic, a voice ascending like machine-press talk. He didn't understand.

The man opened his hand. An offering. She was barely there at the next cross street. Disappearing into the dark. Confused, he thought the man had come to deliver up his prepuce. Arm outstretched. A gift, like the King's shilling. The man opened his hand and in the blasphemy of it he accepted the folding thing.

It was four bills.

You forgot your change, the man said.

What?

Your change.

Oh . . . thanks.

The man turned, shaking his head. The money lay in his hand like a benediction. He put it in his pocket and drank the can in a single sip. When he looked up she had gone.

He ran down the street, drawing air into his lungs in big gasps. Running clumsy in the strides of a high-jumper. She had vanished completely. Turned into one of the side streets. His throat was hoarse, his breathing erratic. The shoes stabbing him along the toes and in the arches. She was nowhere to be seen. He stopped outside a large brick building. A bell tower on the corner. Here the subway emerged in the middle of the road to run on pillars for the rest of the line. Two streets over he could see trees. She could be anywhere. The building told him nothing. It was shut, an immense iron gate closed at the front, with the words: And the Bush Was Not Consumed.

An old man in uniform sat in a booth reading a paper. CANDIDATES DEBATE, said the headline.

Excuse me, you didn't see which way a woman went there? She, uh, left her purse in the store.

The guard rested the paper on his lap.

Young woman you say?

Yes that's right, she must have just gone by.

Mmmm nope.

You must have see her.

Mmmm black girl?

Yeah and she was in a kind of green skirt.

Yeah, she just went right along here, right along.

Thanks.

No bother.

He jogged up the street. The building continued all along the lefthand side. He could see people working in a library. Students. A hill blocked the view to the other side. He ran up it wheezing. Two black men were sitting in chairs underneath a sign that said: J. A. and L. parking, open until midnight every night.

At the peak of the hill he could see another avenue and the lights on in buildings in a distant part of the city. He ran past apartment blocks and black trash bags left on the sidewalk. A housing project faced him, and a school, the windows meshed-in, graffiti below the name board. If she hadn't gone inside an apartment building, she had to be one of the shapes maneuvering through the night air at the bottom of the slope. Seven or eight people to choose from. Three to the left and four to the right. He had to make a choice. A sinistra, he thought and turned left. He ran a little, still trying to be inconspicuous.

At the next block he caught his breath, peering into the gloom. As one of the shapes went under a street light, he saw it. A green skirt. He ran up to within fifty feet. She hadn't looked round.

It was definitely her. He could see the legs and a thin body swaying. He slowed to a walk.

The moon was up. The clouds had all but cleared. He could feel his knuckles tense. He was walking down into a poorer neighborhood. Homeless people bedding down in a park on the other side of the street. Some of them sleeping over leaking steam pipes.

She was ahead only twenty paces. Her keys were jangling in her right hand, she must be close. A sign said: General Grant Houses. The doorway was clean and well kept. A tree in a pot stood lopsided under the arch. She seemed to pause for a moment and then turned and walked into the high rises. As soon as she was through the door he sprinted after her.

He stopped at the building's entrance and walked confidently into the light and through the swing doors. She was already pushing the button on the elevator. He hung back in the shadow of the broken light and watched her. She was breathing heavily from her walk. The lobby was empty, featureless. No mailboxes. Nothing. Directly outside someone was lying on a bench.

He looked at her and her shoulders tensed. She turned round but she couldn't see him. His hands were straight and his fingers crossed to scud her out.

She was so pretty. Her hair sprawled out like a roadmap and her expressive eyes looking round nervously. She turned round and said something to herself.

They were connected by her damp footprints that were already evaporating on the tiled floor. Her feet in small block heels, twitching. Her back was to him now, only one of them aware of the other. The lobby windows were open and over her perfume he could smell the river and the city.

His jacket was heavy, he wanted to take it off.

Yo, someone said outside.

He looked at her feet. Such tiny shoes. A bell sounded. The elevator door opened. She got in. The door jerked closed. He ran over to where she'd been. He watched the clock and saw that the elevator had stopped at the seventh floor. Already the second elevator was there. He pushed the seven button and got in. A pit formed in his stomach as the lift began to rise. He folded his arms and leaned against the wall, his stare focusing hard on the illuminated lights.

He coughed, his breath smelling of peaches in the palm of his hand. From the soda.

The lift rose quickly ticking off the floors as if it all meant nothing. The acceleration of the elevator nauseated him for a moment. The number six was lit and then the elevator stopped.

Shit, he said and pushed on seven.

It didn't go up.

Shit.

He cut through the sliding door and headed for the stairs. Out of breath, blood pumping, he pressed on the sign marked Fire Escape. Falling against the door. His head held tight. Hands up against his ears. Tight. Grinding his teeth. His tongue locked against the roof of his mouth. The blackness dropped like a switchblade.

Jesus Ch—

Hail fell on the monument. He was in another place. What was he doing h—

Will ya look at that. That's desperate, that is. Jesus Christ. I knew it would be like this, so I did.

Gray and pathetic. Cold. A perpetual drizzle hanging over the sky. Fernie against the wall, smoking.

I mean you can't see your hand in front of your face. Boys a dear, I wouldn't like to be out on the water on a day like today, eh?

He skulked in the lee of the massive stone obelisk. He and the weather were allies in misery. Reading off the war dead, jaded and resistant.

Every time I come up here it's foggy.

It's wild, always fucking pissing down.

Bored, he gazed into the mist suspended over the Lough. Sleekit and dour it hovered, intemperate and charged.

Are you not speaking? Don't blame ya. Nothing much to effin say.

The cliff edge faded into a patchwork of green and brown. A kestrel circled overhead, calling out to its mate. Long harsh calls unsettling in the silence.

What do you think that was, that a curlew or something?

No.

One field over, black turf cuttings were cadaverous and empty in the boggy landscape. A tractor oxidizing far below, looking like a Dinky toy.

Look I'm getting a wee bit fed up waiting here. Like a hoor or something. Waiting around, you know. Be bloody snowing next.

Dungy cattle were chewing near the barbed-wire fence. Docile and quiet. Rags flying in tatters along the enclosure.

Take us ages to get back. Tell ya, this is one fuckin eejit place to meet. Should be in a wee bar somewhere.

Yeah. I don't have the time for it either. I've got to go.

Have you decided where?

Aye.

Well?

I'm going to go to America. New York, probably, or San Francisco.

That's where all the fenians go.

That's where I'm going. The cops'll never look for me there.

Aye. Suppose. Its a godless country, though. The cities any-way. You think they know their Bible? All heathens.

He shrugged at Fernie and with damp matches he tried to light a cigarette.

Anyway we should be in a wee bar somewhere warm. And you should be off to the Caribbean or somewhere for fucksake. Ha ha. Them boys have the money. Tell your brother to get you a ticket. We can afford it. Fuck, somewhere like that.

The hood on his duffle coat was heavy from the downpour. He shook it out and tried again with the cigarette.

Carra fucking bean. An those wee hoor nigger girls in the grass skirts, you know. Hoors like lieutenant Ye hoor ye from *Star Trek*. Wild. And they all screw like bunnies. So they do. Like bunnies. Bunnies.

He opened his eyes. The rail was cold steel. A sign on the wall said: fallout shelter. He hadn't drawn breath for half a minute, frozen spastic in mid-inhalation. The stairs went up. He could see the counterweight on the elevator ease its way down the shaft. The window to the outside had been broken. Intractable, the street condensed slowly. Steam rising in columns from the pavement. The indigent moving on towards the park. He looked down. But it was gone. The needle man. A morphology lost in the darkness.

And then, as if his finger had been on the mute button, the sound came on again.

Through the perforation in the building's structure there was talk and the song of cats. Traffic, and shutters coming down on the last remaining grocery store. Inside was the noise from the elevator doors and the lobster crack of feet.

He ran three stairs at a time up the steps, slipping on the raw concrete. He pushed the door to seven and looked down the corridor. A door was closing at apartment 705. He'd lost her. He walked to her apartment. Calm. The corridor was empty and turned on a dog leg. About sixteen flats in all. A wet trail led to the fire escape, the way he'd come. Her door was painted brown and had no name tag. He sat down on the floor, pulled out a cigarette, toyed with it for a moment and then put it back in the pack. He stood up and took a deep breath.

Damn, he said. The elevator was returning to the bottom floor. Rattling unevenly. Someone upstairs was shouting.

Don't you tell me that.

I never . . .

Don't you tell me that.

He raised his hand and looked at it. The half moons on his nails were small and dotted. His fingers formed into a fist. The people above arguing like dogs barking. Their words lost now in the walls. He knocked on the door. Three shorts taps with a space between. He heard the word "shit" from inside and then footsteps coming towards the door.

Who is it? a voice asked. Rich and melodious.

It's the police, he said. His voice, he discovered, was placid and without surprise.

It's the who?

Come on open up, it's the police.

He held the undercover's badge up to the glass and heard her lift the peephole to look. She was deciding.

How much was her life worth?

The lock turned and the door swung open. She was standing there, her shoes off, her hair let down. In her bare feet on pentagon tiling. A chain was between them, connecting the door to the wall. It had been painted over green.

You don't look like no cop.

I want to search these premises.

She paused and looked at him.

What for?

His accent faked, hers slipping back. He could see that her jacket was good material. A couple of hundred dollars at least. He reached in his pocket. She drew closer to the chain to read the print on the badge he'd shown her, but she knew. She knew.

Take the chain off the door, he said. His voice a promise. She hesitated. Unsure of what to do. Unsure how to extricate herself.

In his left hand now the fake gun was pointed at her abdomen. His eyes composed.

Nice and slow, he said. Suddenly she moved to slam the door. Her body a wave of motion. Her hand pushing. She was smart and quick.

He reacted.

He leapt and turned, drop-kicking the door with both of his feet, his body horizontal. Her face flickered. Not fear but resignation. Her mouth opened to yell. The force was crashing. His lungs exhaled into a grunt, primordial, bestial. Her eyes locked. There was a crash and the chain pulled out of the wall, smattering against the door. She was knocked back. He hit the floor, landing almost on his fingertips. She was lying in the entrance. He got up, calm and ready and walked in, closing the door behind him.

The kettle was boiling in the kitchen. He was working at the plastic on her passport with a razor blade. Steam separating it

from the paper. She was watching, hands and feet tied profes-
sionally to the chair.

I need to take some money.

I haven't got shit, she replied.

I can be wild.

She did not reply.

The apartment was bigger than he thought it would be.
Tastefully decorated in reproduction African tribal art. It was
subtle and well laid out. A large computer and monitor domi-
nated one corner. An industrial dot matrix printer sat beside it,
as big as a drinks trolley.

I'll tear this place apart looking for it, top to bottom. You
wouldn't want that would you?

I told you. There's nothing.

Because I wouldn't want to be you if you were lying to
me now.

She said nothing.

He found a fold of bills in among the dust, underneath the
sofa. Fifteen twenties and a fifty. And some more in her purse.
The apartment was a mess. He had torn the computer books
from the shelves, uprooted the carpet and sliced most of the
soft-back chairs. In the five rooms of the flat only the bathroom
was untouched. He had examined the contents of the refrigerator, wanting to eat, but still unable to do so. He put the de-
frosting items back in the ribbed shelves.

He sat beside her on the living room floor staring at the
blank tv. Bruises on her head. The gag in her mouth.

It's all going to be fine just as long as you keep your head.
Her eyes were tight-set. Tears at the back of her pupils. She
was shaking, though it was not cold.

He didn't want her to spasm, but he couldn't release her
and he needed sleep.

You've got to stay calm, it's the only way. His voice had slipped completely. Do you want a drink or anything?

She shook her head. Nose flared, eyebrows arched, resting with her head against the wall, staring at the white ceiling.

He sat at the desk. She only a few inches behind him near the sofa. Still awake, how could she sleep? He got the Yellow Pages from a shelf in front of him and cleared a space on the table. Eight green stick-ups were pinned to the wall, messages in an unreadable scrawl. There was something sad about the place. It was sterile and young. He found the section marked Travel and ripped out the next five pages. On the toilet he picked up a newspaper from the magazine rack. He couldn't concentrate, the words fusing, making no sense. Tiredness was beating on him like a drug. He checked the pajama cord on her feet and the pantyhose ties on her ankles. She couldn't get out.

Do you have any sleeping pills?

She nodded towards the bathroom. He found the tablets in the cabinet by the mirror. Behind the stubble on his face, black rings under his eyes.

Here, I want you to take four of these. They'll help you sleep. She shook her head defiantly, her breasts moving under her blouse.

I'll have to force you otherwise.

She shook her head again.

I mean it, I don't want any trouble. Her eyes, brown and dark, said no. He prized open her mouth with his fingers, holding her jaw apart with half a fist. He put the pills on the back of her throat, on her tonsils. She choked but swallowed them down. He pulled out his fist, kneading the bite marks on his forefinger.

Sonofabitch, fucking sonofabitch, she said, saline collecting at the tear ducts of her eyes. They refracted blue.

Shut up.

He re-gagged her and stared at a print of a Masai warrior. Hair pleated, face intense and demanding, maroon colored. She was still awake, though drowsing over. She swore softly. He was waiting. He was so tired.

Sonofabitch she mumbled over and over in a murmur.

He starting picking up some of the stuff from the floor. Chairs and pillows. A book entitled *Lotus 1-2-3* was not about meditation. He dropped it on the table and checked her over. Her breathing was constant, eyelids fluttering.

She was sweeter now. He went to the bedroom and got a blanket and put it over her legs. In a couple of minutes she was snoring fitfully. He stared at her. A tap was dripping in the kitchen sink. He placed two hands on her right breast cupping it as if it were a bird. The heating system was clanking hollow in the water pipes. He leaned forward and kissed her long forehead. It was smooth and smelled of lemons. He pulled the blanket up to her neck and turned.

Her bed was on the floor. As big as the room. Dust had been swept artfully into the corners. The window was fenced in. He lifted up the latch and shoved across a rusted metal shutter. He pulled up the screen and finally the glass. Below him was an outdoor fire escape. A safety-conscious building, he thought, indoor and outdoor getaways. He climbed out of the apartment, his hand on the metal trackway. It was nearly dry. He sat with his back against the rail looking down seven stories. He could hear the wind. In front of him he could see the buildings on the far side of the river. He was that close. The street was emptying out. The lights in the opposite building were nearly all extinguished. He sat and thought. Flies were making their way towards the bedroom lamp, so he pulled down the screen again. He was isolated now. Sitting up there. Anonymous in the shadows. He lit a cigarette, cupping his hands to protect the flame. She was inside sleeping.

Aircraft engines soared far to the north. Traffic was quieter. The tips of his fingers were numbing. He took a good smoke and held it in his lungs until he thought his chest would burst. Exhaling through his mouth and nose in a choke. He coughed twice more. His teeth began to chatter involuntarily. He threw the cigarette, still burning, way off the rail and watched it drop and disappear. He threw the lighter-gun after it and heard it clatter on the concrete, muffled and deficient of sound, disappointingly so for so symbolic an act. He opened the screen again and swung his legs back in through the window. Levering his thighs on the metal trough for the security shutter. It dug into him. He winced and fell onto the bed. The night behind him at last.

He took off his borrowed clothes in the bathroom and climbed into the shower. He found it hard to stand. The cold water stung his face, getting into his ears. He looked at his long body and deep-set eyes. He grinned at himself and scrubbed with his fingers, removing every last trace of blood and squalor.

After a ten-minute wait he got through to the tv psychic. He was on cable access, Channel 17. The room was bathed in the blue light from the set. She was sleeping behind him. He was sitting on the floor, naked under her bathrobe. He told the man his day and date of birth. And the hour, making allowances for the time difference. His American accent warbled, but better than the phoney Russian of the psychic. He looked good though, he was a bearded man in a crushed velvet, purple hat, with a long hook nose and wild hair. Demonic eyes made him look like Mussorgsky or Rasputin. He asked the man if it was safe to go home and the man said yes. He hung up the phone.

It was later now. Time was dropping like the forming of water marks.

The city came in through the window, its voices speaking of absolution and violence. The man above was pacing in his room, walking the same steps again and again. He could understand.

We're all alone.

He was a foreigner lying on a hostage's bed. Smelling of perfume and reading torn-out pages from her Bible. A book he read a thousand times in Sunday School. This not the King James, its words unfamiliar and lacking resonance.

And she slept, vulnerable and fragile, her neck up, an unmarked face in the oblique light. He rose into a sitting position, his stomach muscles cramping. The room was furnished. In the gloom he could see a cabinet, the drawers pulled out where he had searched for money. Underclothes scattered on the fitted carpet. Jewelry upturned. A mirror slanting. The trivium he had taught this room was one of havoc, ruin and waste. The stench was of violation. The shadows argued still. The heavy elements breaking down. He ran his finger along a furrow in the blanket and pulled the duvet tighter. His head leaning back into the duck-down pillow. The pattern was aztec, he remembered. The gun lay broken on the ground outside. The door was open to the living room. She was trussed. His hands were without color.

Water dropped. A siren wailed. Children turned in beds of covers. People slept. The hungry tapped. Lepers wandered silent in the parallel streets, and in the dark he wondered what her book had been.

PART TWO

" 'Oh there was a woman with a pimple on her bum
    She itched it, itched it, sore
She called for King Billy and he rubbed it with his willy
    And it itched, it itched, no more.'

This traditional street rhyme is of course a parody of the Loyalist song, 'The Sash', which begins with the semi-poetic refrain: 'It is old but it is beautiful, the colors they are fine,' and then deteriorates into a maudlin rant about the decorated sash of an Orangeman from Scotland. The mawkish tone of 'The Sash' makes it unusual amongst the victory anthems of the Northern Protestants, and the children's parody version suggests a moving flexibility among the young to poke fun at the bigoted sensibilities of their elders, albeit for degenerate sexual motivations. Alas, it is apparent that Northern Protestant youth, untouched by the majesty of gaelic culture, is incapable of producing songs with anything approaching the complex and subtle rhymes that are abundant among its peers in the South."

—PROFESSOR RUARI O'LUGHDAIGH, *ULSTER FOLK MUSIC*

CHAPTER SEVEN

It's the summer time and I'm running through the orchard at the back of the cricket field. The dogs are after me and I'm laughing. I'm running like I cannot run and it occurs to me that it isn't real. But the doubts are only a murmur on my forehead and I enjoy the wind on my face and the view down to the Lough. Of the ships and the blue water, and the channel beyond, warm and still like a linen tablecloth. I reach the aqueduct and the dogs are at my heels.

Below me are tiny waterfalls and a museum of pasture, cut off from the meadow.

Get her, get her, the man is shouting, and my friends are telling me to jump to the safety of field. Screaming at me, excited and terrified. I reach the edge. The dogs are up on me. Boxers, with their tails docked and slabbers coming out of their mouths. Snarling.

Jump, come on, they yell, frenzied. The ends of my feet are over the concrete levee. My training shoes. A lace untied.

Come on.

I leap off the aqueduct into the hay at the bottom. It breaks my fall and I bounce up and run to my friends. My skirt tucked up into the back of my dress. My panties mooning him. The dogs can't follow and start to howl and whine, pawing at the air.

Good for nothing mutts, the man says and hits them with his walking stick.

Mister Steensen's a bunion and has a face like a pickled onion, we yell at him.

Eat this, John says and throws a cow pat.

Eat this, I say and throw a handful of muck.

Copycat the barber your daddy fell in the harbor, your mummy's wick and doesn't knit and sucks the end of a dummy tit, John sings the nursery rhyme at me.

I turn. The sun in my eyes. The man swearing and walking back with the dogs. My daddy fell in the harbor?

My daddy?

Come on, it's time to get up.

I'm under the blankets and mummy's face is close.

Come on, it's time to get up.

I open my eyes.

I was up.

You were dreaming.

I wasn't, I was awake. I was just thinking.

Well get up now.

Ok maw, I say like a hillbilly.

Condensation is dripping down the window. Mum takes the smell of flowers with her as she leaves the room. She is already dressed and ready for work. I look at the clock on my desk, but everything is only shapes.

It's a quarter to, mum shouts.

Shapes and longitude. I lie under the duvet cover. Shivering and grumpy to be in the World of Up. I reach out an arm for my glasses on the bookcase, on top of the Jonathan Bardon book.

I put them on. The light is on and the door is open. The clock says twenty to. The space fits inside my eyes. My teeth chatter and I push the blanket down quickly. I reach on the carpet for my slippers. My hand on the rubber soles, the texture so great that I want to put them in my mouth. Instead I sit up and slip them on my feet, grab my dressing gown off the chair and pull it on over my pajamas. Putting the arms in as I stand.

I pull the waistband tight and widen the door. I walk down the hall to the kitchen. There are a couple of letters lying on the mat. In brown envelopes. The radio is on.

And that's a little number from Johnny Cash. And we'll be back in just a mo.

I sit down on the stool at the breakfast bar.

Here you go.

Mum puts a bowl of cornflakes and hot milk in front of me. Less milk than in Alan's. The way I like it. I set the spoon in the forest of dried flakes. She opens the door and throws the butt of her cigarette onto the patio. The cold boggy air comes in, smelling of salt and fertilizer. The jungle of birds scatter, flying up to the fence and the roof of the supermarket. Mostly crows and the yellow tipped seagull that turns the chicken bones inside out.

Drink up all your orange juice, she says, and gives me a half-full glass. She lights another, with the three-for-a-pound lighter. I sink the spoon, drawing up a tiny skull of milk. Mum is at the sink. Mascara on her tired face. She is washing dishes and blowing smoke out the open window. That seems to be all she's having.

Alan, come on now, she shouts.

He grunts from his room.

Come on.

I am, alright?

It's gonna be cold today, below zero, a little warmer along the coast, but black ice warnings are in effect, so beeee careful if you're driving out there, the radio man says.

I rub my eyes and look at the flecks on my fingertips. Little grains of sticky beryl.

There's post, Alan shouts from down the hall.

I suck my fingers clean and take a sip of juice. It is warm on the back of my throat. I'm still not hungry. I push down the cereal and let the spoon float on top of the cornflakes. Balancing it on the rim. Milk invading at the sides and sinking it.

Post.

I know.

The spoon slips, but before it disappears to the bottom of the bowl, I grab it. Mum looks at me sternly. I take a bite of the still crunchy flakes at the edge and drink a spoonful of the sugary milk.

That black ice is tarrible, so it is, the radio man continues.

Mum blows the last of her second cigarette out of the window.

Tarrible, so it is, I mean you think it would have the decency to be white so you could see it, but this oul black ice, powerful sleekit, so it is. Worse than those wee tricky wains that put marleys under your tires. I tell ya, today, if I catch any of youse motorists out there speedin there'll be trouble. So there will.

She stubs out the butt in the ashtray on the window sill and leaves it beside the blown glass dolphin. Ash still rising.

Do youse like Elton John? Well I do and here's a song I know you'll love. It's one of the oldies, "Rocket Man" . . . er coming up right now.

Alan comes in and sits down opposite me. I'm grinning from my coffee. A delirium of sweetness. He is a year and a half older. But different from me completely. His hair is reddish-brown and he has amber freckles all over his pale skin. Like his da, who was a ginger bap, at least as far as I remember. Alan's thinning above his forehead but he brushes it down. He thinks nobody notices. His fat hand reaches for the juice and he drinks it down in one. He burps and we both laugh.

That's so rude, mum says.

Sorry, he replies winking at me.

To cap it off, as he's pouring the coffee he cuts a fart.

Oh Alan, mum says.

Sorry.

Sorry isn't good enough. Do you do that when you're out—what will people think?

I said—

You should be setting a positive example for your sister. Come on. Do you think the, uh, do you think Mrs Thatcher passes wind? Or the Queen?

Alan looks at me and rolls his eyes.

Mum are you saying the Queen doesn't fart? I ask her seriously.

Of course she doesn't. And don't say that word.

You don't think the Queen farts?

No I do not.

But she has to, she's a human.

The Queen would never do something so rude.

Mum let's be clear about this. Are you saying that the Queen is too Royal to fart? Alan chips in.

Yeah mum, she has a special ability, taught to her when she was wee? Like the masons or something? That only those of the Royal blood can know?

I don't want to talk about this, she says.

Yeah you're right, Alan says, nearly laughing. When she was like six years old King George took her into the secret fart-control room of the palace and . . .

That's enough, mum says and by her voice we can tell she means it.

Alan winks at me.

Mmmmm, mum says to herself and I can't help but smile a

137

little. Since moving out of the council estate and getting her new job mum has been keen to distance herself from her past. Trying to be more genteel or something. It's sweet in a way.

Alan burps again but this time neither of us hardly notice. I'm busy playing with my feet. I kick my left foot out of the slipper and wrap my toes round the washer at the bottom of the stand of the breakfast bar. As I eat I lift the washer up and down the pole with my big toe. It's moist. Like ferns. And whiskey cold, but the smooth metal feels good.

I've got what we call a navy spoon. With a yacht on the end. A tiny sail on the handle. The spoon is two mirrors, one is upside down.

Hurry up you two, I have to get going.

Alan finishes his breakfast and goes to the bathroom to get washed. Mum goes into her room to put lipstick on. I eat slowly and run the ring at my feet up and down the metal in time to the music. The pole is slightly bent in the middle and warped from when my brother and me sat on the breakfast bar. We could feel it distort under us. Buckling with a huge cracking sound. But we never told and mum has never noticed. But the washer only goes up half way now. I stop and look at it under the table and see the fracture. Rusting. It worries me because if it breaks we won't be able to get a new one. Mum will go nutso. I stop playing with it and put my slipper back on, having to bend down and use my fingers as a shoe horn. The radio starts playing ads.

Bathroom's free, Alan shouts. I put my breakfast bowl in the sink and run hot water into it. I drink the last of my juice and rinse out the glass.

I go into the bathroom. I pee and take a packet of Tampax out of the cupboard. I am wondering if my period will start today. I am already a few days late. I wash my face with soap and cold water and brush my teeth quickly. I try to comb my hair but it doesn't do any good and it hurts.

Back in the bedroom I put the tv on to listen to *Breakfast News* while I dress. My school uniform is pressed and clean. Nothing new seems to be happening in the world. It's all about the Middle East and the trouble there seems unresolvable. Like here.

My books are all disorganized because I didn't have to go to school yesterday. On Tuesday I only have one class on my timetable and that's History. I've made a deal with my History teacher that I can skip the class if I spend the day working. And I did. I caught up on the Bardon book and *Portrait of an Artist*. But today is busy. I've got three sessions of History, then Physics, then English and finally Art. No free time at all.

It's an unusual combination of subjects to be taking for my A-levels and everyone was against it. Including mum and Alan. Only three subjects actually count for university. They all want me to drop Physics, and it's not my best, but I kind of like it. I pat the text book.

I open the bottom drawer and get the photographs I've taken over the last few weeks and the sketches I've done of America. I get my bag and put in my European History books and my Course 2 Physics book. The Art stuff is over the book of Louis MacNeice poems. And the book on Klimt. I get a little rush when I think of Mr Preston.

Is everybody ready? mum shouts from the hall.

Yeah, I say and turn off the tv. Alan is already waiting in his duffle coat. He sticks his tongue at me.

Beat ya, beat ya, he says.

You are such a child, I say back.

Did you turn your light off? mum says.

No, I forgot.

Well stop footering about and come on.

I run back down the hall and turn off the light, my hand snagging on my *Dukes of Hazzard* poster on the wall. I tear the corner under the blue tack.

Shit. There is a rip halfway down Daisy's face, but better her than one of the fellas.

Mum and Alan are walking down the path. I close the bedroom door and step into the hall. I grab my lunch from the table. I can see through the cellophane that she has made me a jam piece.

The day is bright, with the wind lashed to the telegraph poles. The hedge barely moves. The sun is over County Down and the clouds are wrecked behind the Knockagh. In the garden the dug earth is full of bird shit and white stones. A slater is crawling along the moss between the cracks. I close the front door by lifting up the handle and slamming it. I test to see if the handle has locked. It has, so I turn and swing the bag up onto my back.

I can hear round the corner that mum is having trouble starting the car. It's chilly today. A thorn from the rosebush is on the porch slab. I pick it up and balance it on my nose, like a horn. I lick the bottom and stick it on. I go round the side of the house to the drive. Frost is on the gravel. My head tilted back. Alan is in the front seat with his seat belt on. The starter is wheezing like an old man. I get in the back.

Did you put de-icer in? Alan asks.

Yes.

We could still get the bus, he says sarcastically.

You're not going to get the bus.

But if the engine won't start . . .

It's going to start, it just takes a while.

Alan's eyebrows go up. I have more faith. The car is Jap. I know the engine will kick in eventually. Mum tries it another couple of times.

Don't flood the engine, he says.

Alan please.

Finally the motor shudders into life. Mum pumps the accelerator as exhaust fumes rise in the cold air, blocking the view through the rear window. Alan puts the radio on, turning through the stations until he finds one playing "Black Sabbath." Mum reverses the car slowly, edging it between the pillars and out into the street.

Car coming, I say and she puts the handbrake on.

The car goes past and we angle out into the road. Mum keeping the petrol on to stop us from stalling.

When the car has backed out she puts it carefully into first. She turns right onto Victoria Road and slips in behind a tractor. No one has commented so I take the thorn off my nose. I notice there is a skelf on my thumb. Underneath the skin, a big one. I dig it out with my fingernail. Without it bleeding. I'm pleased. The tractor is going about ten miles an hour. Alan taps the dashboard impatiently.

Overtake it ma.

Hold your horses.

We follow the tractor up to the building site behind the graveyard, and when it turns off we finally get into the fourth gear.

Mum pushes the button on the cigarette lighter.

Give me my bag, she says and I reach it to her from the gap between the seats. One hand on the steering wheel, she hokes out the packet of Rothmans. She puts a cigarette in her mouth and lights it.

My brother flips the station.

You're listening to national radio one. Radio, radio, radio one, the jingle plays.

I suck my thumb where the skelf was.

A boy runs across in front of us.

Ye wee skitter, mum says, braking.

She drops a gear and we turn past Prince Andrew Way. For many years it used to be called Kennedy Way but the strain of having a major road christened after a Catholic president finally proved too much for the local council who changed the name on a split 6 to 5 vote.

I look out at the massive curbs and the new housing developments. Big sheet-glass windows. Bavarian slats and roofs that hide the angles. Odd. The construction is not completed and in the wet the place looks like something from World War I.

Mist has washed the field on the other side of the road. Baird's Mansion and the place where the orchard used to be. From my dream. It's empty now and depressing.

Things flit by the window: a blistered pond, a burned-out car, the swollen teats of a cow. A Shetland pony bedraggled. Chewing on the bog grass. The pony I can understand.

Rag cloth and the remains of plastic bags are on the barbed-wire fence. Like a dog turned inside-out, blowing violent motions in the no wind. Water comes like a river off the new road. Mum accelerates the car up to fifty-five. She has opened the window to blow out the smoke, but the breeze funnels it into the back seat, I can taste it and it smells good. We drive parallel to Love Lane and the golf course. The trees are sparse and the birds weave masses for the branches. Docked. In stacks I can see the cardboard limbs and boats of leaves against the unpainted breeze-block walls. The lane has been widened for the increased traffic to the new estate.

The car slows as we turn onto North Road. The traffic is still comparatively light. The Church of God is in front of us. The spire and oblong of the tabernacle buildings looking strange and alien among the squat council houses.

Mum looks at her watch. I do too. It's just after eight, we're earlier than usual.

You've got your Art project today, haven't ya? she says looking at me in the mirror and wiping a lipstick trace off above her mouth.

I do indeed.

You must be very good, that Mister Preston thinks a lot of you.

I don't say anything to this.

Alan is arseing around with the radio's volume control and mum continues.

I wish you'd let me see your project.

I will when it's done. So I will.

I'd love to go to America, she says almost girlishly.

Aye and me too, Alan says. It's not fair that you got to go and I didn't.

It's the luck of the draw, mum says.

It is not, they just felt sorry for her, Alan grumbles and then turns red. His cheeks twitching.

Alan, mum says, annoyed.

My brother steals a look at me over his shoulder. From his face he is sorry for what he has said. I stick my tongue out at him to make him feel better. He wrinkles up his nose and goes back to fiddling with the radio. Mum throws the cigarette-end out of the window. I watch it fall onto the road and under the wheel of a Mother's Pride bread van.

We get to the end of the road. There is Hope, the sign outside the church says. Above a rainbow in a curvy font. It's a strange thing to announce but I suppose it's necessary in the face of evidence to the contrary. We pass the Inter and stop at the entrance to the Grammar School. A red car has followed us all the way.

I'll take you down the drive, we've got good time today.

We'll be too early, Alan whines.

Yeah, we should have got up later, I join in.

I'll get you up later if you're not careful, mum says, and we all grin at the nonsense of this remark.

She takes it leisurely down the drive and stops the car in the bus-turning circle. In the school buildings the lights are on. White and red and winking like a casino. We get out of the car into the windy morning.

Ooh bit breezy up here, mum says. I hold down my skirt. Alan offers to carry my bag and I say nah.

Ok take care you two. Be good.

Be good yourself, I say back.

And if you can't be good . . . Alan says and waves with both hands.

Oh you, mum says and pulls the door closed. She turns the car and we both wave ironically like little kids until she gets to the end of the driveway. She drives onto North Road and a car the shade of Scotty's shirt comes in to take her place.

We walk down the path past the rugby pitches and the river. Close together. He protective of me, blocking me from the gale.

What do you have first? I ask him.

Computer Studies.

Ach that's a load of oul keek, I say, teasing.

Aye like your face.

If I'd a face like yours I'd teach my arse to speak.

I thought that was your arse speaking.

You were thinking were ya? I thought I heard an unfamil-iar noise.

Ach take a wise wee girl.

We walk over the bridge and into the car park, ripping the piss out of each other until we get to the new school buildings.

See ya later, he says and goes off to meet his friends down

at the football pitch. They play footy every day whatever the weather.

See ya. Wouldn't want to be ya.

I go upstairs to my locker and leave in my Art folder and drawing pencils. I put in my lunch and lock the door. I am the only one in the corridor as I walk to the sixth-form study. I open the door and find the lights are on. It isn't as empty as I was expecting. Keith McGahern is sitting on the desk reading a history book. He is a cute boy, Keith. A bit odd and shy, and he has a scar in the middle of his forehead from a childhood accident. Nice though.

Hiya.

Oh, hiya.

What're you up to?

Ah nothing.

Me too.

I put my bag in the racks at the back of the study where my friends and I usually sit. Keith is in the far corner near the window, where the boys are. Against the wall is the taste of glue and petrol. From a Zippo lighter. My name is mentioned on the desk partition in marker pen. Old news. In the wind outside there is the sound of laughter, a tremble of little girls. The buses must be coming in. I unzip my bag and blow the chalk dust off the desk.

On the wall I can see something and I go over to take a closer look. It's a graffiti drawing of me climbing up the Empire State Building like King Kong. In green felt tip. Done recently. It doesn't look anything like me. But the curly brown hair and specks and hump are enough to make the point. I try to pretend they're just jealous. But it's more than that. I want to think of something else but can't. I'm biting my lip as I hear footsteps on the corridor. As I get out my Physics book to look over my homework, the door opens and Pete comes in. A dopey-looking

145

kid here on a transfer from the Inter. It's the school for pupils who fail their 11 Plus and mostly teaches vocational studies. If you work hard enough sometimes you get promoted up here to the Grammar. But everybody still rakes you for coming from the thick school. The poker chips we made out of paper have PAP written on them, which means Pete's A Prick. And everybody knows what the letters stand for except him.

Hi, he says to Keith.

Hi.

Hello Pete, I say.

Hi there.

He sighs and throws his bag onto the desk.

He sits behind Keith and starts retying his tie, loose hair falling over his face. His nails are long, like sugar scoops. Grappling with the tie as if it's a tricky snake. All three of us sit in silence for a moment in different parts of the room and then: Does anybody want a game of poker? I ask, the words just coming out.

Keith looks up from his book and stares over at me. He seems to think for a second.

Yeah why not? he says. Pete do you wanna play?

Aye alright.

We go to a table and sit down. Keith shuffles the cards like a pro and announces five-card stud. When Laura and the other girls arrive off the Marina bus, I'm playing cards with Pete and Keith at the boys' table. I'm down on the chips, but I can see her face of mild astonishment and that's enough. We're talking about last night's tv. All American shows of course. That's all that's ever on.

Did you see that bit on *Hill Street Blues* where they have the riot?

An he feels up the woman cop?

146   Oh my God I laughed. And she like slaps him or something?

I was fit to be tied, Keith mocks, in a posh English accent.

He's funny that boy, Pete says to me.

I was watching *MASH* on BBC2, it was funny too.

Ach but that's an old show.

Laura and her friends ignore us and sit in the corner. One of them skites my bag across the floor and they laugh at something. Their giggles pitched and menacing.

We play cards until the room begins to fill and the boys want their table back. My PAP chips are almost gone but it doesn't matter.

That was good, Pete says.

Yeah.

The bell goes for assembly and people begin to file out putting their prefect badges on. I begin to get anxious that Sarah won't show up. But she does when the room is nearly empty.

Hey what about ya?

Uh not too bad.

Dja miss the train?

Nah dad give me a lift.

Come on we better go.

Sarah dumps her stuff on the floor and we walk briskly along the corridor to the assembly hall. Kids are already milling about outside the doors.

Where do we go today? I ask her.

Don't know, I forgot to look at the roster.

Let's go behind the first years, they're no trouble.

That's what you think.

We push our way in through the fire doors. The lines are starting to form up. First years at the front nearest the platform and lower sixth at the back. The prefects are dotted about the hall, keeping the lines straight and people in order. All the girls are on the left hand side of the room and the boys on the right.

In the melee I can see that big Louise McMurtry is leaning

up against the wall bars, with an unlit fag in her mouth. Brazen and unconcerned. Chatting with the fourth years. She waves at me and Sarah. Not afraid of jeopardizing her cool.

The sun is out, beams falling from the high windows. Yellow sunflowers of light on the gymnasium floor. Dust is everywhere. And the screaming of kids and laughter. We shove through the crowd to the front of the hall and stand behind the first year girls. Yelling at each other, squeezing their eyes shut and playing. Skinny and looking like dolls in their tiny uniforms. Or like elves, dressed up. Their white socks are pulled up high on their thin legs, past the knees. Most of them are wearing pony tails. Some have Girls Brigade badges and brooches from the Scripture Union. Sarah and I are scruffy by comparison, not wearing our blazers, our top shirt button undone, our ties at rakish angles. And my hair, as always, is everywhere.

The back doors close and the voices drop a decibel. Like a choir on cue. The talk in front is soft and anonymous. Sarah is straightening the row. In the pause I lean my heels on the basketball three point line. There is a hush of whispered silence before the wing doors open and the teachers begin to file onto the stage in front of us. They look strange in their black gowns with multicolored hoods drooping down the back. Like great walking birds under bunched up vestigial wings. They parade in silence onto the platform. About half the staff. Mainly the older ones. Mr Preston not among them. Mr Pilkington, my History teacher is there looking tired. He's a part time peeler, probably out all night. And Jabba, the other Mr Pilkington, my Physics teacher. Bod, and Smiler Smith, Fritz Smith and Jungle Jim. And the two new Geography teachers talking. The surprise is Mrs Gilmour who comes on next, walking confidently.

Sarah is squinting. Is that oul Granny Gilmour? she asks.

Uh huh.

Sheesh.

Sarah and I are both surprised to see her. No one had expected her to come back so soon. She had been away on a "holiday." In fact, recovering from a mental breakdown after her husband was killed by the IRA.

She looks older but ok, she has her hymn book out already. The second and third row fills and finally Mr Synal comes on and sits at the piano, followed by the headmaster, Mr Jason, who stands at the lectern. When everyone has stopped and settled Mr Jason says:

Let us pray.

All the heads bow in front of us.

We thank thee oh Lord for bringing us safely into thy care, for another day. We thank thee for thy goodness and thy—

Sarah taps me on the shoulder.

Did you see Stevenson?

What?

Did you see Stevenson go?

No.

He left just before the prayer at the side door.

Did he?

Yup.

They've joined the church of the Nazarene.

Mister Stevenson?

Aye.

And what does that mean exactly? I say like a tv interviewer.

Well it means he's not allowed to pray with the rest of us.

I'm not praying at all.

Well you know what I mean.

Yeah.

I imagine Mr Stevenson standing outside with the Catholics who are also waiting until the prayer is over. It's a state school but the Catholics here don't like to pray with the rest of us. Neither them nor the weirdo proddy sects. They all have to wait   149 outside. They're probably having a great time. Most Catholics of course are at the Catholic maintained schools. I had to go to one once for an inter school quiz. It was odd. Pictures of the Virgin Mary and a bleeding Jesus all over the place. Gave me the creeps so it did.

I look around the gym. Everyone is pretty much behaving themselves. Over on the boys' side, Keith is pointing his finger at a couple of boys who have their eyes open. Threatening them, only half jokingly. On our side we don't care, as long as they don't talk.

Mr Jason finishes in a placating voice: We humbly ask oh Lord that you help us in the day ahead to do our best, and to give our best, to respect the principles of the school and to give ourselves fully into your loving care, Amen.

Amen some of the girls in front of us whisper.

There is a bout of coughing. The doors beside the climbing frame open and a few girls come in and join the line at the end. Mr Jason looks to the side of the stage. Carol Burgess walks on carrying the Bible and stands at the podium. It is her turn to read the lesson. All the prefects have to do it, at least once. Sarah remembers something and leans close.

Oh my God.

What?

Yesterday when you weren't here. Jesus.

What? What?

Simon McGrath was doing the reading.

Big Simon.

Uh huh and he really screwed up, so he did. He had to say: Why do you a Jew ask a drink of me—a woman of Samaria? But he just couldn't say it. Over and over he kept saying: Why Je, Jew a Jew ask a drink of me. Finally, in front of the whole school, he walked off the stage without finishing.

150   Shit. Why didn't you call me?

I forgot.

Jesus, he must have felt wick.

And he's not in today.

Jeez.

Carol opens the Bible to the appropriate page. I remember when I had to do it, I had to read the parable of the sower. I was nervous. But it went ok.

Carol coughs.

Jesus withdrew with his disciples to the sea. And a great multitude from Galilee followed, she begins.

Two girls in front of me are talking. Sarah taps them on the back and tells them to be quiet.

Also from Judea and Jerusalem and also from beyond the Jordan. And he told his disciples to have a boat ready for him because of the crowd, lest they should crush him.

I wipe sweat from my eyebrows. It is hot in here now. The heat has been on all morning and the sun is warm through the windows. I take out my hanky and dab at my forehead. Carol finishes the reading and walks off the stage. Mr Jason clears his throat theatrically.

We will now sing Hymn Number 3, "Be Thou My Vision," he says. Everyone reaches into their pocket for their hymn book. A groan comes from some of the boys at the emergency exit. Sarah and I found out that they bet on the hymn number every morning. Running a book on the eighty-five hymns that we play. It's been running for some time and has odds and everything.

"Be Thou My Vision" is a popular favorite, so the book must have lost a packet.

In the keen edged fistling I can hear Mr Jason ask somebody to get the announcement sheet from his office. Threads of stories are on my hymn book and little drawings. A dead fish and bicycle wheels. Lizards and the sad outline of ocean liners. Past the blank pages and above the white-out, the hymns themselves are covered in doodles and graffiti. My practice autographs and those of my friends. On the back I've drawn a fat lady singing and a king with bongo drums. I've had it for six years and in the time the drawings have got worse. Less rigorous. Now most of the hymns are illegible. Number 3 is missing in my book, so I have to share with Sarah.

Mr Synal begins on the piano.

We begin to sing.

Be thou my vision, oh Lord of my life, not be all else to me save that thou art . . .

The piano sounds tinny and off-key and I wonder if some-one has put something inside it again, though stunts don't usu-ally happen until the end of term. Last year during assembly Mr Synal had to get up and pull a dead halibut out of the keys. Smitty McCullers got suspended over that but the only proof was that his dad owned the fish shop, and so they had to let him off.

The heat is getting oppressive now and I can see some of the younger girls start to sway. As we get to the fourth verse their necks are glistening with a trace of perspiration. The song is long and Synal is playing really slowly for some reason. I have to pause for breath after every word. My throat is dry and I can see knees weakening as we get to the third verse. Finally a girl falls straight back into the row behind her, on Sarah's side. A second-year puts her hands out and stops the girl from banging her head on the floor. Sarah runs over and when I get there we both carry her out. Sarah lifting her under the legs and me at the shoulders. One of the boys offers to help but I shake my head.

The ancient of days, in Your salvation and in Gods name we praise, the hymn continues.

We heave the girl through the fire door, Sarah opening it

with her arse. We rest outside for a moment and carry her along the corridor, towards the first aid room, but half way down, she revives.

Uh what happened? she says.

We set her down on the corridor floor.

You're ok.

Oh God did I faint or something?

Yeah.

Oh no, I feel wick.

It's alright, I don't think you'll be the only one, it's dead hot in there.

Oh.

We tell her to go to the first aid room and rest there until a teacher comes to see her. When we get back into the assembly hall Mr Jason is in the middle of the announcements.

The rugby team lost by a considerable margin . . . But the score did, er, not reflect the play.

Sarah nudges me.

The girl who fainted comes back in.

The girls hockey team won. They were playing, er, Campbell College and they won by four points to two.

Laura's the captain of the first eleven. She is over at the far wall with Michael Clawson. Beaming.

Congratulations to Laura and all the girls. On another topic, it has come to my attention that a number of people are wandering out of grounds at breaktime or on their lunch hour. I would like to warn anyone who wanders out of school bounds that if they are caught doing it I will treat this offense very seriously indeed. I know it's only a tiny minority of you. But if you do it again, mark well my words. It will be a short walk down the drive for you. A very short walk.

Sarah and I smile at each other. We've got t shirts that say: We Are the Tiny Minority. It's the headmaster's favorite phrase.   153

That and: the short walk down the drive. Which is his euphe-
mism for expulsion. He continues with the announcements in
a tedious monotone.

D'ya wanna hear a geg? Sarah whispers. Heard it yesterday.

Ok but whisper it.

Baby polar bear in the Arctic goes to his mummy and says:
Mummy am I a real polar bear? And she says: Of course you
are. And he goes away and then a day or two later he comes
back and says: Mummy are you sure I'm a real polar bear? And
she says: Yes of course you are. And he nods and goes off. And
then a week later he comes back, and he says: Mummy are you
really sure I'm a polar bear? And she says: Look you really are
a polar bear, why do you keep asking? And he looks at her
sadly and says: Well, it's cos I'm always bloody freezing.

I suppress a laugh and try to think of a joke or else she has
me beat.

That was a good one. But I got a better one I tell her. Alan
told me.

Is it dirty?

Nope.

Ah go ahead anyway.

Okey doke. Ian Paisley is in London in Chinatown.

Does this have to be about Ian Paisley?

Yes.

Why? You know my dad votes for Paisley, I won't be able
to tell it to him.

I don't care it has to be about a militant prod. That's the
whole point of the joke.

Ok. Tell it then.

Ok though you've probably spoiled it.

Just tell the joke for God's sake.

Ok. Paisley's in London in Chinatown and he goes into a

wee shop and he sees a brass rat in the window. Very beautiful, very unusual.

Like me.

Like you. So he asks the owner if he can buy it and the wee Chinky boy says sure. Ten pounds for the rat. A thousand pounds for the story behind it. So Paisley gives him the ten pounds and leaves. Anyway, he's out of the shop five minutes, carrying the brass rat, when suddenly all these rats start to come out of alleys and out of drains and begin following him. He walks on and more and more rats come out. And he starts to run and looks behind him and he sees thousands of rats chasing after him. So he runs faster and faster and more and more rats are behind him. Eventually he gets to Westminster Bridge and there's literally millions of rats after him. He's out of breath, doesn't know what to do. So he throws the brass rat into the Thames. Suddenly all the rats jump in after it and drown. Paisley goes back to the shop and the wee Chinese man sees him and says: You're back for the story huh? And Paisley says: No, I was just wondering if you had a brass Catholic.

She cracks up just as Mr Jason coughs a final time nodding over to the vice principal. The teachers stand and begin to leave the stage. The back doors are opened and the assembly breaks up. We struggle out through the side doors with the rest of the prefects. The rest of the teachers are arriving through the front entrance, some taking a final smoke before coming into the school building. We are being buffeted from all sides and swept up towards the stairs and to the lockers. In the chaos of running kids I can see Mr Preston standing at the side door, a pipe in his hand, emptying the bowl onto the ground, waiting until the anarchy eases so he can come in.

He waves at me through the crowd, the ring on his finger glinting in the sunlight. His smile broad and confident on his face. The parabolas of leaves curling and oul behind his hand and the lines from his eyes spun and delicate and warm. His wave is a slight declination of the fingers and my hand goes up to wave back. But just then we are shoved up the steps by the crowd and the staircase bends round so I can't see him anymore. The first-year boys are running past us, on their way to Geography. One of them pushes Sarah against the railing. She takes a swipe at him but he's gone. She looks at me and shakes her head. She says a word that I don't hear and is staring like she's waiting for a reply to something.

Yes, I say, nodding my head in mock agreement. Her mouth is still expectant, but I can't say anything more, I'm in a kind of daze and busy thinking about someone else.

CHAPTER EIGHT

He smelled the room. Vaseline and jasmine. Animation. Glossolalia.

The headmaster entered and they froze. In the new-found silence the boys performed like clockwork, on a cold floor changing noiselessly. It was to him like a series of mimes. Intransitive and without motivation. Outside the pitch was wet. Frogs on the edges in the rain. The trees with half closed and bare limbs. Even from the school, huge puddles revealed themselves behind the try line. The headmaster slipped out to put on waterproofs. In the interregnum voices addled and someone laughed. The bog washed down to the field, and under the houses, and on to an impartial sea. Four dissenters had formed a quorum for a roughing up. A fat boy with red hair squealed as rolled up towels snapped around him. The room was lost in a bedlam of conversation.

Stop that, that flippin hurts, that does.

It's supposed to.

The socks were royal blue and pulled right up to the knees. The boots were tight. Through the open window the grass was green and sodden, a swathe of color.

A pale intestine of ash was rising from the slate chimneys.

Hey, are we allowed to wear tracksuit bottoms?

Chlorine running out of the leaf blocked drain. Spreading white and poisonous over the tiles outside the changing room. Crows on the stark branches. Cawing in the mist. The Lough melancholy, and purgatory gray.

Hey are you awake?

And the cold funneling through the window, honed and sleekit. His shoulder moved. A hand was on it.

What? he said.

Hey where were you? You're wild boy, I thought you'd passed out or something.

He recovered a smile.

How could I have passed out if I was standing up, eh?

I don't know you could have.

What were you saying anyway?

Ehm I was wondering if we were allowed to wear our track-suit bottoms, because of the cold.

Crazy hair and moon calf eyes, his friend from way back. He didn't even have to look at him.

I don't know, why don't you ask Willy, he replied absently, still staring out at the ships paralyzed, waiting in line by the outer marker.

He doesn't know, he told me to ask you.

Aye, and what am I, the Oracle?

Pilot boats coming down the deep water channel, horses in the wake.

Well do you know or not?

I don't think we are, just ask Davey when he comes back in.

If I wait until he comes everybody else'll be changed and he'll chew my balls off.

A tanker was off the harbor mouth and a coal boat was pouring black smoke everywhere. Contaminating the air.

Well I don't know, I wouldn't wear them anyway, they'll slow you up so they will.

Yeah I suppose so but it's bloody freezing out there.

Yeah.

158   The door opened to the corridor. Mr Lattimer leaned in, his

hand holding onto the outside handle. His blond hair darkening. Davey. No one called him by his surname. He was smaller than most of the boys in the room. A diminutive seemed more appropriate.

Hurry up, the head's coming to watch us today, he said and closed the door. The headmaster would be there and half the whole school. If they won they'd be through to the final.

He tugged at the laces in his left boot, running them between his finger and thumb.

Anybody see that filum last night? a voice said.

Wild. I tell ya.

Week old mud slewed off onto the floor.

What was it about? someone asked.

Doctor Who is on the Earth with the Daleks.

He loosened the rungs of the boot and tugged the lace until it was equal on both sides.

What channel was that on, was that on two?

He took the right side and wrapped it round the sole clockwise and the same with the left, anticlockwise.

No it was on ITV late. You should have seen it. Them Daleks were pretty scary. See, they wanted to get everybody's brains.

They'd have a hard job finding yours.

Very funny I don't think.

With the length reduced he tied the laces in a tight bow and then again into a knot. He tied the other boot and stamped onto the floor to loosen the mud between the studs.

Anyway they were taking everyone's brains and Peter Cushing was Doctor Who.

You saying they had the brains to come all the way across the galaxy in spaceships and yet they still wanted the humans' brains? Why?

159

They were evil. You get it? Ok? Anyway the Daleks were in London and everyone was pretty upset, you know, at the aliens coming and all. But it worked out ok.

He pulled out the divots of mud clinging to the soles and left them like cow pats on the slatted seat.

Glad to hear that. Wouldn't like to think you were having nightmares before the big game.

He rubbed his fingers on his shorts and stood to pull on the number seven shirt. The rain was falling now and the tips of the posts were stirring in the wind . . .

Light flashed in his eyes. He blinked. He looked at his hands. Older. All that time in a split of an eye. That had been the last game of the season. They'd lost. He didn't have an interest in school after that. One thing had led to another. Quitting, looking for a job. Getting work at the old folks home. Falling in with the hard men. And then the incident with his brother. Jail—in and out. All those moments from that moment. The flashing light again. He smiled. The red light glowed. He counted, one, two. The light effervesced again, running in a circle on his retina. His mouth curled down, eyes squinting into the mirror. He sat on the round stool, knees together, impatient. Another flash, he posed for the final time and he was done.

He got out of the booth and waited for the prints.

He went to an art-supply shop after that and then to a drugstore. He had everything he needed now. He went back.

In jail he'd forged some prison documents for an escape that never happened. Out again he'd forged currency, British and Irish and American passports and even a South African one. It was difficult. You had to really know what you were doing. He would change the name to the name of someone he knew in Buffalo, he would change the photograph and insert his own. If he made one mistake . . .

The apartment phone rang twice.

Sally this is Louise, get your ass out of bed and get in here. Frank isn't coming today, remember? I don't care what the excuse is or how you feel, you have to be here.

He worked his photograph in between the plastic of the passport. Delicate. He reminisced.

The second time was an hour before noon.

Sal come on now, this is serious girl. You better get in, or there'll be trouble.

Trouble, he said to the answerphone.

He blinked. White flecks had formed on the fingernails of his hand. They shook when he looked at them. He hadn't eaten for a day. He sat down on a concrete slab and stared out over the reeds. The sun was low in the sky. A thin man was reading a book on deafness, his head shaven and his nose pierced. A couple were leaning on the wire-mesh fence. And between the talk was the low howl of aircraft engines and the penitential croaking of frogs. Frogs. In the hollow of the bullrushes. The bay was somewhere close, perhaps he would see it when the bus came. The faces were all white. Pale and tired looking. He felt the stubble on his chin. He pulled out the passport and the money and checked them a final time. Not the best job he'd ever seen. But it might do.

The sun was setting. Orange raking in lines over the airport. The eastern sky darkening. His feet were more relaxed in the shoes he'd found in the closet. Mans shoes. Size eleven, he had no idea where they'd come from. She hadn't said. She hadn't said anything. He reached and touched a vine lying inert on the ground. The texture was foreign between his fingers, smooth.

It's ridiculous, we've been waiting for nearly twenty minutes, said a bald man in a raincoat.

Yeah tell me about it, the thin man said in imperfect diction. My flight goes in like twenty minutes.

Yeah it's tough.

The frogs were quiet now that people were speaking.

Should have got a cab, a blond-haired boy said sharply. He was wearing flares and a biker jacket, sunflowers painted on the back. He grinned at the boy. His upturned nose and narrow cheeks smiled back. The conversation died.

The bus pulled in at an obtuse angle, the doors on the side hissing open. A chubby girl in a blue uniform asked him where he was going.

Terminal 1.

Ok that'll be stop number 20.

Do you have any luggage? she asked.

No, he said.

He got off the bus and walked up the incline past a man in a motorized wheelchair. The glass on the front windows was dusted and the door screeched as he pushed it open. The building was nearly deserted. Only two of the airline desks were open, two out of twenty and one a flight to Madrid. A hastily drawn sign said: SunTour Airlines has moved to Terminal Five. Security was a fat cop carrying a pistol. Leaning against the far wall reading a tabloid. He stood and stared around the empty building.

The sun inside was hot and the light consummate and dry. The airport a bleached wasteland of tedium and emptied color. On the far wall he saw his flight. A man in a navy-blue blazer was reading a novel with a pink cover. That section of the hall was roped off by red-velvet cord. He had to walk through a metal detector to get in. A Hispanic woman in a bunched black uniform looked to see if he had any luggage. She shrugged when she saw that he had nothing. He walked in slow time and looked down. The path on the floor had patterns like sand dunes soldered onto acetate. The woman frowned at a thread on her dress and turned away from the empty expression on his face. In the tv screen the x-ray machine scanned the air. The floor squeaked as he walked to the desk. The man put down the novel and looked him over. Smiling, his bottom lip quivering down, his teeth like tombstones after heavy weather. Buddy Holly specs. A semicircle of light shone on the grease in his hair.

Hi there, he said.

Uh yeah, hello, I'd like to get a ticket for today's flight.

His voice unsteady for the first few words. The man smiled broader, his eyes blinking unexpectedly. Around him were dregs of other passengers, coming through the double doors on a tourist flight from Lourdes. Oldsters. Refugees in twin sets. People in walking frames and wheelchairs. The cure apparently not as successful as they would have hoped.

The man was talking:

Yes, mmm, you don't have a ticket? he simpered.

No, I want one if there are any available.

The man's fingers tapped impatiently on the desk.

Just let me see now, he said, straining to remain polite. He tapped on a keyboard.

Yes, we have several places available. You should really have purchased a ticket at the charter agency, it's not really my job to issue, but mmm yes I think I can get you a seat today.

Great.

Just fill in this form.

He handed him a raw photostat, the company logo smudged and illegible.

Can I borrow a pen?

As long as I get it back, the man said.

He handed back the form, written in blue ink, block capitals. A document of lies.

Good. Now could I see your passport?

He reached in the pocket of his jacket and deposited the book on the counter.

It got a little wet, he explained.

Did you spill something on it?

No I left it at a friend's in San Francisco and he mailed it to me and that's the way I got it.

Who did he send it with?

Uh, Federal Express I think.

Strange, they're usually pretty good.

His forehead was damp and his hands had clenched themselves together. The man was examining it carefully. You should apply to get a new one, he said.

Yeah.

He placed three fifty-dollar bills on the counter and some other smaller notes.

Is it all right to pay in cash?

What? The man said and looked up. Oh . . . yes, I'll just do your ticket.

He handed back the passport without another look and began typing at the keyboard again.

Smoking or nonsmoking?

Eh, smoking please.

Ok, and would you like a window or an aisle?

I'll take a window. No I'll take an aisle.

Are you sure?

Yes, aisle, you can stretch your legs out more.

That's right, ok, here's your boarding card, gate 19, you'll be called in about an hour.

Thanks.

He looked through the papers in the newsstand. The black girl behind the counter was bored, reading a magazine. A shop next door was selling perfume. It was empty.

A packet of Marlboros, he said.

We run out.

Well what do you have?

What you see there.

He selected a packet and paid in change. The girl went back to her magazine.

I need some matches too, he said.

She reached under the counter and threw him a book.

On the house, she said.

He went through another metal detector into the departure lounge. There was a cafe and a wide-screen tv. He ordered a coffee and sat at the window. The venetian blinds had all been closed. The sun, hot and excessive behind them. He put his finger on the dust and pulled down one of the metal sheets. Harsh fall light reflecting off the flat runways, blinding. He let the blind strip back up and blinked. Red spots lingered under his eyelids for a minute and a half.

He dozed for a while and when he woke light was coming in like projector beams in a cinema. Polarizing. Arcing in thin lines through cracks in the silvered blind. Dust was everywhere. All of it geometry and desert emptiness. This seemed to be the waiting area for passengers on his charter. The only person of color was the man behind the Quiksnak counter. In a red uniform, he stood bored, rearranging tea bags and coffee filters. Amazingly, a bird was flying from the carpet to the iron roof beams. Picking up muffin crumbs in a beak smeared with cranberry and darting between tables. It was trapped between the sealed windows and the revolving door. He had no idea how it had gotten in. Or survived. He watched it as his eyes adjusted to the light. The yellow tiles of the ceiling provided no resting place for the bird, so it had to perch uneasily on the backs of chairs or the neon Budweiser signs above the bar. He watched it flit amongst the tables. It was a sparrow, condemned and trapped in the perpetual light.

A woman sat down opposite him. Young, in a yellow dress. He ignored her. Obdurate and stony-faced, he stared into the coffee cup and watched the grease float in mini continents. Gravity and non-dairy creamer fusing the territories between them. The bird landed a table away on the hump of a plastic bin. The orange of its balance and the dry black of the feathers clashing in a compound grave and leaden.

The woman got up and four people sat down at the empty table.

Would you steal my grave as quick? she said laughing.

They were all men in their forties or fifties. Two were wearing baseball caps. One said USS Valley Forge, gold on a black background. The other showed a green fish leaping. The man nearest him was wearing a brown toupée and a white golfing top, his belly dangling in front of him like a prosthesis. The final man had gone down to the bar counting out money in his hands. The man in the navy hat arose and marched to where the tv stood blank and reflective on a pillar. He pulled over a chair and managed a stiff leg on it. When both legs were on, the chair buckled slightly and trembled. The man was holding onto his back with his left hand and fiddling at the tv with his right. A speaker crackled into life and the set came on. The picture half visible in the dead sunlight. The man grinned, happy and extraneous, and walked back to the table, bowlegged in his brown slacks. All three men turned their chairs and waited for the commercials to end. It was a show about a teenage boy. The men grumbled and turned back to face each other, leaving the tv unwatched and blaring in the air. Like a hard belt tightening.

The fourth man was coming back carrying a tray of cups.

Ok, who was the Bud? You wasn't it, Jase?

Yeah.

And you were the Miller and you just wanted coffee right? Ok, and it's a hot whiskey for me.

The man with the toupée laughed. Hey, I never realized you were going to get hot toddies, would have changed my mind in that case.

The men began to talk, but he was only half listening.

He broke the plastic of the coffee spoon and ran the jagged edge underneath the nail of his thumb.

My brother once told me what it was like, the man with the toupée was saying.

He gouged out black nail-dirt, which gathered on the edge of the spoon like a furrow.

We all had a real good time, Mullagh something. Anyway it was a great time. A verry good time. Finest golf courses in the world . . .

Laughter.

He rolled the dirt between his finger and thumb until it was in a ball.

It'll be six years since I last saw Jonathan.

He placed the dirt ball on the table and flicked it onto the floor.

Well I didn't bring him much. I bought that loose jumper, the gold one, I don't know if it even fits him.

The last two divots of fingernail muck he rolled together and ate. They tasted of nothing.

An old woman wearing a sleeveless dress sat down under the tv and craned her neck up to watch. Her arms were bare and dark, the hint of melanoma around the elbows. She smiled white teeth at the commercials. The tv light reflecting in her bloodshot eyes.

He went to the window and pulled apart the blind and watched the aeroplanes taxi, and the long flat vehicles like slabs of butter, parked or pulling luggage trollies. Where the fence was there were large refueling tanks, reeds, and a shimmering of water at the end of the runway. The sun was still in his eyes when he closed them.

He put hands up to his head. Terraces of skin and dark juices working in the bone.

At the Pepsi sign he opened his eyes. The old woman was gone, the sun was half a disc on the runway, a deeper red. The sky already getting darker in the east. The departure lounge was three-quarters full. The connecting flight from Florida had arrived, transfering passengers who were queuing up at the gate. Others were filing into the lounge or wandering out into the foyer. They were suntanned, crimson and blistered. Most in shorts, stocky and tired after the flight. After a few minutes of excitement the room settled down.

The tv was still loud, the air impatient. Another woman sat in the empty seat opposite. Her skin was grooved and the v of her t shirt was like a package. Lizardeen. Wrapped in linen. He saw the curve of her breast, the white of her underwire bra. She was young, in her early twenties, puppy fat on her thighs. Her eyes a tired blue. Looking over at the signs: Carlsberg and Michelob. A shamrock. Then she turned round and looked at her watch deliberately, making a point of not gazing in his direction.

Up from Florida? he said in his own voice.

Yes, er, yes just arrived.

Long flight, huh?

No, not too bad actually, it was ok.

Good, long one to go though.

Yes I suppose so.

Her tongue snaking as she spoke, indelicate, uncomfortable. Her hand held at her throat, tucking on the skin. She stood and smiled.

Well, she said.

Good trip, he said.

Yes, thanks.

His eyes right into hers, fierce and intimidating. His top lip puckering out cruely. He held her there for a second, almost let her go and deciding against it, and, then, finally, he did. He released her eyes, glancing to her left, the other side of the room where a neon bottle had the word Kool down the middle. When he looked back she was walking towards the door, her spine dividing the t shirt, the bird flitting above her head, her white stilettos wobbling on the carpet. That was stupid, he told himself. He had to be more careful.

Yet another flight had come in. This one merely passing through on its way to Orlando.

And by now the sun was broken on the bay. A cord above the horizon. The city stripped and there in his imaginings. Silhouetted in the heat haze. Stone and dogs, the black sky a work of art. And for him the interior dialogue playing. Voices telling him it wasn't worth the risk. A whole continent was in the west. In the sunset. He could just get up and go. The contrast was obvious. In a few hours the only color he would see would be battleship gray. And the people on the flight. Purchases high on shelves, photographs already marked in albums. Lined and paunchy. Barbarous articulation in their voice. Sweating venom and war stories. Their talk a parody of itself. He was pushing back the chair, standing, half his mind made up and then the announcement came:

Flight 203 is now boarding, the loudspeaker said, and he found himself sitting down again. To hell with the west, he was

169

going back. It was hardly a choice. He watched the plane to Madrid lift, flaps at neutral. Air India behind it, another thirty seconds and it too was up.

Would unaccompanied minors and passengers in rows 1 to 27 please come forward for boarding.

That's us. The men got up, their hand luggage an assortment of sports bags. They walked formally, stiff from sitting. A single coin sitting on the tray as a tip.

He waited for his turn. Feeling his systems get all wired. To relax himself he formed a triangle on the table with the forefingers of his hands. His thumbs were the base and the angles were impossible. More than 180 because his hand wasn't flat. A curve for the corners. He abandoned the triangle, his thumbs dipping into a card shape. The ace of spades. He brought his fingers closer, his thumbs dropping down until the gap disappeared.

Baggage handlers were throwing cases into an open cart. Laughing about something. Arms the color of charcoal.

Would the remaining passengers please come forward for boarding. Thank-you.

The line was thick with people. Cumulus flares over the tunnel to the aircraft. They were being hustled in one by one through the final metal detector and security check. It would take a while.

He walked to the toilet. Frosted glass refracted the last moments of direct sunlight. Woodshavings lay scraped under recent carpentry at the window. The bathroom was small. A tiled floor. Two cubicles, one twice as big for wheelchairs. He stood at the urinal and released the tension in his bladder. His eyes following the cracks in the tile. The loudspeaker was playing music, lite sounds. Prothalamion strains marking the joining of the passengers with the jet. Sickly. He shook the urine from the nape of his foreskin and rolled it down until he was comfortable. The boxers slapped taut and he pulled up his pants. The ceiling was brunette and bowed. He went to the polished metal sink. It was still a peculiar feeling doing this by himself. Blue was everywhere, even between his toes. Like dust. He pulled his fly, the metal stabbing. He looked at the digit, a hole was disappearing. Pale invading where it had been compressed. He pinched the finger between the thumb and forefinger of his left hand, the tip red, the middle white. He let the pressure off and it went back to normal, elastic and tense.

He washed his hands and walked over to the hot-air blower. A man came through the door. Sun on his face like grease. Fat beneath his chin.

The man looked at him and then his jaw dropped.

Wha ye deen hair? the man asked, a huge grin of recognition smearing its way across his face.

There was a puncture in his concentration, a shattering. He had to think fast, the face was familiar but no name came.

Ach, how are ya? he replied.

Nat tay baa wha bout yersel.

The accent was ruthless. Hard to follow.

Ach you know, getting along.

Wha're you up to owr hair?

Me, I'm just working you know.

The floor was wet, water dripping behind him. The accent clearer now. Percolating slowly.

Wher yat?

He took a deep breath.

Uh . . . Just at a firm, you wouldn't have heard of them. I thought yourin shipyard.

Fillings in his back teeth showing when he spoke. The voice easier with every word.

Me, no, is that were you are? Aye, was there three years, butaam on the brew now, you know?

Aye I know how it is; so what, were you on holiday?

171

Aye I'm over with the missus, d'ya know I was married?

I did not.

Two years now.

An evaporating pool of water on the floor now and the roof smoked and pliant. Tiles, he noticed.

Congratulations, any wee ones?

No not yet.

Eyes smiling, brown on green. Henna. A carotid vein pumping underneath the fragile skin.

It's funny seeing you. I hears all sorts of stories about ye.

Yeah? What like?

Nathin really.

Uh, you seem to have a bit of a tan already?

Aye on the sun machine six weeks so I was. Didn't want to look like a total eejit white and all.

Yeah.

So you flying home?

Yeah.

So tell me d'ya like it over here?

It's fine.

Yeah it's our second time. We came over on our honeymoon in December you know. It was a wee bit cooler, it'll be roasting down there now. Hey wait I tell the wife that I saw you. Oh and I'll be on the phone from Orlando tonight, tell everyone that I met ya. You know our Deirdre always had a wee soft spot for ye. Wait'll she hears you're going back. She's not married you know.

Aye, he said quietly.

He had to get out of there, the air was suffocating. His hands were dry and ready and yet he didn't want to do it.

Cool, look here, I have to go, probably see you in the terminal.

Sure will, it's a big oul thing, but I'll find ya and I'll introduce you to the ball and chain.

That'd be great.

Boy it's great to see you.

Look I really have to dash.

Aye no worries, see you outside.

The adams apple on the man's neck moving with a hint of gridelin. Unsuspecting.

Ok.

Yeah ok and I'll see ya later sure. Hey wait got a pen?

Pen?

Yeah, here take mine. Deirdre is at 67093. Call her. Write it down.

Just done it, he said giving the pen back. Listen it was good to see ya after all this time.

Yeah alright, see ya.

Yeah.

He pushed the handle and walked out of the toilet, sweat dropping off his forehead and onto his eyebrows. Shit, he whispered.

His lungs frozen. Muslin on his eyeballs. The walls achromatic. Losing pallor, discoloring. The corridor down to the bathroom empty. He could see the ashen walls smeared. Already. His foot tapping on the floor. Forward he could not go. The mantle breaking up like tea leaves. Civility and poison. The floor bleached, the ceiling closing down. The green of the toilet door drooling out, his options narrowing. Fuck, he said, and pushed on the door of the men's bathroom. Feet were in the cubicle. Trousers pulled down to the ankles. His heart thumping in his head. The loudspeaker nagging. Aircraft through the frosted window. Water flowing in the pipes. The noise of excrement dropping into water.

The cubicle was on a latch. He jumped and kicked it open. Twice in two days.

What the fuck— his friend said. It's you, Jesus what the jesussnfuck are you playing at?

Whips about his knees. He looked at him for a moment. Sorrel eyes. Hair on his forehead, hanging down like a child. Surprise and consternation on his brow.

In a single movement, his hand flat, he struck him on the neck below the chin. Fast. His eyes blinked once, his mouth open, inaudible. A single split in the gray depths. He fell to one side, his head clanking sickeningly on the metal wall. Hands together like a priest.

Sorry, he said.

He looked like a marionette with the head-strings docked. He stared at him only for a second and closed the toilet door. He maneuvered the body off the seat onto the floor and pulled down the seat lid. He stood on the bowl and lifted a polystyrene tile off the ceiling. He found a ventilation space above, about two-foot high. Above that a big metal pipe. His reflection in it a dead shine. It was dark but he could see there would be room. He lowered himself down and lifted the body under the arms and tried to push him up from the waist. His arms slipped. The torso did not move.

Ballacks.

He squatted and put the body over his shoulder in a fireman's lift. It was still warm and clammy. He straightened uneasily, his back searing. Carefully, he stood on the toilet lid. Shaking. A dead man on his shoulder. The world roaring on the outside. He pushed first the head and then the shoulders through the hole he'd made in the ceiling. His vertebrae caterwauling. His arms under the man's ribs, he pushed the neck into the hole and balanced it there, on the edge. The body nearly horizontal. Like a levitation trick you'd see in Vegas. He breathed and the air was sweet, his head less light. He shoved the shoulders into the roof space. If anyone came in now he'd be screwed, he thought, and, like tempted fate the door opened. Swinging on the latch. A bald man entered, looking briefly in the corners and then at the sink, not turning round.

No freekin drinking fountain, the bald man said, spitting the words out to the floor. The bald man pulled open the door and went back out into the corridor.

He sighed with relief and pushed up from the thigh. The body slid over something rough. His stomach was churning, he was a breath away from passing out, the air tense and filled with glass.

Two more shoves and finally there were only the feet left sticking out. He swung the legs until they too disappeared into the cavity. He checked the floor in case anything had fallen out. There was nothing. He put back the tile and sat exhausted on the seat. His arms killing him.

Last call would the final remaining passengers please go to gate 19, flight 203 is now boarding.

He opened the door and checked himself in the mirror, fixing his shirt and hair. He ran to the security check, sucking in air. The attendant looked at his passport and then at him.

It's in a bit of a state, he said.

Yeah I spilled coffee on it and the pages all fluffed out.

You see if you get sent back at the other end we get fined.

Oh.

His lips hardened. The attendant looked over to the supervisor and he yawned and seemed to nod.

Well we'll let you go on but you really should see about getting a new one next time you fly abroad.

Ok, yeah I will, I didn't realize it was as bad as it was.

Ok, off you go.

Two women. In confrontation. Faces inches away. Roan and Naugahyde. He was at the tunnel now. Just waiting for the line to move. The aircraft in the next gate over was disembarking because the woman's husband hadn't boarded. It was the flight to Orlando. The engines were already idling down and the passengers were looking at her with accusations in their faces.

One of the women was crying hysterically. Blond hair, dark in the center of her head. She was sunburnt, doubled over as if from a blow. Standing at the door, her cadmium dress breaking, shabbied, her belly straining against the oversized leather belt. The air hostess towering above her. Her skin bister and composed. Her face a residue of patience. The crying woman leaning on her shoulder, her finger nails long and painted red.

No I don't know where he is, something must have happened.

Tears running through the baby lotion. Her eyes lost, mica, as she turned to face the door. Lost.

I'm sorry, we're going to have to ask you to go for questioning, the stewardess said with a polished brutalism.

The woman moved away. The runway vibrated in the opaque surround.

No, I can't believe this is happening. This isn't happening. Have you checked everywhere, done the intercom . . .

It was not a question.

He just went to the . . . The rest of the sentence was factored into sobs.

The hostess's arm was underneath the woman's elbow easing her towards a door marked Security. He and all his fellow passengers were watching as their line slowly moved. Thankful that this wasn't happening to their flight. That they weren't involved.

I'm sure it's nothing I—

But our luggage is all on board, our presents and everything, already packed, oh god, oh god, please five more minutes.

But the stewardess's eyes were firm.

He looked outside, lights were winking on a jet that was turning in the dark. The taxi-way was full.

I'm sorry but we've looked everywhere, now please.

Her feet were angled in, knees shaking. She had made a ladder in her tights with the heel of her right shoe. A snake of color on her leg. And the eyes once sour and tight were all puffed up.

We'll hold onto your luggage and you can get it back after you go for some questions.

The wife was unoriginal and constant. He knew the type. Presbyterian. Dour. From a wee poor street in East Belfast. Strength made on a basalt Sabbath. She would not be moved by words. They're going to have to drag her, he thought.

No it's all wired up. Jesus. I'm not going without him.

You'll have to—

No. I'm going to wait here. And when he shows up you're going to put us on the next flight to fucking Disneyworld.

I'm going to have to ask you to come in for—

The stewardess gave her a gentle shove.

The woman screamed, her hands clawing against the hostess's blazer, fingers snagging on a gold button.

And then suddenly men with big arms appeared out from nowhere and lifted her up. The arms in leather gloves reaching underneath the woman's breasts and carrying her.

No, no what the faak are ye doing? You fucking buggers, you bloody bastards.

The last of her dignity gone. Eyes black from tears. She lashed out. The hostess's hat fell, her sable hair cascading down her back, her nose upturned with unconcern.

Like a hooked novelty act on a talent show, the woman disappeared into the door and was gone. There was a smattering of applause.

One of them drug smugglers probably, someone said behind him.

Aye you get that sometimes you know.

Aye I do. Remember once our David, he was on his way to Spain, you know and the boy next to him, sick for the whole flight, had to bring him two extra boke bags. Turned out he had a bag of cocaine in his stomach. Sewn in too.

Terrible.

The hostess picked up her hat and smiled as if she had just forgotten to bring someone's sugar for the second time.

The rubbernecking stopped and the line moved faster. He walked down the tunnel and on to his seat on the plane.

Ladies and gentleman, we're next in line for taxiing, the captain said reassuringly after the doors closed. He picked up an Irish newspaper. He read a line from the lead story: O'Brien denied all knowledge of the missing leopard. He put the paper back in the rack.

The plane wasn't that full, so he changed his mind and took a seat at the window.

In a few minutes the engines began to turn. The lights dimmed. The tunnel backed away on wheels. The Fasten Seatbelt sign came on.

He leaned back in the seat and rubbed out the number that was written on his hand.

He landed at five am. A pencil of light on the sullen fields. Peat works on the low hills. Fog diaphanous on the Lough where there were no birds. The smaller lakes were frozen, the mountains malachite and a reflection of weathered topaz, with gulls and black ravens, wee specks among the frost. Across the runway a red cross hung on a military ambulance. He stepped out of the aircraft into the chill of the morning.

Thank you, said the stewardess. The two movies were still playing in his head. A romance about two people who never meet and a film version of a book he'd read but didn't like.

The air bit into him and he walked cautiously down the steps, one hand on the rail. His foot touched the ground without electricity. There was no ceremony. The police were watching. He walked to the terminal, gazing over the silent airport to the cows and sheep awake in the wet grass.

The purpose of your visit? the man asked.

I'm just a tourist.

The dark bottle-green uniform was rich before his eyes, the man's hat pulled down in a peak almost to his nose. Long hairs on his hand. A slate gray face.

A tourist?

Uh huh. I've got relatives here, he said in his American accent.

Your passport's a bit of a sorry state of affairs.

Yeah I know. I spilled coffee on it.

Oh ok. Er, have you any dairy products, eggs, milk and so on, in your luggage or on your person?

Dairy products, er, no.

Have you been on a farm within the last forty-eight hours?

No.

Had any contact with domestic farm animals?

No.

Alright you can go on, next.

Shoes loose on the clean floor. Cobalt at the edges of the furniture. Nothing to declare. Posters: Hertz, Avis and UTV. Thirteen trolleys and a luggage rack. A big sign: The NI Tourist Board Welcomes You to Belfast International Airport.

He drove a stolen car until he found a shore and a cinder beach to lie on. The sand compact and nearly frozen. The tide coiling out to sea. On the limpid coast were the drums of boilers, privateers on the dogwatch between the stays. The sun calloused and coming back. Radar beacons. The sky a honeycomb of plunder. Burnt and treading on the wash. Lacquer had left traces of arrows in the sand and tiny worm holes and lower a place for shells.

Above him the black flanks of the night and remains of the stars were gone in the bonfire of the morning. Away was the coul from him. And there were birds. Geese, silver and inessential. Beautiful. He reached down, and with his hand vaporous and cold, he touched the water. With the brine still on his tongue he walked back to the car, the engine running, the carbon monoxide clouding the sharp levanter from the city.

CHAPTER NINE

We sprint. Up the final steps on the inside of the staircase. Sarah in the lead but only trotting, so I can be close. We get to the lockers on the second floor. There is a circle of faces and arms that slope towards the ground. My head is pounding and I can't see properly. I pause for breath leaning my hand on the metal. Russet is on the edges of the alloy, and the blue paint is the color of a faded Argentinean football strip.

We have to hurry.

Ok.

The History class is in one of the far mobiles near the garden center. It's quite a walk. Sarah goes into the first aisle. When I've caught my breath I go to my locker in the second aisle. It's crowded now with people. Fifth and sixth years trying to get their stuff. My hand takes the shape of a back and I push through. Easily.

It's a studied decency. Everyone makes space for me. Edging out of the way. Unthinking. I turn the key in the t-shaped handle. Screeching, the door opens. My Art tube falls out and I push it back. I lift up my sneakers and get out the book I've borrowed from the history library. Someone touches me on the shoulder and I turn round holding the oversized book in my left hand.

What's that? Big Louise asks.

It's just a book.

I can see that. What's it about?

Uh, oh you know, the uh 1907 dock strike in Belfast, I say to her. I got it from Rob's wee library.

I'm surprised to see her, this is the second time we've talked in a week. The second time in as many years.

The kids are going crazy getting ready for the classes and she has to shout over the noise: Oh my God, you really are a lick, she says.

I am not. You'd love the book. *Orange and Green Together* it's called, and I tell ya the book was even cornier than the title. So it was.

She smirks and reads the back cover out loud.

A well-written account of the pog, er, pog, what is that word?

Poignant. I can't tell if she's joking or not.

Of the poignant and moving story of a time when Catholic and Protestant workers were united together against a brutal system of capital run riot. . . . Jesus.

Gimme that.

We exchange a look. I push my glasses up my face. For some reason we're both about to laugh.

Well look, this is sort of what I wanted to ask you about.

What? I say, genuinely curious.

Well look, you know us retards in the bottom class don't do proper English, right, anyway we're doing this media thing. And you're sorta brainy, being licky and everything and well. You know. I wanted to do this thing about Northern Ireland in the filums, you know, as my project. We all have to do a project.

Northern Ireland in the movies?

Uh huh.

And you want me to help ya?

Just to give me a few ideas.

No problem.

You'll do it?

I will. Why not? That's a cool subject. We never get crap like that. And it should appeal to you rightly. Like, every film made about Northern Ireland in the last ten years has really been prejudiced against Protestants, I mean really prejudiced. Racist even.

What are you talking about?

You know all them films made by Brits or Southern Irish, all of them funded by Channel Four, all of them about the Troubles. As if they know about it. But they're all the same. Micksploitation, I call them.

What do ya mean?

Jesus do you ever go to the pictures?

Yes.

It's wild. None of them have realistic or believable Protestant characters. Prods all portrayed as thick, mindless bigots. Beating up the Catholics, shooting people all the time. Jesus you'd think we were all like the Ku Klux Klan. It's ridiculous.

Look I don't know about all that. We just have to do a wee project about the media. I wanted a few ideas. And anyway you know Mrs House is a fenian, she won't like that sort of thing, so she won't.

Oh God, speaking of mindless bigots.

Hey.

Come on what do you think about that as an idea? The political angle. It'd be interesting. Can you name me one filum made in England with any sympathy towards the Protestants? They hate us over there.

You know Mrs House is English as well.

I know that . . . Look if you don't want my help, Louise . . .

I do. Look . . . Well, you know, I suppose we could give it a go.

So are you on for it?

Ach I'll let you know.

I can work any night except when I go to GB.

You still go to GB?

Yup.

You are the uncoolest girl in school.

Well thank God I've got my natural good looks to fall back on.

Louise laughs at that and slopes off to the toilet, grinning. Later, she says, giving me a kind of an army salute.

Ok is my only response and I'm not sure whether she was serious about the whole thing or not. I can't imagine going over to her house to help her with her homework. I haven't been there since we both left Queen Elizabeth Primary, which is nearly six years ago.

For Jesussake hurry up, Sarah shouts from over on the other side of the lockers.

I hoke through the A3 paper at the back of the locker and find my Physics book. I put both books in the bag and check on my Art stuff for this afternoon. I'm all wired about it.

Despite her yelling I find myself closing my eyes and forgetting about her and Louise. It's really getting close to being late now and all round me is the excitement of kids being driven crazy by the clock. Tiny voices, and bars of music, and the lockers trembling with the slams of boys. The bell is ringing and there is the noise of violins in the music-practice rooms. A scale on a piano. I breathe in slowly. The smells are honey soap and mint from chewing gum. The tops of my legs are hot. And I'm enjoying the sounds and the nearby crush of people.

Come on, Sarah shouts frantically.

But I'm looking at the ant works on the windowsill and the suicidal hum of flies trapped on the flypaper. This is my favorite part of the day. When anything can happen. People are close.

But my back is another dimension that no one touches. Not the little girls, not the prankster boys or the sporty types with the big white torsos. And all this despite the chronic lack of space. It hurts. But today I feel that a kind of love is in the separation.

I think of Art class. My hand checks the photos a final time and I close the locker and turn the key. As the second bell goes, I open my eyes and walk in the running mass of kids to the back stairs. My bag in my left hand swinging, the plastic buttons scraping along the floor.

Sarah isn't there so I figure she must have gone on ahead.

Someone has turned the switch off and the west staircase is a blind spot with no natural light. I step gingerly but not overtly careful in the dark. Two younger boys knock me against the railing. Anonymous and fearless in the blackness.

At the bottom corridor I go out the side door into the fresh air. I walk under the canopy past the dining room. The path here is muddy with footprints. I step over onto the mica stones and trail of talc.

Behind the school buildings and between the garden center and the woods there are twenty mobile classrooms, permanently wedged up on breeze blocks and rusted wheels.

The wind is coming down from the Antrim Plateau rocking the plastic windows and the brown plywood walls, already warped from damp. Felt from the roofs lifted by the gale is scattered on the ground. Two wee lads are using the bigger pieces as frisbees.

All of my teachers say that they hate the mobiles. Getting soaked going out there. The mildew on the ceilings, the cold. But I like them. When we get really heavy rain they get flooded and sometimes they have to hold all the lessons in the assembly hall, which is a lot of fun.

185

When I get to the History mobile the class is going in.

I walk up the steps and close the door. The floor is moving. I sit down at the desk beside Sarah.

Aaaright get your books out, Rob says.

Aaaright get your cocks out, Cyril whispers behind me.

Sarah shakes her head.

I couldn't wait, she whispers.

Forget it.

I open my bag and find my History exercise book and I turn to the place where our notes ended last time. Rob gets up and sits on the end of his desk, pushing the hair back on his head and tapping his watch.

Ok last time we covered the Treaty of Versailles. Today for the first period we're going to look at the other postwar treaties. Which I'm sure you already know all about, being dedicated young people and having read the next chapter in the book . . . And, uh, for the last period we're going to continue with our urban history option on Belfast. Alright?

Rob walks to the front and dims the lights. He turns on the overhead projector. His spidery writing appears on the whiteboard. Without a word we begin to copy down the details of the Treaty of Trianon. Rob talks as we copy. My hand is sore after ten minutes.

After an hour he lets us take a break when we can return our library books and rest our hands. Sarah delves into the back of her bob and pulls out a piece of paper that has been annoying her and which anybody could have fired.

A couple of people set their borrowed books down on his desk. Rob is playing with his lighter.

I have to leave this back, I say to Sarah.

I get up and walk to the front. I dunt a desk by accident. Drawing attention. I leave the book on the overhead projector.

How did you like it? Rob asks.

It was ok.

Ok?

It was good.

It was a very significant time, you know.

Uh huh?

One of the rare occasions when people in this place forgot religion for once. Put other things first.

Yeah, I say, and walk back to my desk not having the heart to tell him that I couldn't get past chapter one.

Aaaright, get your books out, he says, when I have sat down.

Aaaright, Cyril mimics again.

A new slide comes up on the board and we begin to copy.

Our wrists aching and our hands asleep. Finally the bell goes at the end of the third period. Everybody groans in relief.

I'm off to Biology, where are you going? Sarah asks me, packing her stuff.

I've got Physics.

Lucky you. Ha ha.

Its alright.

Sure it is, with J-J-Jabba?

Uh huh . . . Well you've got Jimmy haven't ya?

Aye Jungle Jim.

Didn't he beat the crap outta somebody on Thursday?

Aye Robert, but he doesn't hit the young ladies.

Well you better watch out then.

Funny ha ha.

Anyway I'm off, see ya later.

See ya, wouldn't want to be ya.

Physics is back in the main school building which is another substantial walk, this time against the wind. Some of the boys from History also do Physics and are walking my way, but they get way ahead.

Leaves are blowing under the arches of the garden center.

Rivers of lichen and moss clumps, vitreous and all dried up. I
don't like them and they smell. I take a detour past the caretakers
who're talking and piling the leaves into a wheely bin. They're
talking to each other in a country dialect that's almost
incomprehensible.

Them bays was derty bastes. That oul han with yon hayur.

Wee skitter, so he was. Give me the fingers, wee bain, his
age too?

Yer man's wain, thon fella, in the UDs.

Aye well, bad lot.

Like yon wee dolls da.

Aye her, thawt knew hur, so did. Bad un, so he was.

I get to the classroom late and close the door, thinking that
I will be last. In fact, though, we're all in before Jabba today.
Mike Martin is firing the rugby ball about. Billy is doing his
homework. The ball whizzes past his ear. Michael laughs.

And she's here. Laura. Talking to Jenny, playing with the
white bow on her jumper. Happy. An arid landscape of a smile
on her features. Jabba comes through the door, more flustered-
looking than usual. His tie is over his shoulder and his tinted
glasses are askew. He walks to Laura. Everybody likes her, Jabba
more than most.

Here's that b-book.

Oh thanks, she says.

R-right everyone, t-today we're go, go, g-going to continue
our l-look at quantum ph, physics and the theory of n-non
locality. Oh some, somebody close the door. I'll open the
w-w-window.

I sharpen my pencil onto the floor and pay attention. The
mist on the glass begins to disappear.

A-at the end of the last c-class we s-saw that H–Heisenberg
believed that th, there is no d-deep reality, and that one of
the con, con, consequences of quantum theory is: the act of

m-measurement creates the r-reality. H-however Einstein w-was never happy with this conclusion. Observer-created r-reality didn't make sense for Einstein.

Through the glass I can see anthracite smoke from the power station. The wind is blowing it all over town. In the estates a cortege is snailing its way through the houses, on its way to the new Mulholland Funeral Parlor.

How c-could a m-mouse alter the universe, simply b-by looking at it, Einstein w-wondered.

Fuck we're talking about mice now. A voice beside me says, which I ignore. Laura yawns, stretching her arms full out. Her fingernails glistening in the bulb light. Her face is half turned to the new girl. Her lips pouted in a whisper. Crimson, like the middle band on her tie. Her hair today is like Louise Brooks'. Jabba is pacing over at the far wall, searching for words, trying to remember what we covered last time. The new girl grins and giggles. Laura's eyes are wide and indigo. I have to look away. But the other window is all steamed up, a pool of water on the sill, dripping into the runoff.

My gear is all in front of me. My books, my pencil case. In my homework book is a photograph of me and her and Mr Preston at the art museum. I take it out. We're on either side of him. Holding his hands, it was only last year. Her hair was like that then, my hair was shorter. In the photo we're laughing at something. Not smiling but actually laughing. Mr Preston didn't have his beard, he was lighter. He looked more like the photographs of . . .

So in n-nineteen thirty-f-five, at Princeton in New Jersey, A-America . . . Einstein had l-left Europe b-because of Hitler. He was Jewish. Of c-course . . .

Outside the funeral procession has four cars and a barking dog. A Lhasa.

Of c-course.

I'm a little bored so I gaze out to the front of the school to see if any of the teachers are out having a smoke. One in particular. But there's no one there, only the gray clouds and the random harmonies of light making a plague of shadows on the front square. And, farther down at the tongue of the Lough, Belfast is shrouded in the low fog of a warm front. It's the same oul dirty rain, and the sea birds are just the jumbled targets of the wind.

Every, everyone p-please pay attention.

He's looking at me. I half cock my head thoughtfully, as if I have been ruminating on his words and seeing nothing through the glass.

Er, anyway at Princeton, Einstein, where w-were we, he, er, he d-devised a thought experiment to d-disprove quantum physics. He w-wanted to show that the w-world was r-really real and not dependent on an ob, observer. Einstein showed that w-when two identical photon-detecting experiments are done, under the rules of qu, quantum physics, the re, results of one experrriment seem to e-effect the r-results of the other. This is s-strange. And in f-fact the results of these th, thought experiments, the maths of which wu, we d-don't have to w-worry about, sh, show that there must be s-some interconnectedness b-between the two separate p-particles. Einstein called the c-connection spukehafte Fernwirkungen.

Jabba pauses, relieved to have got the German out. He spells it on the board and I write it down.

This tr, translates as "spooklike actions at a d-distance." You s-see, if the r-results of the two completely s-separate experiments are the s-same then, Einstein said, the p-particles, m-must have b-been s-sending m-messages to each other, f-faster than the s-speed of light. W-which he knew and we know is impossible. It was spooky, almost s-supernatural. Because n-nothing c-can t-travel f-faster than light. And th, this communication over l-long distances, at faster than light, s-simply doesn't m-make sense, so Einstein, concluded, th, there must be something wr, wrong with quantum theory, it m-must be incomplete.

He walks to his desk and takes a drink of water from the sink. Ugh.

N-now, I w-want you to copy this down.

He draws a picture of an apparatus on the blackboard. I turn my book to the next blank page and sketch the diagram in 4H pencil. Carefully, without rubbing anything out.

Beside me, Jane is predictably discontented.

What the hell is this?

Don't know.

This was nothing like the book. I read it, so I did.

Yeah well.

Jesus, I don't know what the hell that man is talking about. He's a real geg. Typical left footer.

Quiet now, Jabba says and clears his throat. In 1964 the physicist J-John B-Bell, from B-Belfast, p-proved that Einstein was incorrect in ass, assuming that s-something was wrong wu, with quantum theory. Again we d-don't n-need the maths. Work d-done s-since 1964 has confirmed Bell's view that qu, quantum theory makes sense because the universe is n-nonlocal. In the ex, experiment on the b-board, the ph, photons both either take the short cut or t-take the d-detour, not both. There-fore after leaving the g-gun each knows in, instantly and nonlo-cally what its twin has done, and it does the same. The particles com, communicate with each other in, instantly no m-matter how far they are apart. And thus ap, apparently b-breaking the rule that nothing can travel f-faster than light.

I'm trying to keep up, because this is interesting. My pencil is blunt and smudgy. I sharpen it a little trying not to make the point too brittle. Two turns does the trick. I touch it with my finger.

Jane is looking at me.

Tell ya, there's no point in writing it down, it still won't make any sense, she says.

Einstein said that f-faster than l-light communication was impossible b-because if it were t-true then c-causes c-could precede effects. The light bulb would turn on before you h-had even s-switched it, and, and, s-so on. Ahm, s-so h-how does this happen? John B-Bell said that it h-happens because the universe is nonlocal. The act of m-measurement depends not only on the observer nearby but on the entire ex, experimental system, the experimental system being the entire universe itself. Everything for Bell is c-connected to everything else. Time itself and every p-particle in the universe.

I put the photograph back into the homework book, along with the photograph of ma shaking hands with Prince Andrew outside the castle. Jabba's hands are on the desk in front. Laura has her head full back. Jane is reading *Just Seventeen*.

The sea is white along the waterfront. The North Channel like a granite bridge all the way from the Lagan to the Clyde. He talks until the bell goes.

C'est la sonnerie, Jane says to herself.

Y-your homework is to r-read to the end of the chapter.

And out I run. To the drinks machine. One shoulder up. Through the silence of the corridor.

I'm there first. I put in twenty pee and press the button for coffee with two sugars. The plastic cup falls down between the grips at an angle. I straighten it just before the whitened coffee begins to pour. When the cup is half full I press the button for hot chocolate. The machine shudders for a second and then the brown chocolate fills the other half of the cup. I do the whole procedure again, as the growing line of first years gets impatient behind me. Sarah shows up with a wheeker of a smile on her face.

Hey look what I got.

She shows me two bars of Nestlé chocolate, holding them up like a victory sign. I give her the cup of coffee-choc.

Where'd ya get that? I ask, as we walk to the exit. Over the tiles, Spanish style. Muddy clouds in the white space of the plaza. She can't hear me. We maneuver our way through the little kids, being careful not to spill our drinks. The glass doors scrape along the ground.

Ugh, I hate that noise she says.

Outside the sun is peeking out and the wind has dropped. We decide to walk down to the river. Impressively two boys are well into a punch-up and its only 11:02. She gives me one of the chocolate bars.

Ok where'd ya get the chocolate?

Jimmy give it to me.

Jimmy who?

Jungle Jim.

Jim McNulty?

Uh huh.

What for?

After Biology he asked me to clean out the animal house.

To clean out the shite?

Yup.

Sheesh he saw you coming wee girl.

Aye he did?

He couldn't pay me enough to clean out all that animal shite.

Yeah well that's you.

We walk past a group of boys playing hide and seek under the mobiles. Red dirt on their trousers, tiny faces crouching in the dark. Near the water two gangs are fighting for the rights to the grass football pitch. Trading insults.

Anyway you're too fat to play footy, so you are. You're so fat you wear two watches cos your arms are in different time zones.

The old jokes are the best, Sarah says. She looks at me.

Are you not eating your chocolate?

I stare at her with deep skepticism.

Did you wash your hands after?

Of course I did.

Ok then I say with mock relief and peel off the wrapper.

Ach you.

We walk along the river. Over the fence is a burned-out car and on the ground two tires and an inner tube. Beer cans and a half a bicycle. I scrunch up the silver paper and throw it down the bank, hoping it will reach the water. But the wind takes it into the black stones under a tree of shopping bags.

Litter bug.

We get to the car park. The young language assistant is smoking a cigar and standing at the barrier. Maybe to deter vandals.

Vee heist doo? Sarah asks, perplexing him.

Vee gates, is what you mean, I say haughtily. He grins and blows a smoke ring for our benefit.

Es geht mir gut, he says.

Yeah well, don't get carried away Fritz, Sarah says.

We turn back and giggle like a couple of kids. We walk the long way back round the front of the school, talking about tv and boys. Sarah tells me a joke about a robot at a golf course. The bell rings for the end of break and we dander back to the lockers. We're both in English next with Mr Norton and he's hardly ever there on time. It's in one of the mobiles near the wood. I burp and feel the chocolate settling in my stomach. I open my locker and dump my Physics and History books on the bottom shelf. Sarah and I share the English books between the two of us.

On the way she carries the big poetry book and I bring along the copy of *Macbeth*.

The wood is still on Ministry of Defense land, even though the army base has long since closed. We wait for him by the wire that passes for a fence. A few trees in, under the sign that now says: Tresp . . . eep . . . Out, the remains of strange graffiti has been painted out.

Tiocfadh ar la, it seems to read, though the letters are unusual and covered with No Surrender in big red paint. Mr Norton's mobile defies its name and sits rusted and motionless under the swaying branches of a sycamore.

Here he comes.

Mr Norton is in his rugby top and cords. Gray chest hairs in the button top. His red beard trimmed on one side only. The headmaster forgives his eccentric dress. He's only just recovering from meningitis and he's a bit crazier than he used to be. Last week he beat himself with the meter ruler because he forgot to bring the Thomas Hardy test. Sarah and I were keekin our whips. He stood up in front of the class and said that he practiced what he preached, and whacked himself twice on the backside with the big wooden ruler. Everyone was too afeared to laugh.

Ah, my children, still thy yelping, he says with a monster smile on his face. His bag jiggling under his arm.

He's in a good mood today, I whisper.

He reaches for his keys and opens the door with his foot.

We go in behind him.

Today we will all have tea, Mr Norton announces and puts the kettle on. We get up and form a line as he gives everyone a mug with the faces of Irish rugby players on the side. It's a small class, only Sarah, me and five others, all girls except for Keith who today, as usual, is sitting at the back away from the   195 rest of us. He isn't in the queue for Earl Grey. The whistle blows and I remember from my trip that in America there were no electric kettles like ours. There we got a pot and boiled it on the stove, the gas igniter clicking the whole time.

Mr Norton hums as he pours out the water. He gives me my mug with Willy Anderson on the side.

You got a good one there, he says.

Huh?

He points at the mug.

Oh.

Willy Anderson? You don't remember?

No sir.

He was the one who was arrested in Argentina for allegedly stealing the Argie flag during the Irish rugby tour. Just before the Falklands War? You don't remember?

I, uh, I don't follow rugby much, sir.

Oh. Well. Never mind.

I'm glowing with embarrassment now. I put in a round Tetley's tea bag and let it float. There is a tautness in the water. The drink is bitter. So I mix in a lot of milk with a plastic spoon and fire in a processed sugar cube. I sit down beside Sarah at a double desk.

Do you think this water's fresh? I ask, for something to say.

Yeah I'm sure it is, she replies, not really paying any attention.

It does my old heart good to see such fresh-faced youth eager to partake of the fountain of knowledge, Mr Norton booms.

Yeah right, Sarah whispers.

Well now. If it were done when tis done, twere well, it were done quickly. So children lets get down to it. In Hogan, turn to the chapter on the war poets. I want today to look at "Dulce et Decorum Est." Judith I would like you to read.

We're still looking for the page as Judith begins. I take a sip of tea. Sarah gets to the right chapter. Mr Norton walks down on exaggerated tiptoes and gives us an extra copy of the book. I take it.

After a minute of Judith's reading, he coughs.

The irony in this poem is heavy-handed wouldn't you agree?, Miss Wilson?

Judith looks flummoxed. I groan to myself knowing he is about to go into one of his usual pet theses, this one about how the war poets were responsible for World War Two.

He does.

You see, the horror of war so generated by these poems led to the atmosphere of appeasement . . .

For a Bible Thumper he talks an awful lot about war, so he does, Sarah whispers.

I don't think this oul shite is even on our syllabus, I whisper back and Sarah nods. She's pretending to be listening. The radiator is rattling. I take another sip of tea and flick through the poems of the book, getting stuck somewhere between "The Cap and Bells" and "Daddy." I read it twice and think that mine was a bad man too.

Was.

Is.

At the end of the period we do some plays and read the parts out loud. Mr Norton is thinking of putting on a radical version of *Pygmalion* where Eliza becomes a Bolshevik. It's all very nihilistic, he says.

We finish with *Nicholas Nickleby* and by then it's already lunchtime.

Sarah eats in the canteen at lunch, so I say cheerio to her and go up to the study with my jam piece. I eat it with another

hot drink. It's packed now. The boys are bolting their sand-
wiches so they can get down and grab the football pitch first. I
sit at my desk. Someone has left a piece of muck on the seat.
I pick it up and set it on the heater. I swipe the remains onto
the floor with my open hand.

Dja like your wee present? It's the voice of Laura with two
of her friends. The new girl and Jenny who plays goalie for the
hockey team. In cahoots. Laughing. I don't turn round.

Are you deaf? She's bloody deaf as well. Bloody deaf. Deaf
as a bloody post.

I take a bite of butter and jam and chew it hard. I swallow
and take a sip of drinking chocolate with no coffee in it this
time. It isn't as sweet. My thoughts converge on my taste buds,
trying to ignore them.

Hey you, Jenny has her hand on the back of my hair. She
tugs it. I set down the chocolate and turn to face her.

Will ya just fucking leave me alone.

In the noise of the room my voice sounds small. We're
backed in the corner. The three girls are standing round me in
a semicircle. Nobody else is paying any attention. I can see
Keith just leave the room. Shit.

Did you swear at me? Jenny says and adjusts her glasses with
her fist. Her gut is over her skirt and I remember the line about
the time zones. And smile despite myself. Her face is red and
unattractive. And the other is a breath behind. Folded and
pretty, her soft arms are for sleeping in. None of us are moving.
The four of us, like actors. The room is hot. The blinds pulled
down. The card game yelling. My head is up against the clayfeel
of the notice board.

I didn't swear at you I reply softly, trying to defuse things.

Well I thought ya fucking did, Jenny says and turns round

to the others to see what happens next.

Laura's face is in a kind of smile. Her eyes are petrol blue now. And rich.

Gorgeous.

Jenny prods me with a stubby finger. Two rings on it, a heart and a piece of glass. She prods me in the ribs.

Stop it.

Or what?

Well, I say and pause. If you touch me again I'll kick your cunt straight through your fat fucking arse.

Jenny pushes me again. I stand up. She's taller than me by about three inches and much heavier. I've seen the boys mimic her with their arms outstretched to look like a trunk. Can I have a bun please, they say behind her back.

Jenny moves close. Her breath has the flavor of oranges. She grabs me by my shoulders, holding down my arms. Laura hasn't said a word. Her smile has flattened out. Jenny presses me up against the wall. Her hands go almost the whole way round my back. Her squeeze is killing me.

She squeezes tighter and I can't breathe.

Her chapped lips open. I close my eyes. Open them again to see what's coming. She draws her fist back. I look at the ridges on her hand. The dirt under her nails. A scar like the letter H. The fist tightens and she is about to beat my crap in, when suddenly the atmosphere changes. I don't know what it is for a second. My breath is held. Jenny has stopped moving and then there's a voice: Is there a problem here?

It's Louise standing against the cabinet, smoking.

With a giant hand she levers the new girl over to one side until she's standing right beside me. Jenny's fingers begin to unclench my hair. Louise touches me on the shoulder blade and I turn to face her. I smile with relief.

Is there a problem here? she asks again.

199

N-no problem, Jenny says. Laura turns and sits back down at her desk. The new girl goes with her. Jenny backs off slowly and it's only when all three are sitting that I see the flick-knife in Louise's hand. She folds it up.

Blunt, she says giving me a grin, for mashing up me tobacco. Thanks.

It's not over yet.

Louise steps past me and walks over to where Jenny's sitting. She points at me.

If she so much as has a headache, I'm coming after you, do you understand?

Jenny puts her hands up in a gesture of placation. Louise grabs Jenny's outstretched finger in her hand and pulls it back perpendicular to her wrist. Even standing where I am I can hear the bones grinding. Jenny's face contorts.

Do I make myself clear?

She pulls the finger back further.

Uh.

Do I make myself fucking clear?

Yes.

Well that's good, so it is.

She releases Jenny.

We're all pals again, she says.

Jenny gets up and walks over to the door. Tears in her eyes. I look over at Laura but she is seemingly engrossed in her book.

Louise grins at me and relights her cigarette.

Are you ok? she asks.

I could have handled it.

Sure you could, she says. Blowing the exhalation up towards the smoke alarm.

Sure I could.

Alright, she says and gives me a wink. Tapping ash onto the floor she walks over towards her friends in the far corner.

Thanks, I say to her back. Her shoulders shrug.

I finish my piece slowly, each bite forced. I'm shaking. When I've waited long enough to show that I'm not upset, I get up and go to the canteen to wait for Sarah. I stand outside talking to the dinner lady who collects the meal tickets. Sarah is pleased to see me.

Hey, how are you?

Ok, what about yourself?

Mmmm, I'd a great lunch. Cauliflower cheese and dessert was apple crumble.

You know what they say?

What do they say?

It makes ya rumble.

What are you talking about wee doll?

Nathin.

Sarah looks at me oddly.

What's up? she asks, her voice deepening with concern. I shake my head.

Have you been gurnin? she persists.

No, I say angrily.

Sure?

Course I'm sure.

Mmmm.

We turn and walk behind the dinner hall back to the English class. We stop at the fence on the edge of the wood.

Let's go into the forest today, I suggest, trying to clear the air.

No way, didn't you hear what Baldy said in assembly? Said we'd get a short walk down the drive.

Ach him and his short walks.

Yeah, Sarah says cheerfully.

Well Jesus you seem in a good mood anyway.

Uh, not especially, in fact I was reading a letter from my pen pal over lunch. It was a bit of a drag. Almost counteracted the effect of the apple crumble.

Jesus you still keep up with your pen pal?

Yeah? Don't you?

What? No. Stopped years ago. Although, now you mention it, when I went to New York in the summer I tried to call her, but she'd moved.

Yours was in New York?

Yeah, I wrote to her for about a year but that was it. Where's yours from?

Well first I also got an American girl. From New Albany, Mississippi, but I used to write her dead long letters and she only wrote me wee short ones back. So I thought, I can't be arsed doing this and I got a different one.

And you still write to her?

Yeah, she's from Poland, a place called Drohobycz.

Jesus that's a mouthful.

Aye. Anyway I got a letter and she's fine.

Does she know Leach?

Leach who?

You know oul Leach Walensa. Solidarity, all that?

It's Lech. And I doubt it. She talks about coming over here, but she's a Catholic, so I don't know.

Jesus you're biased.

No you're biased.

I think not. Don't I listen to the "Undertones" and "That Petrol Emotion" and they're Catholics. And wasn't I with that girl in America?

Yeah well I kissed a Catholic boy when I was on the Isle of Man. What about that?

Oh yeah. I remember that. At least you telling me that.

Yup.

Yup.

Hey, what do you have next after English?

Art. Three Art in a row.

You're lucky, Mister Preston, Jesus, doesn't he look like Sean Connery?

I don't know, I, er, haven't really noticed.

Oh my God, you haven't noticed. He is so cool. All rugged and hunky, so he is. Mmmm. And you heard the stories and everything?

What stories?

That he, uh, you know, wink, wink, say no more?

What? I say exasperated.

That he did the you-know with a couple of last year's sixth-year girls.

Aye he did?

That's what the old jungle drums say.

Who?

I don't know who it was.

No who said it?

Nobody you know.

I don't believe it.

Gospel.

Well who said it?

Can't tell ya, I was sworn to secrecy, so I was.

Ach you're taking a hand out of me.

It's true.

Sure he's married.

Aye and like he's mister man of principle.

I still don't believe it.

What are you, a nun?

Who told ya?

I can't tell ya.

I don't believe ya then.

Suit yourself.

Ach go on.

No.

Go on.

No.

Goo onn.

Alright. It was Dave.

Dave who?

Dave Synal.

Dave fucking Synal, the Music teacher?

Uh huh.

How does he know?

He goes drinking with him.

Mister Preston goes drinking with Mister Synal?

Yup.

Synal is a fruit.

Still go drinking together.

Ach away on.

True.

He's pulling your leg.

True.

Nah, need proof. Names.

Names? You want names? Why do you think Laura used to do so well in his class?

Laura? That's bollicks, she would have told me, she was one of my best friends.

And is she now? And why not? Because you're doing the best in the Art class now. Everybody knows it.

Look, you don't know what you're talking about, so I wouldn't talk about it. Me and Laura fell out because I got to go to America and she was all huffy about it.

That's not it at all. Jesus, you're in a different world.

Yeah its called Planet Earth. You should try it here some time.

Nope. I know. Synal says—

What kind of fucking name is that anyway? Can you trust someone with a name like that? You know how many Synals there are in the phone book? I say trying to change the tack of the conversation.

He said it, she persists.

Ok well just forget it. Just forget it, ok?

I thought you were interested and—

No. I don't care anymore, I shout and pause to get my thoughts together for a minute.

Ok, she says a little hurt at my raised voice.

I look at her and she looks away. I take a breath and clear my head.

Look I'm sorry for shouting, I say.

It's ok.

Ok.

Hey do you want ta hear a geg? she says.

No. No more jokes.

This isn't a joke.

You just said it was.

It's a true story.

A true story?

Yeah.

Ok.

Wee girl goes into the bathroom and sees her da naked. And they're a very religious family so they are.

Are you sure this isn't a joke?

I'm sure.

It sounds like a joke.

It's a story. Anyway they're a Born Again family and the wee girl looks at her da naked and sees his dick and she says:

What's that da? And of course the da is thinking fast so he says: Oh uh, that's just my hedgehog, Sylvia. And she looks at it and thinks for a bit and says: Hedgehog? Christ it's got a huge bloody cock on it hasn't it?

I giggle for a moment and look at her.

That was funny but I thought I told you no more jokes.

Ach your whole life is a joke.

Aye and yours isn't?

True.

Hey do you want to go into the woods or not? I say at last.

She smiles at me. Her hair loose and down over her eyes. She can see I'm het up and she's in the mood to tease.

Maybe.

Do ya or don't ya?

Well . . .

Do ya or don't ya?

I don't know.

For Gods-frigging-sake, do ya or don't ya?

Aye ok.

Good.

Good.

Goooood.

We laugh, and together we juke under the barbed wire and walk past the school boundary line, into the sparse trees.

We are the tiny minority, the tiny minority, we sing over and over. Our feet crunching on the pine cones and her hand slipping into mine.

CHAPTER TEN

On the far side of the Lough he could see houses, a church, the harbor of a small town. Islands, a lighthouse. The land neutered and unforgiving. The bleak hills falling into the water with executionary slackness. And yet . . .

And yet . . . The girl. The mother. The son. And it all beginning with two boys. July 12th. A long time ago.

A long . . .

He looked out at the water and heard the footsteps come slipping over the rocks behind him. He wondered who they would send.

Why have you come back? a familiar voice.

He grinned.

I mean Jesus. We want to know. Some of us . . . we're not exactly pleased to see you.

His smile evened out. How did I get into this? How many years? He threw away a handful of stones and stood without replying.

Jesus. Enough of the silent treatment. It's a question of trust, you see that don't ya?

He turned round and saw his brother's hand patting the lining on his jacket pocket. It was a sign. He shook his head, he wouldn't try anything.

You owe me. I want to see them. You owe me.

The groan of an aircraft. His breath cold. The frost cracking as he shifted from foot to foot.

We owe you nothing. If you've really escaped like you say then you should have disappeared. What are you doing back here?

Christ. I can't believe I'm getting this from my own brother.

Ah don't come that shite with me. It's a question of trust, you have to show us first. What have you been doing all this time?

I went to America, I told youse that much.

Aye but then nothing. Not a squeak out of you.

I'm sure you found out a few wee things.

Aye we heard things but nothing from you.

I didn't want you to hear anything.

Exactly. I mean how do we know you're not a spy or something? . . . Look get one thing straight, I didn't want to do this, I get this phone call at six o'clock in the morning and suddenly you're back in our lives. I didn't want to come. I didn't have to come. You're not a commander anymore. You're nothing now. Nothing.

Not a commander, as if in the UDA there was anything he wanted to command. He stared at him. His face was a drawing of a face, changed with every line. Become hardened over the years.

I called you because I thought you'd help me.

And as they looked at one another he remembered the day. July 12th. A long time ago.

A long . . .

The sash was on the wall and playing in the scullery. It was hot, the streets were boiling with low level ozone and diesel fumes. The pollen count was 600 and making his mother cough. The air reeked of nitrous oxide and nervous energy.

Will you take me with you?

I would ask for level-headedness. We must all strive to remain calm in this most difficult of times.

Will you take me?

The mayor dabbing his bald head in the harsh glare of studio lighting. The police chief almost grinning to the camera. Six tv crews were jostling for position at the front of the podium.

If everyone does his or her job as I expect they will then everything will be fine.

I want to come, Danny said between sneezes.

Shhhh, I'm trying to listen.

Hacks from fifteen countries firing questions from the stalls. And the smell of bacon sizzling in the kitchen. The dark wee house rich with it. His ma poked her head round the corner.

You've had that thing on all morning, you'll fry your brain in front of that oul goggle box, you will, you two should be outside, and you've work to go to, don't you young man.

Ma I can't hear you over the tv.

Irony slipping by the lie down freezer, that was taking up half the space of the dining room.

Are you gonna take me after or not?

Danny's voice in a whisper. Eyes auburn, filled with hero worship. A sneeze.

No, ma'd kill me.

Dan was unconvinced, the room cramped, a kick mark on the window.

She'll kill you anyway.

And now back to our regular program. Delayed fifteen minutes because of the press conference.

Please.

No.

Puhlease.

A line curving into a plea bargain, a smile there, and a promise perhaps to snitch.

Go on. Please.

A kind of threat in his voice—I won't tell if you let me come.

Jesus God. No. Are you deaf wee lad?

He would never tell. He doesn't think like that. Would he? He looked over. Danny's face was sinking. He was looking in at ma.

Are you sure?

Y-yes.

Again the look at ma.

Please, I'll be no trouble.

Jesus. Alright, he said and both of them smiled for opposite reasons. His a grimace.

Meet me outside at one o'clock and we'll see.

Yeaaaa.

I said we'll see, alright?

Aye ok.

Son, I thought I told you to get going, his mother said.

Ma, it's not real work anyway, he replied.

And you young man. You're going to help me clean the wash house.

I can't, I've, uh, diarrhea.

Oh that's a laugh so it is.

Ma I believe him. It's no laugh. People think it's funny, but it's really brown and runny.

Oh get to work you dirty baste.

I'm gone . . .

Running down the alley.

Are you still here?

Skidding on the clay bake. The air sweet with turf and onions frying.

So one o'clock?

His words were under wraps. His wee lips puckering up.

Yes didn't I tell you?

Ok, he paused, aching for a few breaths more. He was so desperate to be close, to be part of things. He was talking to himself: I'll come home and I'll have a shower and then . . . and don't tell anyone.

No, course not.

Mmmm, he said as stern as he could muster.

And here they were together. Aged and different. Bird calls behind them and the lyric of cars. All the stories and dares leading to that one day. The games, the fights and bringing in his own flesh and blood. Bringing ruin.

Dan, I'm not here to cause any trouble.

The name was a token and had been used to up the ante. But Danny boy was a tough guy now.

Neither am I, he said coldly.

He was sitting on the bank. His fingertips were white and pressed into the soil. The grass trembling with color. His eyes narrow and resolute. Perhaps he'd misread him, his expression was steadfast, draped with textual certainties. He seemed unlikely to cave in. They'd learned him to be hard. Maybe, though, it was all an act, maybe Danny was actually afraid of him. How was he expected to cope with something like this? After all this time.

You better not try anything, Dan said like a young Jimmy Cagney. Moving his shoulders in a half swagger the way the assassins do.

And then it occurred to him that of the two of them he was the sane one.

I won't, he said and sighed.

The image of helicopters in the cobalt waters of the septic tank. Hovering. A thousand feet up, cameras slung, recording everything on miles of Super 8. Ports for heavy-caliber machine guns, flares to knock heat-seeking missiles off course. Soldier boys jawing, leaning out the sides, killing time, not on foot patrol and thankful. SLRs resting. Up and out of it all.

In Ulster only the army can fly helicopters. When you hear one it's a sign that something's going on.

He pulled the lid down on the tank and the copters disappeared.

Gideon Bibles were piled in the paper bin. All of them brand new, the Word plain in the protestant stillness. He picked one up, the deaf-mute watching him in the soft parts of the window frame. He dropped it and grabbed a whole handful of books and put them in the bag in his left hand. He resealed it and opened the bin lid. The rubbish had been cleared out of the skip that morning and now he could see a host of maggots crawling along the bottom of the metal bin. Small white worms writhing blind in a decaying smear of hamburger meat, and the blue-gray fatter ones, a more advanced stage of the former he thought. But then doubting himself. Taxonomy not exactly his strong point. At the corner of the bin large green maggots were wrestling slowly over the remains of a bag marked: Excrement and Sanitary Towels only. He was transfixed, and wanted to look further but the putrid smell of decay made him gag and cough a little. He threw in the trash bag, transforming in an instant the creatures' landscape. They went crazy for a moment and then settled down.

He was impressed to see that within a minute all the larvae had reacted to the change in topography as if their world had always looked like that. Continuing on their myriad paths without a hesitation.

Them's the cratturs, he said and pulled hard on the lid handle so that it shuddered closed with a rusty metallic clang.

The helicopters moved farther away, banking over the tower blocks in West Belfast, less than a drone now.

And they too were like the insects, so prevalent you could hardly notice them. Like the fire and the songs of guns. He was aware of the chopper noise only because he'd registered their existence just now with his squinting eyes. Any other time it was just part of the background.

He shut his eyes against the sun.

Yes.

Where were you then brother? When I was working for a living, keeping you and ma.

Where were you then?

Dan clicked his fingers in front of his face.

Jesus, he said. Sometimes I think you're not all there.

His voice muted as the beach lexicon slammed new phrases with the tide. Spray almost touching them. And the cold wind.

Formal and informal the men sat. Ambiguity in their postures. The pair of them. Up from the wet rocks. A cable draped on a mark of sand. An empty bottle. A can of Harp. The water itself, in and out. Canto and uncanto. October embalming its breath on the railway embankment.

Sometimes I think you're too much there.

The older one, nearly half a foot taller. Stones tearing up the earth behind him and farther back the Atlantic like cement beyond the Lough. A tiredness on the littoral part of the beach.

Now what the fuck is that supposed to mean?

His hand a crook. Homicidal, ready to shoot him dead, but he wouldn't be half as fast enough. Deformed or not. The weapon was between them, unmentioned. It didn't mean a thing. His eyelashes were left to gather in the years. He blinked back. His empty belly moved. Arms like a blacksmith, he shuffled up and sat down on a concrete sleeper, his eyes fixed on the water and light reflecting from his fists.

Dan's head was only eggshell thin beside him. But he wouldn't kill him. He needed the information. Whether Dan would try to murder him was another question. But he was standing easy, looking like he'd just slipped from a royal painting by Goya, posed and half malevolent, arms at his sides and thinking he was invulnerable.

He smiled to show that it was all ok.

Back through the doors of the old folks home. Down the corridor, to the second room.

I've just come to empty your bedpan, he said.

Heryou, whawaint, I'm calln the fakin caps.

The words only an approximation of speech.

Fakin caps.

I'm an orderly here. Remember I told you, as part of my Government Jobs Scheme. I was in last week.

The woman muttered something. The room smelled of wild strawberries and dandelions. The words out of her toothless mouth were erratic. He had to construct the dialogue for her in his head.

Bout ye today, y'all right? he tried. She looked back blankly, afraid still of the unknown.

You've seen me before. I'm just here to empty your bedpan, he said. But she didn't say anything. She was leaning on the bed, arms behind her, like matchsticks. Staring vacantly at the wall. Now it seemed she didn't see him at all.

He opened the bathroom door and sought out the red piss-pot that the nurses usually stashed under the sink. This one was full to the brim with cold yellow urine. No feces. He poured the urine into a containment trough and wheeled his trolley out through the door.

I just have to mop your floor now, he said. Gentle.

She began to speak this time in a clear voice, her accent lost in the text, the words an attempt to exorcise him away.

And the Philistines came up yet again and spread out in the valley of Rephaim . . .

The mop into the brown water. It was cold and dirty.

David again gathered all the chosen men of Israel. And they carried the Ark of God upon a new cart.

He squeezed the extra water out of the mop through the strainer on the bucket, don't leave the floor too wet. Matron had told him. She didn't want a fall and a lawsuit on her hands.

And when they came to the threshing floor of Nacon, Uzzah put out his hand to the Ark of God, for the oxen stumbled.

With a straight back he moved the mop laterally over the bathroom floor, remembering to give an extra sweep around the toilet and bedpan area where what the nurses called "bladder accidents" usually happened.

And the anger of the Lord was kindled against Uzzah. And God smote him there because he put his hands forth upon the Ark.

When he had finished he placed the mop back into the bucket and lifted the load with his knees bent. Knees bent, straight back.

On his first day he'd got terrible back cramps with all the bending over. The union guy had told him the proper technique for doing the floors.

Good-bye, thanks, he said and shut the door. Thanks.

Thanks, his brother said, as he offered him a smoke. He turned and looked round at the landscape. There'd been a lot of changes. One desecration on top of another. The power plant still ulcerous and foul, like a stormy mission station. But with it a new chimney, enormous, out of the heave and girders, and the buildings, imperial and grand. Like play blocks, strange and unnatural in the treeless surround. Reminiscent of a first colony on Mars. Ugly black smoke poured out from the broken chimney mouth belching it into the drab canyons of the early day. He knew without looking that the gun was cocked now and pointed at his head. Behind him. In the dark places.

It's freezing, he said, small talk to cover his hands. He did not turn. There was a long twilight over the far shore. He could feel the malice in the air and the first stirrings of traffic on the highway. Interposed were the Irish palm trees. In defiance of latitude and taste.

I don't want any trouble, Dan, he said.

And the voice remote in his ear: You should have thought of that before.

The patience gone now. He looked at the footprints down on the beach. They were his, dissolving in the incoming tide.

The name on the next room was smudged and the patient himself never offered it. The man was assigned to Dr Khan. He had never seen Dr Khan and he knew better than to bother the nurses. The man looked as if he was in his late eighties. His gray hair thin and growing in clumps on his scalp, he was emaciated and jowly, the flesh hanging from his neck like discarded chicken skin on a dinner plate. The room had no cards or decorations. The bed was cramped against the cupboard, the window looking down on the car park. The man was motionless. There was a fine black mold cultivating in several places on his arms and feet. The man's pacemaker visible on his sunken chest. Today he was naked and curled on a chair, a discarded blanket at his feet. Twisted.

Bastard, the man yelled at him. Black bastard. Black bastard, outta here, ya black bastard.

Now now, there'll be none of that carry on, I'm just here to empty your bedpan, he said soothingly.

I'm cold, the man said. The thermometer on the wall said 30 degrees Celsius.

It's a bloody hothouse, he whispered. Already his white t shirt was soaked with sweat around the armpits. You can't be cold on a day like today. If you'd let the nurses put some clothes on you . . .

Black bastard, just like all the rest, the man said, his mouth barely moving. He shrugged and stared at the man's shriveled white legs. He went into the bathroom and got the bedpan.

Black bastard, cunt, hoor cunt, its the 12th today ya fenian shite.

Fuck you, he mouthed as he left the room, spilling a little piss on the carpet as he closed the door.

The next room was worse. A candle of animal fat, damp and grease. Mrs Clare talked too much. About her grandchildren, all doing well at university. He had to listen to her tell him the same stories every time. Butts in the ashtray. He'd only been at the hospital four weeks, but with Mrs Clare it seemed like fucking forever. The old woman smiled as he came in. Ash on the floor. She looked grotesque and comic with her eyepatch and her missing teeth and her jaundiced skin. He didn't want to hear it, he just wanted to finish and get out of there. Today though she was having difficulty speaking and pointed apologetically at her throat.

That's ok, he said.

After he cleared Mrs Clare's he walked up the corridor to

the kitchen with the aim of getting a drink of water, but Sister intercepted him.

Have you finished all the rooms? she said in her Kiwi accent. Patronizing and clipped.

Getting there, he replied, a phony smile wedged on his lips.

Don't take all day about it, she said firmly.

Ha ha, of course not, he said obsequiously. She marched off checking her watch and shaking her head with practiced theatricality.

Bitch, he said when she was out of earshot.

He poured himself a glass of soft processed water and drank it in one go. It was warm but refreshing nevertheless. He ran his hands under the cold tap and splashed some water onto his face. Flies buzzed around the sink trying to land in the plastic marmalade pots that had to be washed and used later for dispensing medicine.

He walked down to the stores room and closed the door. It smelt of must and germicide. It was small and crowded but he could take a break for five minutes without anyone coming in. The regular cleaner had put cartoons on the wall, Snoopy and Charlie Brown. An attempt to lighten the gloom of the five-by-five cubby hole. But it was still skiagraph and somber. A bolt of humor that was lost among the buckets of disinfectant, toilet cleaner and replacement rubbish bags. He lit a cigarette taking a long draft from the filtered Benson & Hedges.

The floor was not a floor and the smoke buzzed him. The cartoons didn't work, having the opposite effect. Making him think about the outside. Snoopy looked demented in his World War One flying gear. He resented the fact that he was cooped up in here with so much happening in the city center. For a job he didn't want, to please his mother. The ghost of his father.

An alarm bell was ringing down the hall. Someone was calling out for a new water jug to replace the one they'd spilled.

He looked at his watch, it was coming up to twelve, just an hour to go. If he could take the heat, then it would be easy.

Time was psychological and slow. He did a few more bed-pans and then wiped down the floor. Sister told him to take the rubbish bags out of all the kitchens and common rooms. It would be another trip to the bins and the day was burning up, the overhang dry and poisonous. Three choppers up now, looking like big flies dueling for the airspace.

Finally one o'clock approached. He went into the store and washed the grime out of his hands, scrubbing away any flecks of fecal tissue that may have slipped underneath the rubber gloves. Matron signed his timesheet and he was out. Her signature was a spider web on the paper but he felt elated, free. He couldn't have felt better if he'd just come out of prison.

He ran outside to where a grin marked the line of the wee bastard's face.

I'm here.

That I can see.

Well. Can I come?

Jeez. Ok, but I know I'll regret it.

UDA, and the words For God & Ulster, painted life-jacket orange. Unpretty. A picture of the Pope with a dog's head.

I've got very explicit orders.

Oh yes?

Orders. The word was telling, faked up like a military unit. Pathetic. The beach was white and tracing the water margin. A couple of ships waiting for the morning go-ahead to the harbor. Shapes crystalline and caked with salt on the tide pools. Every-where his eyes ended in cambrian horizons. The Lough flat and gray like his brother's one good hand. The sun ascending. The sea god calling up the weather. And the last star gone. A hand even now poised on a weapon made in the Holy Land. None of it fitted, not the sky, not his brother, not the strangeness of the birds nor the woad landscape.

Well here we are then.

Yeah here we are.

His brother's eyes were cold and without feeling. The air bristled with static. Along the railway line a freight train was coming.

If you don't tell me why you're here, I'm going to kill you.

And you think you could?

Yes.

He was wrong. He smiled at the water. He could see the far shore and the shore beyond that over the faded drumlins. An artificial poppy was at his feet. Red on the brown earth. A delegation of crushed beer cans lined up on the wall. The tiny headland sloping down perilously to the wet beach. Can this really be you little brother?

They faced each other on the concrete sleeper. Lines of history on both men's faces. How it hurt to speak. To really talk.

Why are you here?

I've told you. I want to see my family. I can't go to the cops, but I know you'll know where they are. You have connections.

What were you doing in America all this time?

You really don't know?

Of course not. Come on, this is no game.

I was arrested in New York. Someone tipped them off. I'm sure you know nothing about that.

I don't, why would you think—

I had no ID. The tip said I was in the drugs trade. They put me in a dump tank on Rikers. I killed my cellmate, pulled the bugger apart.

Jesus.

Think I topped another man and almost another. It was

too much Danny. They put me in a nuthouse. Me. Can you imagine? Me.

He reached into his pocket. The other flinched, tensed, until he pulled out the packet of cigarettes.

The gulls wading. The oyster catchers shoveling sand. He lit a cigarette with a damp box of matches, the nicotine drawing a heaviness into the front part of his head. No surrender, the graffito said.

A fine drizzle was falling out of the low clouds.

I can see it, Danny said.

Aye.

The sun aching on his back. Sweat on his forehead. Four boys were sitting crosslegged in the yard. All were in a kind of uniform of jeans and a once white t shirt. His brother was watching him fill milk bottles with petrol. Pouring it carefully from a green tank. Everyone was intoxicated on the smell. One boy with a crew cut was taking a risky smoke by the fence pole as a sign of cool. He was choking on the tar.

Will you fucking wise up, wee lad, he said to the boy, half mad, half jealous.

You telling me to wise up. Fucksake and who was it brought him along? His finger pointing at Danny.

I mean feel wick.

Ach shut up the pair of ya.

Bloody trying to get this right, ok?

And who are you, the leader? Fernie asked.

Ah come on.

The yard was laid in blocks. Stained and coated with rubbish. A tire hung from a piece of rope on a rusted swing. The grass at the bottom was four feet high. A deflated football and a naked Action Man lay together by the entry. The stainer from the fence was evaporating in the heat, and the smell was pungent, even over the petrol. He grabbed the bottle in his left and poured with his right.

And you were working this morning, weren't ya? In the old biddies home, right? Scotchy said.

Aye, look why don't you concentrate a wee bit more on what you're doing, he replied.

Fuck me, who's the oul sourpuss then? The job getting you down, what, too busy porking the old dears again? Huh?

The boys laughed and he couldn't help but break into a cheesy grin.

Porking the oul dolls. Oul dried snatches and everything. Jesus is that why you're doing that oul jab? Fuck, you must be hard-up boy.

He shook his head. Scotchy, him, everyone friends again.

Ooohweee it must be disgusting.

He had to say something.

It is, uh, only temporary. I'm doing it for something better. Scotchy wasn't impressed.

Shite, for that government scheme sure you have to do six months on shite pay.

He was defensive: Well I've done all that, and if I get through it, I could get into the shipyards on an apprenticeship.

Ach it's a load of oul crap . . .

Hey at least I'm still not at school. Like youse.

Neither will I be in two months when I'm sixteen.

Yeah well until then I advise . . .

A shadow appeared on the yard. A man in a blue sweatshirt was standing by the gate, a red hand tattooed on his face and the letters UDA and UVF on his knuckles.

Are you boys all right? he said deadpan.

Uh huh.

He surveyed the work.

Good, cos we'll need that stuff ready in about forty-five minutes, ok?

Aye, nay probs.

Good and no more fucking messing, he said with a flash of anger.

The man turned and walked back into the alley. The boys were quietly terrified.

Jesus, Duffy said.

Jesus is right.

He went into the house. Inside it was derelict and dark. The windows bricked up with breeze blocks. The interior gutted, blackened wood and a layer of ash on the raw floorboards. The stairs were rotted and dangerous, and no one had been up to the upper floor. He stood in what was once the kitchen and looked out into the yard. The sun was still strong. He urinated into the old sink watching the piss fall into the ancient plumbing and disappear into the still-working drains. The boys were nearly done. Twelve milk bottles were filled with petrol, rags soaking and jammed tightly into the tops. They were moving the bottles carefully into the shade.

Why can't I stay now? Danny was asking.

You just can't.

Why not?

Because you can't.

But why?

Because I say so.

But why?

You just can't, ok? You're too young.

Please.

Look, stop giving me such a fucking hard time here, I let you come here against my better judgment, you think you'd be fucking grateful.

I'll keep out of everybody's way and everything, I will.

Give my head peace, I'm taking a leak for godssake.

His voice was all impatience and rage. He could see tears well up. His brother turned and ran to the gate. He zipped his fly and caught him up in the alley. A cat scrambled out of his way as he tackled him to the ground.

Alright dimwit you can stay. But one bloody whine and I'm sending you home.

His eyes were almost blue in the shade.

The younger man was uncomfortable. He was balanced on the artificial limb that had taken the place of his left hand. Again they were facing each other. Have you the balls, Danny, to kill me, he didn't ask. He didn't have to. Dan was scared of him, but had the cult of violence in every gesture. It was deep in him.

This whole society was sick. He could see that now. Sick and indifferent to it all. They had their hard wee God: white and dour and manifest. Their country crawling with believers. The homogeneity of it was crippling.

Beside him the expanse of water wasn't a view but a way to herd him in and make him claustrophobic. It was almost too much.

Three days ago he couldn't wipe his arse. And now the fate of his kindred was in his hands. If Dan tried to shoot him, he wouldn't be quick enough and he'd be killed. His brother was so careless, sitting too close, with even the safety on. Danny had forgotten what he had been. And still was.

His elbows were tense from waiting, poised. He rubbed his eyes and read off the messages on the bridge: Linda and Barry, Claudy Loves John, Mary-Anne's a slut. ATWD scrawled with a paint brush below the railway sign. Onto the paint proof wall. ATWD. He thought for a moment. That was a new one to him. He started to get up. Alert and circumspect. His shadow also rose. Any Taig Will Do, that must be it. The gun was in his brother's hand pointing at his chest, almost touching it. It was about seven am, there was still no one about.

You will do as I say, Dan in comedy staccato, you vill do.

Or you'll whack me, huh Dan?

The joke was lost in the anger in Dan's face.

That's enough. We're going to my car, it's just in the car park there. I've had enough of this bullshit. You've told me nothing. I've been patient. You're sitting there dreaming. Well we'll see what the boys can get out of you.

He put hands on hips and shook his head.

An interrogation huh? You think I'd let you do that to me? You think I let youse touch me?

I don't think you have any choice.

But the choice was there. His neck could break just like any other man's. And he was so stupidly close. Hadn't he learned anything? He thought for a moment and then he smiled and there was real affection in it.

Ok, he said and put his hands up as if in surrender.

Don't attract attention. Just keep them where I can see them.

They walked back up the shore.

Ahead steam was rising from the cooling towers of the power station. The sulfur lamps were winking out. Their feet resounding on the cast-iron railway bridge. Even with the weight of both of them the torque on the box girders was next to nothing.

The city baked under the four o'clock sun. The tide was high and the gray waters of the Lough were into the storm drains. Where the traffic did not flow the air was heavy with the smell of shit. The boys were waiting at the fence. The plan was to loose a few stones off into the side street. Inflame the situation.

And then draw the riot down through the alley. The police line was thin at that point. The cops were already overstretched. With the crowd in the blind alley, the boys were to throw the petrol bombs.

We should get a lot of the taig bastards, the man in the moustache said before he went.

Jesus it's hotter than a hoor's cunt out there, Fernie said.

They were on a low roof, in shadow, the bottles wrapped under tarpaulin. The army were still up in their helicopters but they'd never see them.

A vent was pouring hot air from the fish and chip shop below making them sweat like pigs.

You think those boys would close, what with the march and everything, Scotchy said to break the silence. He looked at him. With ginger hair and freckles and two big gaps between his front teeth, he was one ugly child.

Scotchy, nathin staps them chip-shop fellas. Those Chinky boys, Jesus, they're even open on Christmas, Fernie explained.

Aye they are? Scotchy was skeptical.

They are right enough. Sure they don't believe in it.

Don't believe in what?

In Christmas, what do you think?

An Associated Press photographer had positioned himself at the corner of the road, near a police Land Rover.

See that boy there, betya he's keekin his whips, someone said pointing out the photographer.

He turned towards his brother and touched him on the arm.

Are you sure you're alright?

His brother pushed away his hand.

Course, he said indignantly.

If you don't want to stay you don't have to.

I'm dead on, just leave me alone.

Look I . . .

I'm bloody all right, just leave me alone.

His brother lay down on the hot roof and put his arms under his chin. On the road they could see the first of the banners starting to appear. A pipe band kitted out in Catholic green was playing a tune on piccolos and snare drums.

His own boys started singing a song on the roof as a challenge to the rebel music.

There were fenians to the left, there were fenians to the right. Good King Billy in the middle and he's looking for a fight. But the Pope said no and we'll have another go on the twelfth of July in the marrr-nin . . .

His back itched like crazy and he was afraid and could not be seen to be afraid. Occasionally the others would turn round to look at him for reassurance. He smiled.

So what you're saying is that the bloody Chinks don't believe in Jesus or anything? Scotchy asked when the singing petered out.

No they don't, are you thick or what? Lutz said.

Scotchy was appalled: For fucksake that's worse than the fucking fenians.

The Chinks are fenians, Duffy said.

Bollicks, they're no more taig than I am, Fernie said.

Big Lutz laughed: I tell ya Fernie, I've always been suspicious about you.

He could see that Danny wanted to give him another chance. They were waiting to cross the road. Other men would be waiting in the car and by then it would be too late.

Look, why do you want to see them?   **227**

I just do. I have to.

How come the cops never got your prints through Interpol, how come you were never deported?

I don't know. They thought I was a yank. I never spoke, never told them a thing. There was no ID. Why would they look abroad? Besides my records back home were all juvenile. Sealed.

How did you get out?

I escaped.

Escaped?

That's right.

Danny looked dubious for a moment and then smiled, as if remembering something.

Well I wouldn't put it past you. You were three times out of the borstal. You were the boy, Danny said.

I was the boy.

What they call you?

Steve McQueen.

Yeah.

They both laughed at that and he turned and looked at his younger brother. Danny's laugh was still higher and lighter than his. Still the kid. He wanted to reach out and touch him. Put his arm round him.

What if I tell you where your family is? What then? Dan said quietly.

You know where they're at?

I don't see them but I could find out easily.

I knew you were the man. If you told me, that would be it, Dan. Youse owe me Dan and that would be it.

Danny shook his head.

But then what? What are your plans for after that?

I haven't thought that far ahead.

They were waiting until the light went red. Rush hour

started earlier than he remembered. The cars were small and the driving poor. The sea air was still cold.

Danny who's with you in the car? he asked.

Just a couple of lads. Good pair. Old friends.

He tensed as Danny put the weapon in his pocket still aiming it at the small of his back. He remembered working for a Mexican man once in the city. Always dodging the INS. Ready to drop things in a moment. Escopeta grande, the man would have said. Now. Go. Run.

A truck rattled past at sixty-five. The words Crazy Prices on the side. The light went from green to amber and then to red. And the gun was still there. Clearly Danny hadn't been satisfied. But what else could he have said?

You haven't thought that far ahead?

No.

They crossed, caught now between the castle and the power station.

I know you better than that.

No. He shook his head. You don't.

Fernie had from nowhere produced a bottle of Bushmill's whiskey. He should pull authority now, he thought. Fernie unscrewed the cap and drank the warm liquid without a face. Scotchy looked at him. Fernie passed the bottle over to Duffy and Lutz. He shrugged to show that he didn't care.

You want to hear a joke? Fernie asked.

He wanted to say: No jokes and put the bloody bottle down, but he didn't.

How do you stop a fenian drowning?

No one answered.

You take your foot off his head.

Fernie laughed and Duffy passed on the bottle.

In another five minutes everyone was singing again. This time a real racket:

Have you heard of the battle of the Shankill, where most of the fighting was done . . .

Someone was dancing out of the shade. The Catholic march was getting pretty close. It was a protest rally against the larger Protestant marches taking place in the city. It was an affront to the Protestants. A challenge. It had been decided that it would have to end in chaos and they were going to be a big part of it.

His eyes were half shut. The music out of tune and unpleasant to him. His teeth stinging from the cheap liquor. The empty bottle broken on the pavement ten feet below.

Who was shot by the barrel of a gun . . .

The singing went on, loud enough to bring the owner of the shop out to look down the street. His Korean features trying to figure out where it was coming from and then his tiny frame scuttling back in, on the wave of a cop.

As he lay on the battle field a dying dying dying, with the blood pouring down from his head, he turned to the man that had shot him and these are the words that he said, we'll fight for no surrender . . .

His voice was hoarse. He had been joining in. Scotchy was lying on his back making bicycle moves with his feet.

We'll fight for no surrender, we'll fight to guard these walls . . .

I feel sick, a voice said behind him in the light, plaintive and small.

Oh Jesus, he said. You just go right ahead, but if you're gonna puke don't get any on your clothes.

He could see everything now.

The Kennedys' house had gone. The sign said: Rest Home For the Aged. The car park and supermarket were about the same.

The broken light in the middle was yellowed and rusted. Glass dotted around the concrete. The news agent in the corner was opening. Two cars were in the car park, frost on both their windows. A man was letting his dog take a shit on the grass outside the bungalows. They walked towards a red BMW. Two men were inside.

There was no point in wasting his words. Danny had decided now, and he stopped and faced him.

Listen, Danny said abruptly, this isn't about us. I do what I'm told and that's the difference between you and me.

There's a lot more than that, he said in a whisper.

The house at the corner had a yellow hedge and a broken wall. A fence separated it from the supermarket. Faded letters were on the fence: Free Anthony, Sloane and Mitchell. More of their crowd.

Heat poured out from the car and he climbed into the backseat beside a man in a red anorak. The man had his hand in his pocket, not even near pointing the weapon at him. The amateurish nature of the situation was almost laughable.

I don't think he's working for the cops, Dan said.

Well you just watch it anyway, pal, we don't want any trouble, a man said to him.

He was tired and the voices were little more than an irritant.

The third man got in and sandwiched him in the middle.

He could sleep here, he thought. He was tired. His eyes closed. Trains ran on the inside of his eyelids, long and fast, the windows gultering past at a hundred miles per hour. They'd been running for as long as he could remember. He wanted to tell his brother about them, but when his mouth opened it was dry.

When the attack came the police had been unprepared. The lead men fired stones into the crowd and ran down the alley to the getaway car. They were followed by about fifteen marchers throwing stones, trying to hit the car as it sped off. Most of them were spread out standing about a third of the way down, opposite the chip shop. The cops had closed ranks again and were taking no more notice of the incident. It seemed to be over. The car was gone and the crowd was walking back to the main procession. Someone threw a lazy stone at the chip shop window but it didn't break.

Ok boys this is it, bloody it, are you ready?

The boys looked at him. Most of them were half tore. They were all terrified.

Let me show you again. He took a bottle from the stack and lit the rag with his cigarette lighter. He waited until it was burning well before hurling it off the roof, being careful to hold it by the bottom. It hit the ground and exploded in a sheet of flame that caught a long-haired man on the leg.

Get cracking you bastards, he shouted.

The boys responded and began to light up and fire the milk bottles.

The bottles flew through the air and blew up in the alley with dull whooshes of flame and breaking glass. Screams and panic sounded from below. Total confusion was breaking out, people running for cover from the fire.

They're killing us, a woman shouted to the police.

On the roof, yelled another.

He saw a man running, his upper torso in flames, others rolling on the ground. Still more panic-frozen as the blasts went off round them.

Quick boys, he shouted. Come on. Faster.

They'd fired off nearly all the petrol bombs into the alley and were getting ready to go, when suddenly there was someone on the next-door roof with a gun in his hand. He'd climbed up the outside ladder. Pop, the gun sounded. Barely a noise at all. Everybody was stupefied.

Wee Duffy had kept his cool and threw a molotov right at the shooter. It exploded prematurely, throwing Duffy back, his hair on fire. Scotchy put it out with his hands. Fernie threw another petrol bomb and, just as the man was taking aim again, it caught him right on the back.

He ignited in a torch of flame and fell screaming onto the pavement. The boys stood there open-mouthed. The man's jacket crackling and his skin melting before their eyes. The police were in the alley by now.

Up on the roof, the people were screaming. Up there on the roof.

Come on let's get out of here, for Chrissake, he shouted, snapping them out of it.

We still have more to do, Fernie said.

Come on to fuck, you're crazy, big lad. Let's go.

They climbed down the back of the roof and ran to the other side of the road where a van was supposed to be waiting. They jumped over the partition wall and turned the corner. When they got there the van wasn't there.

Oh shit, Duffy said, and froze.

Just run you dumb fuckers, just run, he ordered.

The police were on the roof and shouting at them.

Come back or we'll shoot, this is the police.

But before anyone could think a baton round came whizzing down the alley bouncing off the ground and skittering to a halt in the grating.

They're shooting, the black bastards are shooting.

Run.

And then he felt it. A crunch. The body beside him crumpled up sickeningly. He ran on, and then stopped and turned. 233

Danny was lying on the road. His arm mangled beside him and lying there, at an impossible angle.

Don't leave me.

I won't. You boys go on, quick.

What about— Scotchy began.

Run you stupid fucker.

He put both his hands up and kneeled down in the blood that was running into his brother's hair. The sandy fringe was covered. Two fat cops were coming towards him. Their faces hidden behind the helmets of their riot gear. Running closer, their bodies blocking out the light from the end of the alley.

It's just a kid, one of them said. The other was holding the plastic bullet gun.

Shit, he said. That's just great.

We need an ambulance here now, someone said, the voices melting together.

A radio replied in a crackle of noise: Roger.

Whats the boy's name?

I, er, I . . .

You're in a lot of fucking trouble.

There's people dying over there, who was responsible for this?

I don't know anything, he said, his voice quiet.

Come on son.

Yeah come on.

I don't know anything, he said again, and he knew that this was not a lie.

He was secure in his brother's car. The men sitting on either side of him were afraid. Their guns jamming nervously into his side. They had driven out of the car park and were at the traffic lights. His brother was driving, much to his surprise. The car adapted for an artificial limb. It stank of soporific cigarette smoke. He was so tired. The car turned onto the dual carriageway.

The murky weather was clearing and the last of the lights had gone out. Somewhere behind the drizzle the sun had risen.

Do you recognize me? the man to his left asked.

No.

McGurk, Jimmy McGurk.

Still don't . . .

Scotchy McGurk. Been how many years since we were messers together? Eh? And we started the same day in the shipyard. D'ya remember? Right after ya got out of the youth custody center?

Quite a reunion, he said.

So it's the famous mad dog, McGurk said. Jesus. I didn't think I was going to see you when I went to bed last night.

I didn't think you thought at all, Scotchy.

Scotchy swallowed. I'm not one bit afeared of you, he said.

I'm sure you're not.

Shut up in the back there, Danny said from the front seat.

They accelerated along the highway, the gears changing erratically. As the car passed the police station he knew this was his last chance. They were probably going to kill him. He could kick the door open, get out. But then the whole thing would have been for nothing.

Fuck it, he said and closed his eyes for the duration of the ride.

CHAPTER ELEVEN

Boys are playing. In the funnel of wind between the mobiles. I look outside. The light is oblique and fractured. The wee skitters are out early, throwing stones at each other. A clatter of wains all the way down to the school buildings. The bell rings, tinny and distant. A nervous reaction ripples through the class.

Riotous movement and then sighs and a collective groan of relief. I can say nothing. My throat is constricted. A junction of thoughts in my head. An overwhelming desire to go. Perspiration on my neck.

He coughs into the wedding ring on his left hand.

Ok, everyone that's about it for today, remember to get your competition drawings in by the weekend.

People are already footering with their gear. Putting on their blazers. Talking. Excited. Getting up. In a second the door is open.

His eyes down, he pushes the seat back. And places his palms on the arms of the chair. My left hand is up over my forehead, shielding my face, my right hand putting the pencils into my pencil case. I know what's coming. He gets up from the chair and walks over to me.

His voice is unnecessarily loud.

Er, I'd like you to stay behind and we'll go over your American project.

I look up.

Just for a couple of minutes, he says. Trying to sound distracted. Casual.

Yeah, fine, I say. Our eyes avoiding each other.

Good, it'll only take a moment. I'll, er, give you a lift home if you miss the bus.

For their benefit. For hers. Not that he need have bothered, most of the class is up and out. No one is paying any attention. They want to get home. None of them says good-bye and the last girl out shuts the inner door behind her. Her hand tugging on the knob. Swinging it. It closes with a bang. I hear her feet vibrate down the steps.

Laughter.

The wee thing, somebody says outside.

The mobile shudders for a second more and the room is silent.

Mr Preston grabs a chair, turns it backward and sits in front of me, his legs straddling the edges of my desk, his elbows on the wood. I notice the leather patches on his sleeve.

Just a moment, he says and takes off the corduroy jacket, throwing it carelessly on the radiator.

You brought the photographs? he asks. Gray in his eyebrows. Hard air between us. His voice is the accent of the 1930's BBC. Flat and studied. And syllables that clip themselves. For him it is the artificial memory of a place. I swallow and force myself to blink.

In the motionless room his arms, by contrast, are eager and animated. A pause of unreflection. Ligneous eyes. Indifferent like an urge to murder, a kind of machinery of movement and the charm that falls to the boundary of my face. It takes me in. But I remember that he's like this all the time, and everything is relative. It is nothing to do with me. I should relax. And yet I'm sitting on my hands. Unsure of how they got under my skirt. They're damp and dissolving into the plastic of the seat.

He runs his fingers through his long hair and smiles at me.

Yes I say, as if the pause between his question and my reply were no time at all.

Oh wait a minute.

He stands up again and walks to his desk in an undeniable swagger. His confidence erases the room behind him. Through my speech, I think I am inoculated against him. But I'm not. He bends down, in the silence. In the juke of clouds and the flutter of bin liners. There is a viscosity to his actions, raw in the face and wild like someone from the faery tales. He pulls out a pack of cigarettes. It says Winston on the side. He fails to conjure flame out of his box of matches. He looks at me chagrined, the way the prophets of Baal must have looked at old Elijah.

Bugger.

He strikes again. This time he gets it. The matches are a fleck above the weather. He lights the cigarette and draws long on it. His cheeks hollowing as he breathes in. Funny how the cig paper is always white. Bleached. White against the white of his fingertip.

The smoke coming out of his nostrils as he speaks.

I'll just pull the blinds down so we can see better, there's an awful lot of light in here.

Uh huh.

He brushes ash off his jeans and walks to the window. His sneakers squeaking. Union Jack on the heel. Blackened out on the shoes of taigs. Taig—Catholic I mean. I'm sweating. In the harsh capsule of heated air. He stands at the first window and pulls the string of the roller blind, tugging it below the level of the window so it won't shoot back up.

239

Get the photographs out while I'm doing this.

Ok.

I reach into my bag and pull out the file. Cardboard folded over on itself.

With every blanked out window the room is getting darker. People walking, the dregs of the school idling for the exits, the last ones to get out are Monkey Miller's French class, who've been kept behind.

A couple of traumatized boys walking through the mud with their ties askew and their shirt tails out, looking like victims of some terrible disaster.

I hate that woman, one says.

It's collective punishment keeping the whole class behind because of Sammy McIlroy's note, not fair, agrees his friend.

What was on the note?

Joke. What's the difference between snot and cauliflower?

Kids won't eat cauliflower.

Yeah, an oldie. Tell ya, I just hate her.

Elle est, er, une chienne parfait?

Une?

Oui.

Ein hund?

En français.

Ich weiss es nicht.

He closes the open window and the conversation disappears. Perfect bitch, is what the kid was after. A salope.

I look away from the windows. The walls of the class are decorated with first-year frescos and a realist portrait done by one of the fifth-year girls, for her O level. Portrait. Someone who I don't know, but the auburn burns and the blond streak are his.

Under the blackboard is Laura's abstract sculpture of a horse. Steel twisted and arc welded into a skeletal bird of the land. It is beautiful and violent, the horse, a stallion, the lines stretched out to a gallop. Punctures of light on the metal. Reflecting even in the gloom. So incredible that no one says she could have done it on her own. He pulls down the last blind and takes out his key. I am looking at him, expressionless I think. But clearly I betray something, for Mr Preston grins with reassurance.

So we won't be disturbed, he says. The key turns in the door. The room is dark with only the angle-poise lamp turned on.

It's too murky now, he remarks. Nao, the way he says it.

He turns on the overhead lights and sits beside me.

Can I, he inquires and uses the metal lid of my pencil case as an ashtray.

I've opened the folder. He splays out the collection of Polaroids on the desk. I lean back in the chair waiting for him to say something. Watching his eyes. His right hand flat on the edge of the chair, near my elbow, the cigarette in his mouth.

Well, he says and looks at me. His face all muscled up and tight.

Well, these are merciless. Merciless and marvelous. You've done really well. These are excellent.

He picks up the photographs and examines them closely.

I should really take my contact lenses out to see these better, I mean they're terrific. The texture, the colors. Oh.

He thinks for a second.

And of course nobody knows what you were doing, this is our secret, our project?

No my, er, ma thinks I'm working on, like, my drawings of America.

Ha ha.

My face must show the hurt, for he touches my arm soothingly.

Not that your line drawings aren't good. They're excellent.

241

It's hard to believe that in just a week you seem to have captured the essence of the place. New York's vibrancy, the uh, architectural extravagance. No, those works are good, vital, charged with life. Just a week. Wonderful. Jolly good.

His hand is resting on mine.

But, we can't possibly use them for anything special. They're nice, but the clichés are obvious. Try and deconstruct them and what would happen? The critics, they, er . . . Even in this provincial outpost of civilization. Your drawings. They're captured by stereotypes and they would assume that you are, that we are too. Imagine what they would say. Protestant and Catholic children coming together in a foreign land? Oh dear its dull. Hackneyed. It's old hat. I mean so what? Nobody gets called a, what's the word, a uh, a fenian or a jaffa for a week. But nothing changes when they come back. Does that have an impact? Do the drawings you made have an impact? I mean qui bono, or is it, cui bono . . . whatever, who benefits, that's what Cicero would have asked, who benefits. Er, they're good but . . . Look I . . .

He squeezes my finger and pauses to think. He's lost me. I am wondering why he is talking about Bono from "U2," but I don't really care. He's carried away and with his hair brushed back he does look a little like Sean Connery.

What we're doing is important. Your photographs and the ones I've taken. I've even thought of a name for the book.

Uh huh?

I'm going to call it *The Things We Do*. You see? There's a pun in the title, what do you think?

It's good, I geddit.

Now this will do something. It's the last taboo. Your photographs of, it's such an ugly word, excrement, are uh bursting with color, and shape, and form.

He holds one up. He is excited, talking quickly.

Ah look at these, look at these. No, no, this is the real thing. This is great.

He bangs his fist on the table still holding the picture. Canyons of sound reverberating off the hard surfaces. He whispers conspiratorially: These are so good.

I want to say something. I don't want him to take the piss. I want to be sure.

Do you really think they're good?

Still facing me, with the desk between us, he puts his big hands on my shoulders. The cigarette smoke trails between the lenses of my glasses into my eyes. I shrink down a little so that he will not have to touch my back.

The moment is uncomfortable. His eyes are eating into mine. His fingernails are yellowed. Something of the outdoors about him and faded aftershave. And harsh tobacco, not like ma's. As he presses I'm swarming in his touch.

The callouses on his hand I can feel. The smoky breath like Causeway Whiskey. The table is full of cracks. His smell syenite and peeler green. Black, and voracious are the lines between us.

He pulls his right hand away and puts the cigarette in his mouth. He reclasps my shoulder with a better grip. Both hands on opposite shoulders. Like he's giving me a pep talk. It almost hurts. Something has changed. His movements are robotic and artificial. Rehearsed. In chunks of time, with thought in them. Despite his enthusiasm, there is a control there, in that head. I am aware that he is not known to be tactile. Among the teachers. The world is crowding close. An orchestra of noise from the central heating. Figurines and alphabets. He has surrounded me. I'm enclosed, like an island by Christo. He is holding the cigarette between his front teeth and shaking his head with a kind of poisonousness.

Come on. Why do you think I asked you? You. Your talent shines through your work.

He pulls me closer, my stomach being compressed against the rim of the table.

Ugh, I say out loud.

Mmm.

He lets me go and I sit back. He takes a drag on his cigarette and blows the smoke towards the window. I push the chair with my toes. It scrapes along the floor.

And you did the documentation? he asks, business like.

Oh yes.

Good.

Suddenly, like the shark in *Jaws,* he brings up one arm from below the desk and pats me on the side of the head.

You did everything I asked, didn't you?

I lean forward and his shirt sleeve flops from my shoulder to the chair. A puppet limb. I am relieved. My face is red. I breathe in slowly and bring out the folder with the descriptions. Art Project, it says on the cover. The "j" is over a rubbed out "g." I show him the notes.

I gave each picture a number and . . .

He takes the papers greedily.

Oh yes I see, very good, and this is what you ate before you shat every time, right?

Yeah, everything I . . .

And drank too. Uh huh? One bottle makes you bigger, one makes you smaller. Ha ha. That right?

He turns and waits for a reply but I can only smile.

You don't know what I'm talking about do you? It doesn't matter. Anyway this is good. It's good. You'll get full credit in the book of course. I'm thinking about the layout. A large book, coffee-table size. Imagine it. Eh? On the one side the photograph and on the other your detailed description of what you ate and a witty commentary that I'll write. Not that it'll be completely tongue in cheek but I want it to be entertaining. Jolly. Yes. Serious but also fun. *The Things We Do*, ha.

He smirks and I can see the caps in the back of his teeth. He shifts around in the seat so that he is sitting close to me. The chair perpendicular to my desk. His feet on the T shaped legs. My knees are trembling. He sets the camera on the floor making more space for the photographs as he lays them out.

You don't? he asks as he pulls out the packet of cigarettes.

No.

Wise. Very wise. If I were your age I wouldn't start. No you wouldn't catch me.

He lights himself another and sits back comfortably. He is relaxed. His free hand is under the table, tapping on his leg.

So, er, he begins to say but is interrupted by a cough.

Sorry, he splutters out, blowing ash everywhere. Tiny intersections of gray landing on the table and the floor.

I don't really care. My knuckles are tight and sweat is on the tops of my thighs. I am forcing myself to breathe slowly. Outside I can hear singing. His eyes are looking into mine. Unblinking. I have to look away. Down the class to the sculpture. It makes me wonder. I am about to speak when he puts the cigarette in his mouth and clasps my hand in a cold grip. My fingers damp and his like a dried-up stone. The stem of a breath frozen on my lips.

I look over for an explanation but his profile is a stockade of smoke and his other arm is under the table. Concealed and moving.

So, tell me about how you did them? he asks, still holding me.

H-how I did what? I say and I am not afraid of his touch. Being of this world and no other. Once I kissed a boy in a play. I remember. It was wet. He was my child, and for three nights he slipped me the tongue, before Macbeth's henchmen burst in to kill us. It was the trauma of the moment maybe.

When you dropped your load.

What?

I'm talking about the bog. The shit house.

Mister Pres I—

When you shat.

I—

Excreted. Laid your scats.

I still don't—

When thou didst beshit thyself.

Really I—

Tell me how it felt, I need to know, for the book.

His hand is squeezing mine tighter and the cigarette is drooping ash down onto his tie. He sees it but does nothing. I do not know if he is serious. His eyes are a lens of concentration. His face is lost to the windows and the door.

I—

Come on, I need to know. What was it like? A big log between your legs? Like this one?

He picks up one of the Polaroids. A sepia turd, with pock marks and a valley where it split on my tail bone.

This one.

He pushes the photograph up to my nose.

What did it feel like? Big huh? I need to know. Big, yes. All symbolism you know. Like class last week. Phallic. Eh? Phallic between your little legs. Phallic, like a big . . . Come on what was it like? Eh?

I think that he's joking. His head is turned away. But there is spittle on his lips. I'm feeling chilled. But it has to be a joke.

Well, I can't remember any off hand, I . . .

Imagine. Tell me. Come on.

He turns round and leans forward. In a twitch. His teeth together. The veins are sticking out on the skin of his arm, below the rolled up sleeve. He burps and his breath smells of coffee and stale tobacco.

You can tell me, he says, his voice rising. He stops and takes a long drag. Letting go of me. I take my hand and rub it. Blood flowing back into the fingers. Pins and needles starting up.

You can tell me. This time he is quieter, more charming.

I smile and he smirks back seeing that I am not upset.

You know you're a very pretty girl, he says.

I begin to blush again. In the room there seems to be a quiet understanding. Of the pictures and the art supplies. Bearing witness. Against the wall there is a midgee. Or a spot on my glasses. I want to check and see.

Very pretty.

He puts his hand on my neck. His body angling round. The chair behind couping over on the floor. With a gentle crash.

Oh dear, he says, sounding foreign. Alien. From across the sheugh. His voice spinning through and turning me over. His mouth biting itself. I tremble from his touch. So close to my spine. Grasping the back of my neck. Under my hair.

No, no, you're special. I've always thought so.

Uh huh?

Yeah you're a ducky. A little ducky. And you are pretty. Really pretty.

He winks and half cocks his head. It's like a gesture he has practiced in the mirror. The tendons in my leg are branding irons. My underclothes are sticking to my skin. His hand moves down and strokes my back, on the curve. I shake him off and softly say no.

What?

No.

What? he says, his voice rising once again.

Please don't touch me there, I know you're just being nice and everything . . .

Ha ha. If only you knew. I'm not being nice. You really are pretty. You're more than a pretty girl in fact. You're a beautiful young woman. Ah how does that go . . .

He clears his throat and looks me up and down. Like an inspection at Girls Brigade.

Was in great letters set affliction. But the greatness shew'd the owner—George Herbert. Do you understand?

The word affliction unsettles me. I bite my lip. He shakes his head. Vipers on the split ends of his hair. I don't like it and his face is hungry. His eyes narrow. I close my eyes and his nails are on my back again. Under my sweater and up against my shirt. I am breathing shallow like I'm swimming. In tiny pants. My cheeks are hot and red.

You don't follow. It doesn't matter. Doesn't matter. Nothing matters. Just tell me what it felt like. Just tell me.

As he speaks he is stroking me. Trying to soothe me. Compounds of thoughts in his fingertips. And somehow I'm to blame. If he is frustrated. Annoyed. At my stupidity.

Tell me how it felt.

I'm not sure I know what you mean.

Just tell me how it felt. The turd. What did it feel like coming out, he says, tenser but not unrestrained.

I am getting anxious and a little flustered. Confused at the feeling in my back and legs. Like the feeling in the train but scarier. I look away from him, at the room. The desk is framed within a frame. I am in the chair. Locked. In the air are crunching jaws of hands. And I am here. Between the wild horse and the spiders at the back. And I know now what I want to do. I know. I want to go. I want to say piss off. I want to say. I want. I want to shout. I want . . .

Come to my, or aidez-moi and hilfe. I want . . .

The t-turd? I say. My voice breaking up, in the trickle of sound. Minute in the presence of his.

Yeah the turd, he says, impatient. Grimmer now. Wordless messages in the pauses. His mouth a talking of coldness. I try to wriggle out. Out from under his goalie's hands, but he clamps me harder with a cemetery grip.

The big wet greasy turd between your legs. What were you like eh? What were you like?

I—

On the toilet, your legs crossed. On the bog. Your little, little panties down at your little ankles.

He laughs. Bitter, like a tractor starting up. The air is stale. Our bodies weave in the gravity between ourselves. Closer. And his other hand is down at his groin.

Your tiny panties. Your wee panties. Wee. Wee. That's your word. Wee white panties. And what else is it you people say? Wee white. Wee white. Whips? Huh? That's it. Wee white whips. Down at your ankles and your wee bum squeezed. Is that what it was like eh? Eh? Tell me.

His other hand is squeezing my shoulder and then my back. That hurts.

No it doesn't. What about that turd, that didn't hurt? I'll bet it didn't. No. That felt good. That big turd in your tight wee bum. Your Irish arse. Tiny arse. How did that get through? Eh? How? Your fucking little Irish arse.

Sir you're hurting me I try to say, but my throat is dry. His mouth is breathing out cigarette smoke. His hand squeezing. His other hand on his trousers, pushing down until the knuckles are white.

I'm pressed up against the desk. Waiting. The slow pace of his breathing. I need a getaway. To the high ground. Outside to the wheely bin and between the milk churns. It isn't any fun any more. Your head's a marley, Mister P- the craic's gone. If I could tell him I—

Come on.

Sir . . .

Tap, tap.

Shut up. Tell me. Come on. You want to. Tell me. You think you're the first? Ha. Come on. Come on. Shit. Come on.

Tap.

I want—

Tap.

Shut up. Shut up. Tell me. About the turd. Huge feeking turd, cock, bladdy hell, fuck. Cock, fuck. Oh.

Tap, tap, tap.

He is gripping my back and nearly choking me. Grunting. Really pushing me. My face is almost at the desk, my nose touching. His hand an agony on my shoulders. His other hand is trying to get under my panties, I try to struggle out. Writhe. But I can't move. I can't.

No you don't. Tell me about that slutty wee arse of yours. Slutty wee arse. That big fucking stooly. Tell me about that.

I—

He squeezes, shoves me on the desk.

Slutty wee arse, slutty. Oh . . .

His breathing faster, more intense.

Schmutty wee faaking hearse.

Turd.

Tap, tap, tap.

My eyes are heavy and I think that he is right about me. Slutty. Wee.

The sculpture up against the wall. I'm seeing things. Hyperventilating. Living honey behind my head. I feel like the boy who swallowed his tongue. That time in the playground. My epiglottis is swollen up.

Arse.

Not the first. No. White. No. The bear of the dark. The train. The chimney. Boiling up. And my teeth are in a jump cut. And his arm is pushing down. Digits. Five. The pure and the classical. Like a charge. My tibia and on my fibula. Nectars in the protractors of my muscle. And drums of pressure. Building. And he's gone as far as he can go. Pushing. Taut. His body is grainy, trying to pull down my . . . Strong like a girder. Growing. Building.

And then it comes.

Suddenly.

Burst like Cuchulain. Howling and huge on the Black Pigs Dyke. My head pounding like a warpspasm of bees and crocodiles. And I'm standing up and screaming. Throwing his arm back like it was made of gossamer.

Fuck, I shout. My whole face contorting. Standing there.

Fuck, fucker, fuck. Fuuuuck.

My hands clenched to my sides. Standing. Yelling at the top of my voice. He sitting. Aghast. With his mouth open stupidly, like a bit player on a daytime soap.

Mister Preston?

Another voice.

Mister Preston?

It is outside the door. An older man. Da?

Go away, he yells, go away.

Uh, Mister P-Preston, its m-me. Mister Pilkington.

Bollicks, he mutters and stands up. He looks at me still standing there, shaking and still.

Sit down, he commands and points with a finger. He fixes a smile, walks to the door and pushes his hair back. He turns the key and with a flourish pulls it open. Grinning.

Jim, good to see you. What brings you out here to the wilds?

I-is there a-anything wrong I, I thought I—

Rehearsals for our performance-art piece. Startling. I assure you. Oh you two know each other.

Uh, y-yes, she's in my Ph, Physics class, I t-teach . . .   251

Very bright girl, Mr Preston says, in a tone that is hushed and convincingly sincere, very bright indeed.

Y-yes, she is, a . . .

Insightful too. Her. Er, sit down.

Mr Pilkington sits at the desk. Mr Preston turns to me and mouths: Put the photographs away.

I pretend not to understand.

He turns back to Mr Pilkington.

So what can I do for ya Jim?

Well, I, ah . . .

Jabba is trying to look at me round the body of Mr Preston, who is carefully standing in front of him. To stop him coming down the classroom.

I, ah. W-well what h-happened w-was, I, ah. T-to cut a l-long, a l-long, ah. Well they let down all f-four of my t-tires. I was w-wondering if you c-could give me a l-lift. I s-saw your car is s-still here.

Those little brats. Worse every year. But isn't the garage coming out for your car, the AA or something?

N-not till t-tomorrow.

Mr Preston's brow is furrowed. He turns and grabs his jacket.

We were just leaving anyway, he says. He looks at me.

Uh, just set those, er, photographs on the desk and I'll get them tomorrow, come on.

I stand up and grab my pencil case throwing it into the bag and then remembering about the cigarette ash.

Photographs? Jabba asks.

Set designs, Mr Preston says.

Jabba gets up sadly from the chair, pushing the glasses back on his forehead.

Well I don't w-want to rush you, he says.

No we were finished, Mr Preston says coldly.

I pick up my bag and sling it over my shoulder. I tuck my shirt in as I follow behind the two men. Mr Preston locks the door. And we walk, all three of us, to the car park. None of us talking.

We climb into Mr Preston's big Volvo. I sit in the back. He starts the diesel engine. Jabba gets into the front and fiddles with the seatbelt. I'm looking out of the window, compressing my bag. It feels light, the only time in the last month the camera hasn't been in there. Jabba's Volkswagen is the only other car left in the car park. Sagging on the flats. I pull up my white socks and straighten my skirt.

The car inches carefully out of the parking space, keeping within the lines even though nothing else is near. We turn and head for the lower driveway.

Jabba has been looking at me furtively in the wing mirror. I am concentrating on the moon shapes on my fingernails. I pick at a piece of skin on my thumb, scratching until it's smooth.

He turns round in the seat and gives me a friendly smile.

S-so, y-you're in a play?

I do not answer. Mr Preston laughs.

Ha ha, we don't like to talk about it. It's not good stage karma he says, cheerfully.

Oh, Jabba says.

And it's not really a play, it's performance art.

I see.

In fourth gear Mr Preston speeds down the drive. The car skids at the stop sign. Once we are at the exit he puts the indicator on to turn left. A school bus is passing, blue and packed.

We'll go along the top road and let you off first, Jim, ok?

No no, I d-don't mind, I'm in n-no rush at all.

No, it's ok. It'll be best for—

No, I'll w-wait, he says firmly.

Ok, Mr Preston says gruffly. He turns right onto the North Road. We go past the Inter, and I see a couple of kids smoking cigarettes just outside the gate.

The atmosphere in the car is strained. Mr Preston has the radio turned off. He's not his usual sarcastic self. I look and find that he is staring at me in the rearview mirror. Glowering.

I look out of the window. Through the corner of my eye I can see him grimace over at Jabba. He is furious.

So Jim, what nonsense were you filling my star pupil with today? More of that quantum physics time-traveling mumbo jumbo?

W-well, it's n-nothing quite—

Don't give me that. They're cutting our budget and you chaps go round filling young heads with all that quasimystical ten dimensional, string theory gobbledygook. Load of nonsense.

Mr Preston is grinning. I can see that he is trying to divert the conversation into an argument. Jabba is too genial to be baited. He tilts his head back to me.

T-today, wu, what were we looking at? he asks me. I shrug my shoulders.

Come on, what w-were we l-looking at? he asks again.

Dunno, lots of stuff.

Well, says Mr Preston sarcastically, clearly it made a big impression.

Come on, w-what in p-particular?

Well, uhm. We did nonlocality and, er, the Heisenberg uncertainty principle, I reply, talking to the back of his head. Right to the bald spot. Still not looking in the mirror.

See, Mr Preston scoffs, I mean what's that all about, uncertainty principle, nonlocality. Ha. Codswallop like I say. Doesn't mean anything. Nobody's proved any of this stuff is real. Isn't that right? All theory. Am I not correct? Theory. Aesthetic dreams. That's my business in Art and yet you guys get all the big bucks. Load of nonsense. It's a disgrace actually.

Mr Pilkington coughs and pushes the glasses up on his nose.

W-well, a-actually it's not. N-not t-to go into details. To-day's class, f-for ex, ah. Just one ex, example it's ah, well accepted by some theorists that any n-number of uni, universes are c-created, by ob, observers. Ah, ah and we, c-can't know which one we, we're in, un, until we actually l-look. Or for instance o-only l-last y-year– the Bell i-inequality was shown t-to be . . .

You've done it. My point exactly, I mean what does that mean? What you've just said. Think about it. What does it actually mean? It doesn't mean anything. You to me are Bishop Berkeley and I am Doctor Johnson refuting you thus: Mr Preston hits the dashboard with his hand and laughs.

Neither Jabba nor I know what he's referring to, so Mr Pilkington continues: No these are i-important questions, whether the u-universe is observer c-created and c-contingent or pre d-destined by—

You see Jim. Again. No connection with the place we're living in now. No connection with the real world.

Mr Preston is driving fast now. At least fifty-five on a single-lane road. He slows to put it into second as he turns off onto Prince Andrew Way. The big car corners like a moose.

There is.

What?

It's my voice talking. Much to my surprise.

There is a connection with the real world, I say confidently. Mr Preston is looking at me over his shoulder incredulously, with half a sneer on his face.

Oh yes? he says.

As far as I get it, quantum physics says that the world is real   255 but nonlocal, everything depends on everything else, that's what it means. Its atemporal and nonlocal.

V-very good, Mr Pilkington says.

Well, Mr Preston laughs, that makes a lot of sense.

He pulls the Volvo into the car park near my house.

It is almost dark. I pull the lock up on the door and unbuckle my seatbelt. The sun is setting behind the McGuire's chicken yard.

R-reality, Jabba says and then his voice trails off.

I open the car door. Jabba has pivoted round to me and his face is smiling. Billowing the lines on his face like a sail. An ink stain on his shirt. Mr Preston is lighting a cigarette, his mouth turned down in a scowl. Jabba is looking at the space between me and the door. He puts a greasy finger on the lens of his glasses. I copy the gesture, fixing mine. Plumes of smoke. A Garfield on the window and a zebra hanging down. I open the door. Like Schrödinger opens the box. The planes are over the Lough. Are you afeared of flying? asked the girl. The girl beside me on the trip to JFK. Are you afeared? No, I'm afraid of falling, I told her. Flying's fine. I reach for my bag. Who needs him. Jabba's grin is broadening. My foot is half way onto the tarmac. It takes the pressure of my leg. The wind is cold on my thigh. Over near the chippy I can see a car with its lights on.

Take care, Jabba says.

Don't worry.

I close the door and wait for them to drive off. Mr Preston revs up and stalls the engine. The setting sun is at my back and the breeze is up against my spine. Golden loops of reflections are in the window panes. Shop owners are pulling down the shutters and exposing the graffiti. The line at the chip shop bends until it is in front of the off license. In the dark Mr

Preston is hammering at the choke and the cigarette lighter. Jabba is frozen in his tweed jacket. And my hand is on the plastic grip of my bag. I am standing. I turn and notice the car. The car that is not there. I do not see anyone. Not the hair, not the face, not the eyes.

The fingers over the steering wheel. And the man breathing out, with the lights on. There is a screech of brakes on the Marine Highway. The snarl of a fast car. A jet over the water banking for the airport. The froth of diesel in the air. And I'm looking.

The car that is not there. The man that is not there.

The Volvo's engine flares into life. Mr Preston winds down the window.

Remember we'll talk more about this tomorrow.

He reaches out and discreetly grabs my wrist.

Remember?

The car that is not there.

Remember?

The man who is not . . .

Re . . .

In the darkness. The insanity of seagulls and the basking sharks. The salt air. The seaweed, and the jellyfish. He will not save me. Smell of the beach. The black of the wood and the grass repeating on itself. He will not save me. For I will save myself.

I pull my arm down sharply.

Aaaow.

See ya, I say and turn.

Wouldn't.

And walk.

Want.

One foot in front of the other.

To be ya.

And the car is driving off. And I can see his face in a smile. The one that isn't there.

Mum is waiting in the kitchen.

Sarah's called you twice, she says.

I'll call her.

I drop my bag and walk into the hall. I dial the number.

Hi, it's me, I say.

Well, aren't you the girl?

What?

Never thought you had it in ya.

What? What?

Remember that foul mouthed wee mucker who was on the train the other day?

Aye, what about him?

Well I saw him today, and he was desperate to get your phone number.

You didn't give it to him?

Of course not.

Oh . . . good.

Terrible wee fella, so he is.

Aye, I know.

He rides the train two days a week now, so we're bound to run into him unfortunately.

You were talking to him?

Briefly, he's got an apprenticeship in Kilroot, he's an electrician in the power station. Dunnow how he got that so young. Anyway he's totally smitten, poor wee crattur. Coarse as fuck like.

Yeah.

So how'd your Art thing go?

Well . . .

What?

Ach . . .

What?

To tell you the truth . . .

What? What?

I think I'm dropping Art.

You're dropping Art. Why?

Uh, it's just too much work.

Yeah. Well. I guess so. Suppose you have to drop something. Stop being so licky all the time.

I better go on anyway, ma's getting the dinner ready.

Ok see ya tomorrow, just wanted to tell you about that cheeky wee skitter and everything. You femme fatal you.

Thanks. I'm glad you did . . . so I can avoid him and all.

Dead on, see ya later alligator.

In a while face like bile.

I put the phone down and walk into the kitchen. In the time it took to talk the sun has set. I look at the wet footprints on the floor. Mine. She hasn't seen the mess yet.

Two pans bubbling on the stove. Peas and meat. The *Belfast Telegraph* on the breakfast bar. Water dripping. The radio playing Hank Williams. An ingot of a tune over the noise of the extractor fan. Mum cutting up potatoes. A blanket of dark outside. The great scoop of night over the Lough and the Antrim Hills. Moths against the door. Fluttering. The moon at the kitchen window. I walk to the door and look at it through the glass. Mum turns.

Oh ya ganch ya. That's bad luck so it is. Don't you remember, nanny used to say that. Greeting the new moon through the window. Tut, tut.

I cannot open my mouth. My lips are all dried up. My granny used to say that. I touch the pane. Bad luck so it is. Sirens on the highway. Bad. A crescent near the chimney. Luck.

She looks at my face. Grins. And with a palm touches my hair.

Bad luck. Except of course when it isn't, she says. And her arms are cool with the comfort of the truth.

CHAPTER TWELVE

He was tied to a chair in a black room. Five men were crowded close. Their breath smelling of stale whiskey and tobacco. Gristle. All of them. Former comrades. Hard men. UDA.

It's a question of trust, one said.

How do we know? said another.

We've had so many undercover cops they were practically running the show a few years back, a third.

Unintentionally comic. Excited, jumping in their shoes at the prospect of a real live interrogation.

The wall was covered with Scottish and Ulster flags and a small portrait of King Billy crossing the Boyne. On the far wall a naked girl was pasted incongruously beside a memorial plaque for the Battle of the Somme.

The men were heavy and slow. He knew them all. His hands tight behind him on the chair in a sloppy knot. Every one packed a weapon. Guns stuffed between the folds of fat in their jeans. Eroticized violence in their gestures.

The light was in his eyes.

Jesus, it was all so amateur.

They had lit him a cigarette. His brother was standing at the door, not looking. They hadn't talked since the car ride. His brother the stranger, not him.

Fat moved. Tattooes faded. In came beer and cheap vodka. Playing cards with teenage girls on them.

Christ, he thought, and this is the high command. He wished he was a human bomb and could take the lot of them.

But he couldn't, not if he wanted to see the wains, just once.

It's a question of integrity.

Yeah. Integrity.

It's not that we don't trust you. But the burden of proof is on you.

Aye that's right. See you do this thing for us tomorrow. Just a wee thing. So it is. You'll be with a couple of boys you already know. From the old days.

But the old days are the new days, don't they see, he thought and his eyes blinked to make them go away.

Listen it'll all be over in a morning and then tomorrow afternoon we'll take you up the coast. To see your kids, your wife. Ex-wife, I should say.

What do you think?

It makes sense, come on.

He looked at them and nodded. I'll do it, he said.

He had to admire their ingenuity. It was a good plan. If he kneecapped a child then he couldn't possibly be a government agent. No undercover would want to incriminate themself that way.

But it was the act itself.

I need to get some rest, he said.

For a couple of hours, someone said.

They took him to another part of the house. A blue door with a bolt on it. He was pushed in gently. There was no light inside and the windows were bricked up. There was a mattress on the floor.

He lay down and climbed naked under a blanket of dyed wool. The door behind him closed heavily. The men with guns outside. Half drunk and listening to the hit parade on

Radio One.

The room was small and cold and the only light now was a horizontal line under the door. He tried to get some rest, but the blanket was a covering of barbs and sleep came slowly.

They turned the light on in the garage and he walked over to the workbench. It was years since he was here last. The small room was cluttered with odds and ends, some tools, garden furniture but mostly junk. Everything was covered with a thick layer of dust. He'd once given the order that this room was never to be cleaned. Not because he wasn't fastidious (in fact in those days he prided himself that he was neat and precise) but because the dirt seemed to soften the edges. The sharp metal tools could be terrifying sometimes. The thin veil of dust was almost a feminizing influence. A softening.

Little had changed. A rack of Armalites was on the wall. Black and shined. Magazine cases in a box, bolted. A tin of WD-40. A tub of mercury. Autumn sunlight splayed in through the garage windows, harsh and vulgar, fragmenting the room into hot and cooler sections. He chose a shady corner and set to work disinfecting the drill bits. Two men watched him from the door, both young and unknown to him, tapping their pistols at their sides. He dropped three of the long twisted pieces of precision steel into the white spirit. They bubbled there for a moment. With his fingers he cleaned the metal. The clotted remains of the last job floated to the top and hung on his cuticles. Flecks of someone else's skin and dried blood.

He plugged the electric drill into the wall and tested it for a second. It revolved sickeningly with a high whine. Christ, he gagged on the smell of paraffin. He let his finger drop from the trigger and the revolutions slowed until the drill came quietly to a stop. He checked the hammer-function button and when he was satisfied that everything was ok he put the drill, his

263

gloves and the drill bits into a canvas bag. He was ready now. He looked at the men. When do we go?

We're waiting for a phone call, one of them said.

The call came half an hour later. Two men he knew showed up soon after, in a hijacked taxi. Fernie coming over and Scotchy staying in the car.

What about ye? Fernie was saying, still the big man, six four at least, over three hundred pounds, and clumsy too. Danny probably only kept him around because he was useful at the physical stuff. He shook Fernie's hand and he slapped him on the back.

Ready to rumble ye boy, ya? he said jovially, his loud voice echoing down the back streets.

Aye.

Jesus you're a sight for the sore eyes.

Long time, no see, as they say.

Yeah, long time.

Jesus man let me look at you. I thought you were dead. Heard your ma passed on, nice wee doll too.

Fernie wasn't quite the same. Too familiar now and too flippant, but he let it pass. Scotchy was adjusting the mirror in the driver's seat of the taxi and smoking on a Dunhill. He was nervous, you could tell. Maybe something had gone wrong already.

Hey, good to see ya again, Scotchy shouted over feebly.

Yeah.

Fernie laughed.

S'pose you been fuckin away since you got out. I was desperate for it when I got out of the Kesh. Jesus I screwed three weemin in the same night, so I did. One of them was this Paki doll, fuck she was wild boy. Wild.

He forced himself calm and walked out of the garage into the dour morning. The men at the doorway spoke into a radio.

The sky was gray and the air chill. Damp hung on the gable. He climbed into the taxicab.

When Fernie joined him in the back, Scotchy slipped the car into gear. His head was thundering. He still hadn't eaten anything.

The whole island was swimming. One big bog of dirt and mushrooms. Scotchy let his foot off the clutch too quickly. The engine roared.

Shit, Scotchy moaned. Fernie chuckled and his laugh had a message in it. He lit himself a cigarette.

Is everything alright there Scotchy, he asked, looking at the little man's rodent face in the car mirror.

Scotchy turned and gave a twitchy gap-toothed smile.

S'fine, he managed.

Good well let's get going, he said in a monotone.

One of the men who'd been watching him waved. More than a good-bye. He nodded back. Soon, he thought. The car drove off and he was alone with the two of them. No one was following. The early road was all emptied space and clear milk bottles on the doorsteps of the houses. Wrecks of a sunrise and, on the road, black earth from the construction sites.

He had to admit it was a smart setup they had him in. He was hanging by a thread and these two idiots would kill him as soon as look at him.

Colder than a witch's tit out there today, the big man muttered.

Aye.

Like yon time we were on the Knockagh just before you went? 'Member?

I remember.

Fuck. Seems like yesterday. I was telling you to go to the Caribbean. 'Member that?

Aye.

On the road were winter flies and Catholic girls. Swarming. Waiting for the school bus.

Cold then, cold now.

Aye it is indeed, said Scotchy.

He looked at the two men carefully. All the color was out of Scotchy's cheeks, drained and anxious, his smile a rifle. The other looked the same as he remembered him last—well fed and full of bluster. Those had been crazy times. When he was just too well known and he had to get out. Had to. And Fernie was only a little older looking, heavier round the cheeks perhaps and with his hair shaved into an almost skinhead to conceal the baldness. Scotchy was giving him a look in the mirror every couple of seconds.

You look done in, Scotchy, he said. Get any sleep?

Aye. I'm fine. Just the cold boss, that's all.

Boss. He'd said. That was interesting, perhaps he still had some clout. His belly groaned.

Where'd you jack the taxi? he said to cover the sound.

They stopped at a traffic light. Fernie was clearly itching to tell the story. He grinned broadly.

Jesus boy you should have seen us, he said. We go in cool as you please. It's this oul boy and we tell him to take us to the river, so he did.

He rubbed the rings under his eyes and ran the evaporating white spirit through his hair. He stretched his back and tensed and untensed his thigh.

Really short guy, practically a bloody dwarf so he was. Anyway he's driving along talking about the tv, some soap opera shite he's on about you know. We're talking back, as you do, and I pull out the old pump-action. Shits his pants, literally. So he does. Fucking shit himself so he did. Shite smell everywhere, my gawd, despret.

Fernie doubled up and even Scotchy managed a laugh.

That right? he said.

Scotchy looked back. Aye it is. We threw him out of the fucking cab and told him we'd drive ourselves.

I tell you boy you missed a hoot, Fernie said slapping him on the arm.

Sounds like it, he said. The whole thing ringing untrue. Fernie's eyes widened, stung by what he took to be a lack of enthusiasm.

Fuckssake boy, what are you like, too much of the oul arse banditry in the clink, he said, turned you into a right oul cunt. Fernie laughed loudly at his own joke. He couldn't help but smile, just a little. And then, trying to ease the tension, he let his doubts about the morning drift and broke into a grin that he hoped would reassure the both of them.

Belfast was in fall. Orange highlights were on the foliage and a thin coating of ice clung to the pavements. It was still early. Only a few cars moved, exhaust fumes pouring into the cold air. The city was drab and damp and tinted cinder. Red-bricked houses slumbering in tight little terraces and murder holes, graffiti marking out the boundaries of the territories between them. King Billy the icon of the Protestant streets and the Hunger Strikers in the Catholic. He felt sorry for them. For the wains in gray beds sleeping under peat fires and the black slate roofs; all of them tight and together in a protective huddle under the whispers of the Cave Hill and Divis and the Black Mountain.

All of them lost.

Close one, Fernie said, as an army Land Rover drove past ignoring them completely, the khaki paint almost concealing the cardinal lettering on the plate-armored side. Stop Murder: Use the Confidential Telephone, it said. He had to strain to read it, the words not designed for the red-green color blind.

As the Land Rover turned he could see giant billboards advertising cigarettes.

Purple silk with cuts in it. Rothmans had a poster right beside it and Marlboro was opposite.

Dying for a smoke, he thought, but neither Fernie nor Scotchy offered and he didn't feel like asking.

They passed the shipyard on Queens Island. Silent and idle. The aureolin tint of the cranes blurring before him. He'd worked there once. Cover for a real job. It had been easy. You went in, did your thing and went home again. No worries.

Harland and Wolff the black letters said on the side of the warehouse. They took a turn by the river and then the taxi drove over the Lagan and into the other half of the city.

So it's good to be home, right? Fernie asked.

He nodded.

Yeah.

And then he thought about it.

No.

These were the streets. These were the people. But it was not home. He didn't feel the affinity. Who were they? This bunch. This tribe from which he came. Prods in Ireland. Jaffas. He looked at Fernie and grinned. It was like living in a time warp. Religious wars. How could they not realize the pointlessness of it all?

Couldn't they see?

How could they? With their pariah eyes and the schizophrenic noose of their allegiance. Split between loving England and hating it. Booing the English at football games and mourning when their soldiers died. These people who didn't even know if they wanted to be called Irish or not. Stateless. Orphans of history with only their mad religion to give them any identity
at all.

He could see all this now that he had been away. The lie of his life. He looked round him and shook his head.

And then he thought and reversed himself. For even so this was still the place to be, where you could speak and be at ease, as much a home as any sinner had in the world.

Yeah, he said, it's good.

Fernie yawned and spoke: Aye it's great. I was in London for three months, almost kilt myself from missing it. Me and some boy went on a wild bender throughout Kilburn. He was from Derry. Found out later he was a fenian, but he was a good lad.

I see.

And the things are going well with you are they? Fernie asked, almost sounding as if he was interested.

They're ok.

Good.

And then after a sufficient pause: You know I don't know why you wanna pester the big boys when they're doing so much for ya. I mean why are you making waves? Giving them grief?

Fernie had said all this with a certain deliberateness. As if it had been rehearsed. And it was for them the big question. Was he a friend or was he an enemy?

He knew the answer now.

The seat was hard.

The shirt was up and across his belly. His fist was pressing into it to keep away the groans. The bridge sliding sideways over the Lagan like a giant crocodile. He couldn't answer. All I want to do is see my fam— . . . They wouldn't understand. A giant billboard on the far bank read: Multiple Sclerosis Does Not Just Kill. How could he explain without making it sound like betrayal. Like quitting. How could you ease yourself out? It wasn't an easy thing to say.

No. He couldn't tell them. How could he when he knew, knowing Fernie and Scotchy, that they still had the fire in them? That he was the only balanced one in the car. In back-street Belfast there was a saying for when you got lifted: whatever you say, say nothing. Say natin.

And it was right. Silence was best, since you can't tell anything to a man possessed.

He shook his head and finally cadged a cigarette.

And still they drove. Back through the west of the city, through a space ringing with the roar of helicopters and the pillar boxes spray-painted lavender. The curbstones white and gold. A lone dog sniffed at a glass-smashed bus shelter. Dead faces stared out from murals on the wall.

His lips and tongue were chapped and dry.

Smash the H blocks, an old graffito said in the shell of buildings. The ashen space of a tenement. The pillow of a face. The cold kitchens, the rubble. A sign said: Buger Sams, the "r" missing. Starsky and Hutch staring through the streaks and the stones, and a man called Pulverize.

Over the Blackwater and everywhere the architecture of loss was on the Falls Road. And then turning again. His eyes heavy under the concrete of the railways. The crosstown bridges and the debris scattered over the lunar landscape. The slum clearance stark and cold, adorned with the latent fury of EU ready cash.

Here he could see the intersections of his life, this narrative out of context.

His past a dream. His incarceration nothing more than a fable.

They drove past a beer poster and boarded-up back-to-backs, a surreal and lonely world outside. Lazy violence, all of it romanticized by distance, sly bookies' shops, razor wire on the hospital walls, an army post behind three lines of fencing and the abandoned building sites like galleries of memory, slashed with scrawls and promises of retribution. His sense of place confused by Scotchy's route among the parallel and un-complicated dregs of streets.

He wound down the window to get some air. A kind of absolution coming with the cold of it and the dingy morning breath of factory smoke that snaked and strained among the alleys.

He closed his eyes. Letting the carriages take him back.

That last day on the run he'd been in his apartment. The men outside the door were goons from Langley, Virginia, and from the cops and the local DEA. Hammers had come through the door and in a second he was on the floor, his face examining the gap between the tiles. His hands cuffed behind him.

A stick smacked into the side of his head and then as if time was on the ff button he was in the holding cell, confined. His jaw locked. His legs in iron. His fingers clutching the fingers of his cell mate. The man's eyes on the wrong side of his head. His small intestine spelling out the word: riverrun. The guards throwing up when they saw what he had done . . .

And that wasn't even the worst.

In any case he took the memory and whetted it for what soon he would have to do. But it was harder now. The carcasses were piling up and almost smothering him. He leaned on the door in the back of the taxi and tried to get a breath.

Outside, creatures of the air were resting on the telephone wires. Cratturs. He blinked and his head was spinning. Half the world was black and half the world was nitroglycerine. There were sunbeams and the light was harnessed and put to use, shining off the backs of pedestrians and roofs and the somber faces of the clergy.

There was a shake in his hands and a nagging pain of rheu-matism in his limbs.

Never forsake the blue skys of Ultser, a sign said, a pochle of syllables. They were over the Farset now as if it were a mystery tour. The only other vehicle they'd passed in the last five minutes was a milk float running on battery power.

They had given him an overcoat and old clothes to wear, a black sweater and jeans. Adidas training shoes. He was muffled up like a Russian and the day wasn't even really cold. Never mind what Scotchy said.

He shivered despite himself.

Fernie spat onto the taxi floor and looked at him: We're the last of the oul gang, so we are, Fernie said. You know that? All the rest are in the clink or pushing up the oul proverbials. Us and Dan of course. You know Duffy's dead, and Lutz.

Is that right?

It is. All them gone. Abroad or inside or six feet down. Lutz topped himself, the big eejit.

Sad.

Aye but you're here. The big cheese.

Was.

Aye in the past but I'm still surprised they haven't splashed your story over all the newspapers. You escape and all and you being so big and everything.

Aye you're practically famous, Scotchy said, chipping in his dialogue.

Yeah like Elvis.

No seriously. There was a whole page about ya once in the *Tele* and didn't they have a story about you on the six o'clock news? And that picture from, uh, that time we were over the fuckin border. Huh?

What's your point, Fernie?

No point. Relax. Just remarking that you're dead well-known, so you are. And now we're hearing nathin. You break out of the clink and nobody says nathin. You're not on tv, not in the papers. It's funny, so it is. It doesn't make any sense.

It doesn't make sense if what you've said is true—was what Fernie had wanted to say.

It was all clear now. Their trust was casino real, and he realized that they hadn't believed a fucking word. He cursed inward. Jesus. He should have held something back.

I explained it all. They never found any ID. So no one knew who I was.

Aye that's what you said, I forgot, Fernie replied.

The taxi turned left over the bridge and ran along the Markets. Scotchy secure now that they weren't being followed. Fresh wreathes on the railings at a check point. They were gone, the trees he remembered here. Black stubs on the sidewalk. Scotchy's quiff brushed over a bald spot, and he adjusting the dial on the heater. The soldiers at the check point were asleep at their post, a snoozing invader in a pincer between the buildings. The car startled them. A swab of malachite and copper. A boy with a painted minstrel face. Another with a radio, sweating in a kevlar sandwich. Six green bonfires. Scotchy wound the window down. The river was unpacked and smelling. Mackies Factory as silent as the Wee Yard. The soldier waved the car through with a dip of his rifle.

They turned next down towards the peace line. A bunch of flowers had been left outside the Law Courts.

Fuck the Pope, a wall said. Fuck the Queen, said another, not a million miles away. Green paint had been thrown at a mural of The Man on the White Horse, a brave thing to do— people had been assassinated for less. He could tell they were close to the house. Scotchy was picking at his arm, Fernie's grin was off his face.

You better have this, Fernie said, and handed him a gun. It

was unloaded. When he looked up Fernie and Scotchy were staring out of the window. The pistol was an old Browning revolver. He toyed with the hammer and the chamber and put it in his jacket. He counted off the street names, one by one. Jericho. Bethlehem.

I've got a joke for ya, Fernie said.

They passed a big new police station he hadn't seen before. It had a wall three feet thick. The fence was bent to bounce off mortars or coffee jars filled with Semtex and six-inch nails.

Ya ready?

Sure.

Why do they keep a bucket of shit at an Italian wedding?

I don't know.

The policeman at the gate post looked at him through the window of the guard hut. A shock of blond under the bottle green of his hat. His brow was furrowed with thoughts of bullets and of hand grenades. How will I hurt you, he thought. How? Not today, not by the hair of my chinny chin chin.

To keep the flies off the bride.

The taxi began to slow. Scotchy was in second gear. From the numbers he could see that the house was at the end of the terrace.

Want to hear another?

When they got there it was identikit to all the others. Two bedrooms, white stone, the tiny garden neat and trimmed, roses growing along the path. Fernie playing with his machine gun. He was pulling the balaclava down over his face.

The car stopped and they climbed out. The engine running. Scotchy nervous on the accelerator. Tarpaulin flapping on the roof of the house next door.

Hey boy do you want to hear another?

Another what?

They were walking down the path and then he and Fernie

were ringing the doorbell, looking innocent and relaxed. Like they'd come to read the electricity meter. A bicycle was leaning against the wall and there was a jam piece in the middle of the grass.

Another joke, what do you think?

The bell was ringing. Fernie's Kalashnikov leaning against the door, filed, with a sawn-off support. With the letters AK-OK chiseled in the wood.

What do you call an Italian virgin?

The door was made of timber and frosted glass. He could see through. Letters were in the hallway. Lilac and primrose yellow on the carpet.

I don't know.

A girl who can run faster than her brother.

A woman answered the door opening it slowly. She was fat, fifty, face hidden by a large pair of glasses. Lines deep on her lips. A smoker's brow.

Mrs McGann? he asked.

Yass, she answered speaking through her nose.

We've come for your son.

He's nat in at tha moment, yiel heff to try—

She was cut off as he pushed her to one side, knocking her glasses off onto the porch.

I'll check upstairs, he yelled to Fernie.

He ran up the narrow carpeted staircase past pictures of the Giants Causeway, the Manchester United 1958 squad and the "Mona Lisa." He pulled out the pistol and kicked in the door at the top of the stairs. It was a pink bathroom. Chintz wraps and a crushed-velvet cover on the toilet. A heart cushion and a wicker basket. The room was empty, the window open and drawing in the cold. He exited and, hugging the wall, walked along the landing. He opened the next door along which turned out to be the airing cupboard. Stacked with towels and linen.

275

There were two doors left, they would both be bedrooms. He kicked in the one nearest to him. It was a child's room, there were bookshelves filled with comics, posters of soccer players on the wall, the duvet on the bed had two long-haired wrestlers printed on it. A fourteen-year-old boy was lying on the floor playing a board game with a girl who was a little younger. Both children had dirty blond hair. The boy in t shirt and jeans. The girl in a sweater and hockey skirt. On her way to school. A fan was blowing the girl's hair into her face. The room was hot from the central heating. His fingers tensed.

The windows were steamed up, condensation gathering on the wooden sill. Everyone froze for a moment. Their actions slowed down to a few frames a second. The boy turned his head. He was still leaning on his elbows, his upturned nose and big eyes wrinkled-up in surprise. The children looked alike, brother and sister. The girl, on the verge of yelling, let her grip go on a piece of toy money she was holding. A slip. He watched as it caught a current from the fan and blew up into the air. The cards on the floor said Chance and Community Chest. The bill, tumbling through the air. It fell onto the board between a boot and a car. He wanted to speak but his throat was too dry for words. He seemed unsure of what to do. He blinked. Get a grip. He drew the gun and pointed it at the child.

Get up, he said softly. We're not going to hurt you.

The boy rose slowly. Passive. His sister burst into tears. It's ok, he told her. They're not going to hurt me, he said embracing the lie for her sake.

He led the boy back into the landing. The mother was screaming downstairs. The carpet was muddied from his shoes.

Where are you taking my son . . . she was crying over and over. He heard Fernie say something and then a slap and then the woman was silent. The boy stumbled on the stairs. The glass table at the bottom was broken. The woman was lying on the floor.

Ma, the boy said.

She's alright, come on ye wee fuck, Fernie growled and pushed him from the neck. They ran down the path into the waiting car.

I haven't done anything, what are you doing? the boy said, as the taxi bumped along at fifty-five.

Shat up you're only making it worse, thieving wee bastard, we'll teach ye to steal, so we will, Fernie muttered.

But you've got the wrong person, really I haven't done . . .

Shut the fuck up. Fernie shouted and slapped him across the face with the butt of his pistol. It was only a slap but it drew blood.

He glowered at Fernie as the boy burst into tears. They rode the rest of the way to the safehouse in silence.

Fernie held the kid by the legs while Scotchy sat on his struggling arms. The warehouse was big and empty.

You haven't been here before have ya? It's like, it's like a dead-on place for hiding jacked cars and stuff. An taking wee shites who're liable to make a lot of noise, Scotchy said.

The generator had been turned on that morning. Cooking the air and spitting diesel.

They didn't know, but he had been here before. He'd killed a man here once. A squealer. Whacked. Another life ago, when he believed.

Oil that had leaked into the concrete was starting to evaporate in the hot baking air, giving off an evil smell. The roof was leaking water into two massive drums that were close to overflowing. Litter clogged the corners, swept there and left.

Beer cans with naked women on the side. Cigarette packets. Bags of cement. Sandbags stacked against the blocked-up south entrance. He kicked aside a stack of empty boxes from the Chinky and brushed dust from the electricity socket on the wall.

He plugged in the drill and as he fitted the broadest bit into the hub the kid began to scream.

Shut up, Scotchy said.

His back was up and he didn't care.

Let him fucking yell, he said, before Fernie kicked the boy quiet.

He squeezed on the trigger but the drill didn't start. The other two men looked at him.

What's up? asked Scotchy with a tremolo in his voice.

Dunno. He looked at the drill curiously and then smiled.

Forgot, you have to press the red button on the side, works as an extra safety, he said, and gently squeezed on the grip. The drill kicked into life with a quiet rhythmic hum.

Shit no, the kid hollered, louder this time. Fernie thumped him with his fist nearly rendering him unconscious.

Don't knock him out, this has to hurt so he'll remember, Scotchy said, slowly, like he was reading lines from a script. The boy began to thrash his legs as he brought the drill close to his kneecaps.

Got a lively one here, someone said, maybe Scotchy, he wasn't listening, his mind focused on the job at hand. The men were holding the boy down, stopping the struggling.

You want to hear a geg?

He put one knee on the boy's shin and the other on the cold floor, and with a well-practiced precision he drove the drill laterally into the boy's left kneecap.

What do you call a nigger in a suit?

The bit penetrated the skin remarkably easily, getting tangled for just a moment on a piece of thread from his jeans.

The defendant.

The blue denim quickly discolored as it absorbed the blood that began to ooze out of the wound. He pulled out the drill fast before blood could clog the mechanism.

Dja geddit? I've got another.

His first incision had been a good one, he had driven through right to the cartilage. He had three more to do on the left knee before he could move to the right: an incision laterally from the other side—the inside leg—and then straight through the patella from the front and back; he would need to put the drill on hammer function for that, going through bone was always tricky.

What do you say to a nigger with a job? . . . Big Mac and fries please, d'ya get that?

He tried to stay away. Cold and detached. It was easy, if he could remember. He clicked off the drill and watched as it blurred down to a halt.

Jesus boy you're no fun, you laugh at nothing.

He checked the drill but the bit was fine so he turned it on again. The sun was out now, dreary light spilling from the high windows catching the dust particles as they fell and rose, spinning on thermals from the generator. He shifted his position to the other side of the child, leaning on the boy's good knee while he passively drove the drill again into the bloody one. The long electricity cable was in his way so he had to stop halfway through and throw it over Fernie's head.

I guess they were right about ya.

The drill ripped through the skin around the patella like it was crepe paper and drove awkwardly into the bone.

See this part, it's the worst, dead difficult this part. Fernie to Scotchy. It's like, you know, have you ever tried to hammer a nail into a porcelain toilet seat? The curve, you know.

What the fuck were you doing hammering nails into bog seats?, Scotchy said.

The boy limp now, quiet. Resigned or deadened from the pain. This part was tricky.

It's a analgee thing.

Fernie was right. This was difficult, but he'd done this many times before when he was younger. He was a master of sorts. The kid was lucky in a way. His victims could usually walk in six weeks, sometimes without a limp.

An anal what?

Your arse is an anal.

Ha ha.

Analogy that's it, a analogy alright?

All it took was patience. Like keyhole surgery. He avoided the nerves and major blood vessels. Even though he couldn't see properly underneath the red gore, which had been once the boy's white leg. He didn't need to see, he moved the drill by instinct. Not looking at him. The boy's eyes pleading pointlessly. There was nothing he could do. Everything was quiet now, complete hush, the boy yelling again in silence, Fernie talking in silence. Outside even the morning had its ears stopped. He could hear nothing. Not the banter, not the whine from the drill, not the drone of choppers. Chinooks over the hills. Or the two men moving back.

Alone in a noiseless world. The open mouth screamed as the drill destroyed a nerve ending. Blood drooling. Scotchy saying something. The drill spinning.

I think it's time.

The warehouse a prism of his concentration. The seconds slow and measured. He breathed, adjusted the handle, drove in a little further. Blood sprayed onto his t shirt.

Uh huh.

A hammer clicked. He stopped for a second and watched as a drop of sweat fell from his forehead. Catching the light, refracting it slightly. The boy's cheeks brimmed with tears. He tilted the rag child on his side to roll him over on his back. Then he noticed that no one was holding him.

Pandemonium.

A catastrophe of noise between his ears.

Eyes fazed. An eruption. His ear drum blown to bits. For an instant, razorbladed off a second he heard for real, and saw the face of a man holding a gun. He wasn't smiling. Gold in the middle of the mouth. Insanity in the torn cloth of his expression. He was numb. Fernie and Scotchy were staring at him, backing off. As if he were contagious. From the noise a window had fallen in. The clouds on tack. Fernie's finger was on the trigger. Eyebrows looped. On a bender. Blood pouring out onto the floor, pouring by the pint load. He looked down. There was a hole in the boy's chest the size of a football. Glass on his tongue. Smoke coming from the end of Fernie's gun. The boy was gasping for air but his lungs were lying in pieces on the floor.

He almost laughed. Through the gap the sun was like a lemon rind and the roof an echo of the ground. The boy's face was dotted with his own insides, a banquet of spidershapes. He blinked once, slowly.

There's been a change of plan, Scotchy said, his voice deepened with authority.

My brother has given me up. Both men were ten feet away and pointing weapons at him. Fernie had the big gun that had made all the noise, an S and W special. Huge. The Kalashnikov hanging over his shoulder.

I'm sorry we have to do this and all.

You killed the wee lad.

Ach he was a wee shite.

He was fourteen.

The first shot took him on the shoulder from Scotchy's semiautomatic. It burned and pushed him on his arse. It made his head swim, a swamp in the crackle of his optic nerve. He couldn't see, and he didn't move in the wake of the firearm. He was just sitting there like an aunt sally.

Die ya bastard, die.

A second shot took him in the gut, again a small round.

Fernie fired the revolver with a boom that made his ears ring. The bullet punched a hole in the metal drum behind him, cracking it in half, spilling gallons of stagnant water onto the floor. Pouring out like a dam burst.

Fuck, Scotchy shouted, you missed him, so you did. You stupid fuck.

He felt the muscles in his ankles. Tensed. Still sitting but adrenaline carousing now in the jungle of endorphins.

Ah shaddup ye whiney wee toerag.

The problem with these boys, he told himself, is that they talk too much. He threw the drill behind him and jumped for the sandbags by the door. Scotchy fired another shot. A lifetime too slow. He reached the sandbags as the drill hit the water. The power socket on the wall exploded with a massive electrical discharge and a bolt of flame. Fernie's body hammered against the roof beam as if propelled by some invisible force. His hair standing up like a fright wig, his fingernails black. He pummeled into the metal support, his head splitting open like a melon.

The spill had not reached Scotchy, but as he turned from staring at his dead partner, a sandbag took him in the face knocking the gun out of his hand. The generator was on fire. The room was acrid, blinding him. Scotchy fell and hit the concrete with his head.

He picked up the gun and pointed it into Scotchy's left eye socket, pushing it hard against the eyelid.

Where are they? he asked.

Scotchy terrified. I don't know, I don't know, shit I . . .

He pushed harder feeling something crunch.

Scotchy yelled: I don't know fucking anything, I don't know sweet fuck all. Oh please please, holy fuck please.

Ok. My brother's house, where's that?

Scotchy was choking, his eye was white from the pressure. What?

My brother. Where does he live?

Thirty-five Craigavon Street.

You sure? I wouldn't want to find out that you've been lying.

No Christ I wouldn't.

Good.

He pulled the trigger, the sound muffled by the soft tissue in Scotchy's skull. Blood and brain exploded out the back of his head in a v shape. The left half of his face caving in like a leper's. A smile on his broken teeth. His other eye staring in a half wink.

Outside he found a Ford escort. The side of the warehouse was on fire and beginning to attract attention. But time was short. He broke open the lock and climbed in.

The clock said eleven am when he pulled the car outside the house on Craigavon Street. It was a big white detached affair with a mock porch and a patio. Milk bottles were on the step with a note in them. The gate was cast-iron and painted black. It swung on a heavy mechanism that creaked when he pushed it open. He walked up the path. A sodden garden to his left, a fresh-dug flowerbed to his right. Roses pruned for the winter. Moss between the paving slabs. He followed the path round the side to another gate that led to the back. It was high and bolted from the other side. A thick hedge surrounded the garden. He put his foot on the beam and hoisted himself up. His shoe slipping. He put his hands on the top of the gate and pulled himself onto his stomach. A pain was there and bloodslime.

As he swung down onto the grass a doberman pincher tore into his leg knocking him over. A huge dog and vicious with it, but snarling, not barking, which was good. Its jaws took a hold on a chunk of his ankle. Grinding towards the bone. He was on his back, the dog at his leg. His upper body free. He thumped the animal on the eye. His knuckles scraping on its pupil. It winced and backed off, its tail drooping. Quickly he thumped it again on its flat head and again behind the ear. The dog was winded, momentarily stunned. Whining in little frothy groans. Blood was on its long tongue. Its legs splayed, as if it were on ice. He climbed on its back. His knees straddling its rib cage. He put his arm under its head and pulled back hard until its neck cracked like a dry stick snapping.

He broke open the back door with his second kick. He held the automatic in his hand and walked through the kitchen. The table cluttered with tools and a cylinder head from a motorbike. The cupboards were grease-stained. He opened the door to the hall and headed up the stairs, keeping low, holding the gun in both hands.

Did you hear that? a voice said.

What?

Did you hear that?

A woman and a man. He kicked open the bedroom door and turned on the light.

One move and I'll kill you both.

The woman screamed.

Shit, his brother said. She was about seventeen, blond and face contorted with fear. Ugly in the morning. He crossed the room, feet on the shag pile. She was looking at him. Her jaw locked. Beside the bed was a pink dresser and a wooden cupboard, the wood swirl in the shape of a railway tunnel. Behind him a blocked-up fireplace. He walked over to her side of the bed. Her scalp eggshell thin. Her white hands up protectively.

No please, I, don't . . .

He hit her on the head with the pistol butt. His brother flinched but didn't speak. She slumped straight back.

Ok motherfucker you better tell me what I want to know.

They were strangers now but perhaps it was always so. His brother was calm, his skin white against the cream sheets. He waggled the gun.

So you topped the boys, I thought you might.

It was bravado. There was no real awareness that death was in the room.

Bullshit, you thought I'd be lying in a sheugh somewhere by now. With a hole in my head.

He stood with his legs apart.

No I reckoned you'd—

Don't, my patience is . . . They killed the boy, you know, a boy. His rage hard to contain. The hypocrisy written on his fingernails. He was part of it. We don't progress morally at all. We don't change. He moved closer to the bed, his foot on the prosthetic limb that was lying on the floor.

That wasn't in their orders, they were supposed to put the drop on ya and let the kid go, he said, his eyes narrow and not fully awake. Perhaps he thought this was all a dream.

You reckon I'm just off the boat, he said. Well I tell ya. Now I don't give two fucks. I've come a long way. I don't have . . . I want to know where they are.

You've been shot, his brother said. And his childhood was

285

in the room. Nah you missed me. He was taken aback. Did not. He looked down. Did so. His shirtfront was drenched with red. Not. So. His shoulder was half numb, his head heavy. He had lost a lot of blood to his coat and trousers. His hands. I don't give a flying f . . . He sighed. Just tell me. Weary. The carpet softer than his bones.

Tell me and I won't kill you.

He put a light plastic plate in his mouth. It was white with breadcrumbs. He looked in the drinks cabinet and picked out a bottle of Bushmills whiskey. He unscrewed the lid. It was half full. He took a swig and poured the bottle onto the two wounds in his stomach and shoulder.

On feek, he said between gritted teeth. The plate broke, shards in his mouth. He spat. He dropped the bottle and the gun. He pulled a black sweater over the bloody t shirt. The fire was the hurt. When the girl wakes the carpet will be wet with vomit and the brains of her lover. He walked into the kitchen and put his mouth under the faucet and drank. Water running onto his face. Through the window the garden was decorated with a swing and the body of the dog. His legs were swaying. A Lundy tendency made him want to sit down and call the peelers. The kitchen tiles were smears and footprints. He pushed on the door and walked into the hall. Horse brasses on the wall and a painting of stallions. A poster of a woman playing tennis, her arse naked. He leaned on the aquamarine wallpaper, changing it forever. He opened the front and walked down the garden. The postman was next door. He jogged to the car. It took everything he had just to stand up, let alone run. Drive. The engine started and the streets went back behind him. The city that was gorged up by the mud and the belches of the Lagan.

Yesterday's light in the back of his throat. The gray morning clearing from the radio beacons on the Cave Hill.

Nine notches in his head. The streets were fluid and the air was seething with him coming. He smiled and put his fingers behind his own head, like the horned god. His fists like mastiff dogs. A handful of words on the radio.

You're listening to afternoon talk with Ivan Martin and Richard Young.

His trousers like a reddle man. The atmosphere heavy and in curves. Vats of water on the M5. Gulls wading in the purple mud. Erato and Orpheus. Lyr, the god of the sea, behind the clouds.

The headlines today.

Children flattened in the queue for buses. The perfume a heady blend of gastric juice and cordite. The traffic was all in the other direction, going into town.

A bomb on the outskirts of the city last night killed two people. Two men have been charged with membership of a proscribed organization.

His temples bumped and crazy and the Lough was flowing counterfeit along the highway. The middle distance had the shore and the trees, the power station on the bay.

The weather is wintry with some heavy showers. So watch it on the roads. Ohhhkay, today's talking point brought to you by Guinness issss: violence. Of course we know all about violence here in Province. Shootings, bombings. You name it. But why is it that for many people violence is seen as the only answer?

Jesus, he said.

He put his hand on the bloody gear stick sliding it into

287

four. He accelerated the car up to the speed limit. 60 here on the carriageway.

Our first guest, Doctor Ernest Beck, the author of a new book, *Violence and Redemption,* argues that masculinity is imaged as violence too often in our media culture. Think about that Martin. Anyway, he'll be joining us in just a minute. And we hope to talk later to Professor Ruari O'Lughdaigh who argues in his new book, *The Sins of the Fathers,* that violence in Ulster is perpetuated by folk anthems and songs. Well well well. And— I'm reading the blurb here—the problem is ritualized hatred passed from one generation to the next. The problem is too many big words if you ask me.

He drove quickly. Through the suburbs and up the coast and finally round the bend to the town of C–. The harbor choked with mud and lobster boats, the highway clear, the mad stoplights always green. Lyr from the glens and the wild ocean. He drove past the castle and along the dual carriageway. Accelerating past the police station and turning at last into the big housing estate.

Again he was in the car park. He was so close yesterday. If only he'd known that the family hadn't moved very far. It was the house with the yellow hedge behind the supermarket.

It was too late. His life was on the steering wheel and the foot pedals. The machine gun was ten miles away. He kept the engine ticking over. The coal truck spitting bricks as it passed. The air was freezing. Frost on the pavements like gray hairs.

And we're through to the Professor. On the line live from Dublin. Go ahead sir . . . Am I on? Oh yes. Ivan. Er. Good morning. Good afternoon I mean. I'm on? Well from my perspective in Dublin the main problem with Protestant . . .

He turned the radio off and now there were only birds.

Chimneys spewed ash onto the rooftops. There was gravel on the tarmac. A rooster with its head pecked in. A boy with a box and a claw picking up litter. Behind him, a hundred yards back, the news agent was busy. He recognized the owner from way back. He slumped down in the seat, his collar up. His face light. Limpid and serene. Jayzus bay doan dain tfiel tget ap ssam pataters in yehr trec-tur. The wind slanting through the tv aerials. A different voice. Tadae weir goan ta dae inegration ba parts. To some integrals there is no solution. A football on wet concrete. The rain on. Black trousers sprayed with mud. Blazers apart. 600 seconds is all the time they have. Under the city were a million lab rats and a thousand beetles for every man. And he missed the faces, constructed of the sun.

A big Volvo pulled in, two cars in front of him. The door opened. And, as if by a miracle, there she was. Low and a burst of drop-down red. The girl. Her back was making of itself. We all fall down. We all . . . He held the gun. Her bag was at her side and her arm was in the grip of a man still sitting in the car. She turned and looked and they saw each other. He smiled at the bird shadow and the line of the high tide. The sea in ambush. And the blue was just the hush in her iris.

Of course. That's where it was the whole time. She jerked down her arm and the man said, aoww. Her skirt was pleated and her legs skipped. His finger was elongated and did not bend. A shillelagh made of blackthorn. She turned back. Mi pistola hermoso. The floor of the car was Christmas color.

His eyes closed.

It isn't the . . . he said.

His lips pursed and lengthened.

A tanker moved on the gray sea. A bird flew. Cattle were at the ragged-up fences. Her mouth was the song of the bear in the woods.

§

This is not the end.

To me, we live in a deep reality. Mr Pilkington didn't explain things very well but I believe he was right. The late Belfast physicist John Bell said that we exist in a world that is nonlocal, where everything depends on everything else, and each entity in the universe is linked together under the phenomenal surface. And since this is the best interpretation we have, I think Bell's formulation was right. Everything that was or is, or will be, is joined and woven together in the superluminal fabric of deep reality.

This kind of holism used to make me optimistic. But morals don't come from metaphysics and in my homeland everything is measured not in the homogeneity of things but rather in the degrees of difference.

And although the Province is a mystery to me now, troubled and fractured like no other place I know, I remember that time with great exactness.

It's hard to understand and harder still to explain, but within the singular ways of the town of C–, one thing is clear: something did happen to us in those four days leading up to Halloween. We were touched. By what or whom I can't say. But it was there, and I was changed.

I did drop Art. Shortly after, Mr Preston left to teach at the University.

As you can probably guess I went on to study physics. On the mainland. I got out and I'm now a teacher.

I get letters from time to time. Sarah is married and living on a farm. My brother is in the police and happy. My mother works for the civil service with a group of ladies she really likes. She is still alone and she still misses da, though I think she's reconciled to the belief that we probably won't ever hear tell of him again.

There were lots of rumors once that he'd been seen. But the paramilitaries take care of their own and nothing ever came of it. None of us talk of it or him.

To be honest, though, I miss da too but tell myself I don't need him.

I live abroad now and in a kind of exile.

I can't ever go back because it's all just too much for me. Its too fervid a place. Ulster. Hard. There's too intense a feeling there. Like you're living on a wire.

Sometimes though I do miss it. I miss the voices. The iron expressions of the people. I miss the rain on the buildings. The grim faces of the big storm clouds and, perhaps most of all, where I lived—close to the hills and the aged gray music of the water on the sea. I dream about it.

I dream about his island.

And when I wake I tell myself that this is not the end, and one day I'll go back, for, in this world and in the other, all things are surely possible.

"This neglect then of rhyme so little is to be taken for a defect though it may seem so perhaps to vulgar readers, that it rather is to be esteemed an example set . . . of ancient liberty recovered . . . from the troublesome and modern bondage of rhyming."

—JOHN MILTON, *PARADISE LOST*, "THE VERSE"

GLOSSARY

BOG	toilet	OUL HAND	hardened con
BOKE	vomit	PEELER	policeman
CLEG	horse fly	PIECE	white bread
COUL	cold		sandwich
CRAIC	fun	POCHLE	shambles
CULTCHIE	hick, yokel	PROD	Protestant
DANDER	walk	SCUNNERED	annoyed
DUNT	bump	SHEUGH	ditch; body of
EEJIT	idiot		water
FENIAN	Catholic (derog)	SKELF	splinter
FOOTER	fiddle; waste time	SKITE	dodge
FOOTY	football	SKITTER	rascal
GANCH	idiot	SLATER	wood louse
GANDER	look	SLEEKIT	cunning
GEG	joke	TAIG	Catholic (derog)
GLIPE	oaf	TIG	tag
GULTER	laugh/pour out	TOP	kill
GURN	cry	UDA	Ulster Defence
HOKE	rummage for		Assoc. (an illegal
HOOR	whore		Protestant para-
JAFFA	Protestant (derog)		military group)
JUKE	dodge	UVF	Ulster Volunteer
KEEK	crap		Force (an illegal
KNOCKED	stolen		Protestant para-
LICK	teacher's pet		military group)
MARLEY	marble	WAIN	child
MINGING	dirty	WHEEKER	great
MITCH	play truant	WHIPS	underpants
ORANGE MAN	Protestant mason	WICK	terrible